WICKED LADY

LADY ANNE STUART—as ruthless as she was ravishing, she proved an irresistible temptation to the best and worst of men in the Carolinas . . .

RAOUL DE POLIGNAC—the dashing young French officer who joined the fight for freedom only to be forced to choose between ideals and his compelling lust for Lady Anne.

ADAM RUTLEDGE—the kind of rugged individual so essential to the Revolutionary spirit. He decided to teach the scandalous English "lady" some manners.

STEPHEN SAYRE—a man without a conscience, a spy and a traitor—he held Lady Anne in his corrupting power.

BARON VON POELLNITZ—Lady Anne's adoring husband. Benign and generous, he was tragically blind to his wife's treachery.

Wicked Lady

Inglis Fletcher

BANTAM BOOKS · TORONTO · NEW YORK · LONDON

WICKED LADY

*A Bantam Book / published by arrangement with
The Bobbs-Merrill Company, Inc.*

PRINTING HISTORY
*Bobbs-Merrill edition published May 1962
2nd printing . . . . July 1962
Bantam edition / January 1976*

To the Citizens of Chowan County and the Town on Queen Anne's Creek, whose ancestors have furnished me with the material for this and other books.

Contents

Foreword

This is a novel without a hero or a heroine. The soldiers of the American Revolution are the heros; the women of Edenton are the heroines.

The book is both fact and fiction, but I have been guided by the rule advanced by Sir Walter Scott that the novelist's first duty is to "tell a story." To that end I have clung only to the fixed dates of battles, and have introduced incidents that occurred a year or even two years before or after the *events* when I thought they would enhance the story.

So if it is history, as typified by dates, that the reader seeks, I advise him to read the historians of the period. In this novel he will find only people, and the experiences that made them great or small according to their natures.

For source material I have leaned heavily on *The Life and Correspondence of James Iredell,* edited by Griffith J. McRee. New York: Appleton Co., 1858; *Originals Abroad,* by Warren Hunting Smith. New Haven: Yale University Press, 1952; *Booklet 14,* by Charles N. Hatch, Jr. Washington: National Park Services, private records of the *Von Poellnitz Family in America.*

My thanks to Dr. E. Lawrency Lee, History Department of The Citadel, Charleston, South Carolina, for his valuable assistance in research; and to my daughter-in-law, Gladys Fletcher, for typing the manuscript.

INGLIS FLETCHER

Bandon Plantation
Edenton, North Carolina

I

Pembroke

The August sun was sinking in red glory behind the tall pines of John's Island. Waterfowl skimmed across the quiet waters of Pembroke Creek where it flowed into Albemarle Sound. Along the shores of the creek, the south boundary of the plantation, tall reeds hid the nests of the blue heron and white cranes standing knee-deep in the waters of the pocosin to guard their young. A flight of ducks were winging northward over the waters of Edenton Bay to a familiar refuge on the Chowan River, where with shrill cries and a great flapping of wings, they settled down to feed in a sheltered cove for the night. The babble of children's voices came from the quarters line. In the waters of the creek a fish leaped from time to time. The cattle were lowing in the meadow; the hounds barking in their kennels. It was the familiar pattern of sound at the end of a summer day.

The Negro slaves walking down the path that led from the tobacco beds to the kitchen were talking of the day's work and the night's rest to come. Snatches of song broke into their chatter, for ahead of them was rest —and a good supper in Dulcey's kitchen. The smoke of the kitchen fires rose thin against the crimsoning sky, filling the warm air with the acrid odor of the pitch pine burning in the great brick fireplace.

The workers stopped out by the pump to plunge

1

hands and arms and grimy faces into the wash tubs. They all knew better than to carry dust and dirt into "Miss Dulcey's" clean kitchen.

Old Dulcey sat on a high stool near the fireplace, her bright calico skirt flowing down to the floor like a gaily colored Persian shawl. The vari-colored silk turban that bound her head designated her position in the household as one of importance. The firelogs burned brightly. From a swinging crane swayed an iron kettle of soup. Iron skillets and pots sizzled with frying pork and bubbled with boiling greens. Sweet potatoes and corn pone lay roasting in the warm ashes.

She greeted the field hands as they came in: a sharp word here, a kind word to the very old and the very young, and a warning to all to wipe their feet on the tow sack at the door.

"Get you goin'," she called out. "The white folks is dining in style tonight and I want you out of the way might fast."

"Yes, ma'am," the men answered. "Yes, ma'am."

"You, Sam!" she yelled suddenly, pointing at a yellow boy near the door. "Tak' dose corn pone out of your shirt front and put them on the hearth. You ain't goin' to steal off of Dulcey!"

The boy shook with terror at the sound of her shrill voice. He laid the pone on the hearth.

"Tain't fit for ought but the swine now," she shouted. "What for you think you steal from Dulcey? You think my eyes too old to see?"

"No, ma'am, Miss Dulcey, no ma'am. I think you sees real good. I takin' the pone for Granny. She's sick in the bed and she surely does like your corn pone."

Dulcey dropped her belligerent tone. "Your Gran' sick, boy? Why didn't you say so? Take the pone and I'll send her down a bowl of soup."

The boy grabbed the pone from the hearth. Thrusting them into his shirt, he darted out of the kitchen.

The hands laughed. "You make yourself a cross old cat, Dulcey, but you as kind as a kitten," an old man called out.

"Shut your big mouth, Ebon. You talk too much!"
Her words were rough but her voice was mild, and she
joined in the laughter.

In the big house Marianne Cabarrus was giving the
house servants their instructions before the dinner guests
arrived. Her housemaid, Promicy, had already laid the
table with the silver and crystal Marianne had brought
from France. In the center was a low crystal bowl, over-
flowing with the delicate Queen Anne's lace that grew
by the roadsides. Marianne was pleased with the arrangement. No one else in the county would have thought of
using a wild flower for a table decoration.

"Promicy, the decoration is very pretty," Marianne
Cabarrus said.

"Thank you, ma'am. I remembered you liked them
when I fixed them last year."

"So you did, when we were entertaining the Governor."

"Yes, ma'am. He was a nice gentleman. He gave
me a crown!"

Like all other slaves, Promicy would have remembered a gift of money. But Marianne was sure that Governor Burke had tipped Promicy only because she had
been so confused by the honor of helping Samuel, the
butler, wait on the Governor that she had worn a hat the
whole evening.

The table decoration was typical of the way Marianne had adapted herself to the ways of the landlords
of North Carolina, and to their love of the land and
their respect for it. To them land meant freedom, and
everything, even the wild flowers, that came from it was a
symbol to them of their mastery of the wilderness and
their essential control of the colony they had built.

When Marianne had first come to the Albemarle as
the young, beautiful wife of Josiah Bodley, the people of
Edenton had gossiped about her. "A typical Frenchwoman," they said. "She'll never be happy married to
that old man and living in this small place. Not after
Paris and London, she won't." True, Josiah Bodley was

old enough to be her father, but he was respected as the land agent of Lord Granville. Being connected with the land, he was entitled, so the people of Edenton thought, to a wife worthy of him and of Pembroke Plantation.

Marianne had surprised them. She seemed to regret nothing of her life in the capitals of Europe. She settled down to plantation life with ease, and acquired a reputation for hospitality even in that region, where hospitality was ranked among the cardinal virtues. She made old Josiah Bodley comfortable until he died a few years after their marriage. Compelled, not unwillingly, to change their suspicions of her, the villagers who tended to suspect all "foreigners," had come to love and admire her. They did not know that she had originally come from a village in France not much different from their own.

A good many planters from around Edenton had courted the young widow Bodley. Her charm and beauty enticed them, but the rich lands of Pembroke were an equal allurement. If only those fertile acres might be added to their own! The bachelors of Edenton itself cast longing eyes at the comeliness of Marianne Bodley and the crop-laden fields of Pembroke. Marianne's widowhood was not lonely.

Still, much as she had conformed to the life of the colony, she had secretly hankered for the time-tempered tenderness of her native land and its people. She returned to France for a visit. When she came back to her own plantation in North Carolina, she was married to Stephen Cabarrus, a handsome young merchant from her native town.

At first, Stephen Cabarrus had objected to living at Pembroke, but in the end he had given way to her pleading. "With one promise from you, my dear," he said firmly. "That you will not talk of your life here with Bodley. I want you to forget that entirely. This is to be a new life—with me."

Marianne promised readily. She had respected Josiah Bodley, nothing more. She loved Stephen.

"Just you alone, Stephen," she told him. "It is you I adore."

That had been five years before. Their life together had since belonged to the present—and to the future. The past was never mentioned. There had been no children, a regret to both of them, and it was Marianne who suggested that Stephen write to his sister in Paris, asking her to allow her young daughter Penelope to come to them. At first the idea was not to the liking of Stephen's sister. Then their uncle Cabarrus, the great Spanish banker and head of the family, used his influence to change her mind. Penelope had come to live in America.

Penelope seemed almost childlike compared with the Edenton girls of her age. In contrast to the more mature beauty of Marianne, she was underdeveloped, but the possibilities were there for beauty, as Marianne told her husband. Not only beauty but common sense, which is important in a wife.

"What would you do without *your* wife's common sense?" she asked Stephen.

"I don't know, my dearest, how I ever existed before I had you," Stephen answered, "but Penelope will never be you, and I confess I don't see the hidden beauty in her. She is a nice, sweet French girl . . ."

"And will make some man an excellent wife," Marianne finished.

Stephen looked at his wife with admiration and love in his eyes. Marianne was tall and slender. She walked with grace, and she had a melodious voice. Her eyes were dark and limpid. She showed her Latin blood in her energy, her flashing smile and her quick impulsive manner.

"We must look for a husband for her," Marianne said. "A nice American with a large plantation."

Stephen laughed. "Let's not think of marriage at present, my dearest. Penelope is only seventeen."

Marianne spoke quickly. "Seventeen? Why, I was only sixteen . . ." She paused suddenly, remembering her promise not to speak of her life with Josiah Bodley. "Oh, Stephen, I forgot—I am sorry."

Stephen did not answer, but he patted her hand before he left the room.

Marianne remembered the incident now as she crossed the broad hall. She was thinking about the attractive young Frenchman, Count Raoul de Polignac, who was one of their house guests. The other guest from France was his guardian, the Duc de Braille, an older man. She had no fears about Penelope taking a fancy for him.

But what if Penelope should take a fancy for young Raoul? She could not allow that. Penelope must marry an American. Besides, she would only break her heart over Raoul. He would not look at her; she was too young, too immature. He was at an age when his interest would be in an older woman, not a girl like Penelope.

Marianne had worried about the situation ever since the two French visitors had arrived to stay with them, bearing letters from Stephen's uncle, the influential banker Cabarrus. Like hundreds of other French officers, they had come to America to take part in the great revolution for freedom. Now they were waiting for the Governor of North Carolina to assign them to regiments.

Besides the two french officers, Count Cosmo de' Medici was also their guest. An old friend of the family, he had come from Williamsburg in Virginia the day before to recruit dragoons for his company, which he had organized at the beginning of the Revolution. Like the many Frenchmen who had followed Count de Rochambeau and General Lafayette to America, Captain de' Medici had come from Italy, inspired by the new ideas of Liberty and Freedom that had caught the fancy of young men all over Europe. Marianne had no fears that Penelope would be attracted to Cosmo, but Raoul was a threat to her plan to have the girl fall in love with one of the young planters around Edenton.

The dinner Stephen Cabarrus was giving that night was to introduce the Duc de Braille and Count de Polignac to what Marianne called "Edenton's Great." Ever since his guests had arrived from France, Stephen had tried to arrange such a dinner, but until now it had been difficult to get all the Edenton men together at the same time.

Judge James Iredell had been riding circuit in the western part of the state. Dr. Hugh Williamson had been with his field hospital in the Great Dismal, or in Philadelphia. William Hooper, although he lived in Hillsborough, spent so much time with the Iredells that he was almost considered an Edentonian. Samuel Johnstone and Charles Johnson were cousins, originally from Scotland, and were all over the state as members of the Assembly. All these men had reputations as patriots far beyond the confines of North Carolina. It was for that reason Marianne called them "Edenton's Great." Her title clung to them.

A goodly company, Marianne thought, as she went up the broad stairs to her chamber—brilliant men, unusual to find in a little village of six hundred souls.

She found that her woman had laid her bath. After it, she selected a rose-colored taffeta from her wardrobe. It was a gown she had had sent from France that very spring. She thought the color enlivened her skin and flattered her. She wanted to look her best for her husband's guests that night. Although she would not dine with them, she would receive them in the great room, which she had made into a true French drawing room, and make them welcome to Pembroke.

She stood before the long glass, smoothing out the voluminous folds of the silk, tucking in the Mechlin lace modestly to cover her rounded bosom more fully, and giving a final twist to the two long curls of dark hair that hung over her white shoulder.

She glanced at the little French clock on the mantelpiece. It was almost seven. The guests had been invited for eight. She hoped Stephen would be home in time and not have to dress after the guests arrived. She had tried to persuade him not to ride out to his river Plantation, but this was his regular day for visiting with his overlooker, and so he was bound to go.

With another glance at the clock she rang for Stephen's body-servant, Puti, to prepare his bath and lay out his clothes. Puti came so promptly that Marianne was sure that he had been waiting in the back hall.

Puti had been with Stephen ever since he had come to North Carolina. The only Mohammedan of all the plantation slaves, he felt himself above the others, who came from Guinea. He often told them of his adventures in crossing Africa on the Great Slave Road, which extended from the east coast to the west. From Dar-es-Salaam to Lobito they had traveled on foot. Thousands upon thousands had been driven across the road by their Arab masters to be sold to the traders waiting for them at the bay, and transported to the southern plantations of America.

Puti wore the red tarboosh that designated his religion. His house uniform, a Zouave jacket of scarlet cloth embroidered in gold that came from Spain, he wore over a long white cotton robe. He called himself *capita,* which meant "the captain," and he kept the house servants in line. He actually obeyed only Stephen, his *Bwana,* or "master." From Marianne he took merely orders of small importance about household matters, although he showed her deference and called her *Memsahib,* which means "mistress."

After Marianne had given him orders about Stephen's clothes, she walked out through the long French doors to the upper gallery in the ell, from which she could view the broad reaches of Pembroke Creek beyond the garden that surrounded the plantation house. The slanting rays of the afterglow had turned the dark waters of the Creek into a scarlet path of light. The border of pine trees gave off a clean, fresh fragrance. How calm, how peaceful it was! All nature seemed to be resting in beauty.

The thought came to her with disturbing poignancy. This was a time of war. Across the border in Virginia and as far north as New York men were fighting and dying. Across the state line in South Carolina, cities were held by the British, and battles were being fought. Even in North Carolina, the British held the city of Wilmington and the river ports.

She thought of soldiers who might never look at another sunset. War and the horror of war were everywhere about them. Yet the sun set each day in quiet beauty as the night before her eyes. She brushed away a tear as she heard the joyful barking of the dogs welcoming their master home. A moment later Stephen's step was on the stairs. She went back quickly to the bedroom to welcome her husband. Her heart beat faster, as it always did when Stephen came into the room. The quality of his smile, the glance of his brilliant eyes enveloped her with the warmth of his affection and love.

He was a tall man, over six feet, slim and graceful in his movements. He used to tell her that in his youth, when he had visited his banker uncle in Spain, he practiced twirling a bullfighter's cape, and was determined to spend his life in the bull ring, bowing to the thundering crowd that applauded his agility until he placed his sword in exactly the right spot to stop the trumpeting bull in its tracks. At first, a plantation in America had seemed a sadly ironic realization of that dream. But he had made a high place for himself—he had become a member of the council and speaker of the Assembly— and had forgotten the dream of his youth.

As Marianne felt his lips on hers she knew the same thrill she had experienced when first he wooed her in the garden of his uncle's house in Paris. "I will always be your lover," he had told her then. She withdrew reluctantly from Stephen's arms, her slim hands straightening her dark curls.

"Darling, I had Puti lay out your gray brocade coat. I thought you should celebrate for your visitors from France and show them that you are no back-country-man."

Stephen bent to kiss her throat "You are the best of wives."

Marianne smiled, pleased at his praise. "Hurry

now! The Edenton men will soon be here and you must be in the drawing room to greet them. Is Mr. Hooper coming?"

"Yes, he is still at Iredell's. He has just come from Hillsborough. We will hear from him of the progress of our army in Virginia."

"Will the army come through Edenton?" Alarm came into Marianne's dark eyes. "Stephen, I'm afraid!"

He put his arm about her trim waist. "Hooper thinks not. He believes Cornwallis and his troops will march from Wilmington through the middle of the state to Virginia. It looks as if the British are gathering around Williamsburg."

"Stephen, sometimes I wish you had stayed out of this war. You didn't have to take sides. You are really a foreigner."

He put his fingers across her lips. "Never say that, even in jest. I am an American. I believe with all my heart in this revolt against the indignities of the British. So does every Frenchman who has any thought for freedom. Look at all the French who have come to help fight for liberty!"

She said: "I wish the Governor would find someplace for these young Frenchmen to fight. Waiting has made them discouraged and unhappy."

"Never fear, the Governor will place them. I think Cosmo de' Medici will offer some of them a place in his dragoons."

"I am glad. It is sad to see them sailing all the way from France, full of eagerness to fight for us and finding no place waiting for them. But hurry, you know Judge Iredell is always on time or a little ahead. I'll go down and see that Promicy doesn't get too excited and put out the wrong wine glasses."

Stephen laughed as he stripped off his clothes, got into the foot tub and began to sponge his lithe body with warm suds.

Promptly at the stroke of eight he joined Marianne in the drawing room, which was decorated in the French style, much different from the simpler American rooms in other plantation houses. Presently they heard a boat bump against the landing, saw lanterns bob up and down as slaves ran down the platform to help the guests from the pirogue.

Marianne told Stephen that she would not dine with them. "Let it be a man's affair. It is sure to be political and I know nothing of politics."

Stephen laughed. "You are joking, my dear. Do you think I would be Speaker of the House if you had not used your blandishments on the members?"

Marianne blushed. "Am I as obvious as that?"

"Only to observing eyes, my dear. The men are all envious of my beautiful wife whose only thought is for my comfort and the management of my household."

"Let us keep it that way. I can't abide a managing wife."

"Never fear. It is the iron hand in the velvet glove."

Marianne laughed. "The Gallic touch—I like that." She moved to stand before the fireplace to greet her husband's guests.

"A beautiful background for a beautiful woman," Judge James Iredell said as he lifted her hand to his lips. "You make me think of the French Court in the days of the great Louis."

Marianne dimpled. "Judge, I vow you are a true ladies' man. You say exactly the correct things to please us."

"He says what the rest of us are thinking," Samuel Johnstone's gruff voice broke in. "Jemmy is learning things since he rides the circuit. I swear he wasn't as adept when he was ruling the custom house."

"How do you think I won your sister Hannah, Sam? By talking about the crops?"

The two men went on to speak to the French visitors. Dr. Hugh Williamson moved up to talk to his hostess. They were friends of long standing, owing to Marianne's interest in the doctor's field hospital on the Dismal Canal, which was being highly praised by every officer in the American army. She had scraped lint and wound innumerable bandages for him throughout the war.

"I'll have more lint for you next week," she said. "I'm teaching my Negro women to roll bandages."

"Good—very good, my dear. I think I'll be needing them before long."

Marianne put her hand on the doctor's arm. "Do you think there will be a great battle in Virginia?"

"So it would seem. I have no orders as yet, but I am ready to move out of the Dismal at any time now."

"I am afraid, doctor. I am so afraid."

He laid his great hand over her tiny one. "I don't mind saying that I have my fears also. But we have good leaders in General Washington and the French Rochambeau. Let us hope they are wise in their plans."

"But General Washington is far away in New York."

Dr. Williamson bent over and spoke in a low tone. "Perhaps he is not so far away as the British think, my dear, but don't speak aloud of this. Not one word!"

Stephen came up to escort the doctor and the other men to the dining room, where Samuel and Puti and Promicy were standing against the wall, waiting to serve them.

Marianne looked in on the guests as they seated themselves at the table. She had planned the seating so that Judge Iredell would be next to the Duc de Braille. The Duc wished to reach the ear of General Washington. What better way than through his close friend, James Iredell? William Hooper, the member of Congress from Hillsborough, was just beyond, so that he could enter the conversation. Next to him was Dr. Williamson.

Samuel Johnstone, Cosmo de' Medici and Charles Johnson were deep in conversation. Probably Cosmo was telling the senator about his company, the first dragoons in Washington's army. He was justifiably proud of his men.

She heard Cosmo say: "Four of my best men were from western North Carolina—Drury Bass, George

Chambers, Withe Span and Moses Upchurch. They enlisted in Franklin county in '75, when I took over for Captain Jones. They were with me at Brandywine Creek. Good men, all of them."

Johnstone said: "You can count on the North Carolinians. They make good soldiers, but they are like my own countrymen, the Scots, in that they want a light hand on the bridle."

De' Medici laughed. "That I found out in the beginning. We Italians are like that also. Individualists, my father used to tell me. They follow but they won't be driven." His darkly handsome face, with the classic de' Medici nose, looked thoughtful. "Perhaps that is the secret shared by the great generals—lead with a light hand."

Samuel Johnstone leaned toward him. "Have you heard where General Washington's army is?"

"I don't know. Surrounding New York the last I heard."

At that moment Stephen tapped a spoon against his wine glass. "Judge Iredell has a letter from Pierce Butler of South Carolina to the Continental Congress. I've persuaded him to read it to you. I'm sure you will all be interested to hear what goes on in Philadelphia."

All eyes turned toward James Iredell. He was small in stature, but a man of large views and broad interests. When he spoke, everyone listened, for he commanded respect. He was admired for his ability, loved for his gentle spirit and kindly ways.

He turned the page in his hand. "I'm not sure that I should read you a personal letter."

The men urged him to read it. He agreed only to abstract certain parts he considered of interest and importance to them.

The letter deplored the reaction in Europe to the persecuting spirit manifested to the "miserable Tories." It urged mercy and forgiveness as "Godlike virtues." Then Butler stated that he had "proposed to the legislature to negotiate a loan in Europe, and establish a public bank."

"If your State," Butler concluded, "does not shortly fall on some plan of finance to restore her lost credit, she must suffer much, and the citizens feel great distress." He ended by urging Iredell to come to Philadelphia.

As he finished, Iredell leaned forward. "There are men here who think it is unimportant to have the respect and good will of foreign countries. I am not one of them. We are fighting for individual rights and liberties. We are also fighting as an example for other countries. We need not only their support but their interest in how we will maintain the liberties we are fighting for by way of laws."

Sam Johnstone's harsh voice broke the silence that followed. Politically he was the most important man in North Carolina, but he was a dour Scot, a member of the famous Annandale family. People feared him. "I am afraid," he said, "that we shall have to wait a long time before we establish proper courts of law. We have battles to win and a land to make free before law is established."

Charles Johnson of Bandon took up the argument. "Sam, you always throw cold water. Damn it, why can't we still work under English common law?"

Johnstone smiled wryly. "We can. Indeed we can. But at the moment we must find a way to get me back into Congress in Philadelphia. Butler is right. North Carolina must be represented."

The Duc de Braille spoke for the French officers, who had been silent. "If our Admiral de Grasse has his way, we will sail north and blockade the Chesapeake. That will bottle up the British at Yorktown." He made an inclusive gesture with his hands. "It will be the end of Cornwallis, if only Washington will leave off surrounding New York and get down to Virginia to join General Lafayette."

Williamson said: "The rumor has it that Washington is marching."

Stephen Cabarrus motioned to Samuel to fill the wine glasses. "I am more worried about Craig, the English commander in the southern part of North Carolina," he said. "He is devastating Wilmington. If he should take a notion to move north, we would be directly in his path."

Johnstone laughed. "What would happen to our Edenton ladies who have swarmed to Windsor? Craig might march through that town and confiscate all their goods and chattels."

Iredell looked at his brother-in-law. "Your family never moved across the Chowan, Sam. You think Cornwallis will not come this way?"

Samuel Johnstone lit a clay pipe. "I don't like the idea that any British general could drive me and my family out of my house. My house is my castle." He puffed a cloud of smoke before his face.

James Iredell took up Pierce Butler's letter again. "What do you think we can do about the enmity of the North against the South?"

Johnstone answered angrily: "I can't understand the animosity of the North toward the South. The New England delegates try at every turn to defeat the South. We have no such feeling toward them. You can see by our voting records."

"Perhaps there is jealousy toward the Southern gentlemen because they are envious," the Duc de Braille ventured. "I notice they do not have the gracious hospitality of you Southerners."

Stephen laughed. "It's the climate. How can one be gracious in a snow country? It takes our pleasant southern breezes to make for hospitality and friendship."

Iredell took a sip of wine before he spoke. "Have you had any late dispatches from France, Stephen? What is the situation there?"

"Nothing of especial interest. Nothing like the raids of our Admiral John Paul Jones in '79 along the English and Scotch coasts."

"A most successful maneuver that was," de' Medici said thoughtfully. "A surprise attack leaves the enemy in confusion. Strike and be gone."

There was a moment's silence at the table. Samuel

passed quietly around filling the wine glasses with burgundy.

The Italian turned to Johnstone. "I have heard much of the success of your brave Admiral, and I also have heard that he owes everything to your Edenton citizen, Mr. Hewes."

"You can hear anything these days," Johnstone replied. "Hewes happened to be the head of the committee of marine affairs. He knew where to seek out the ships he needed. John Paul Jones owes nothing to anyone but John Paul Jones. I am sure if Mr. Hewes were alive tonight he would say the same thing."

"I did not know that," de' Medici said. "I was thinking about the story that when John Paul arrived here in Edenton from the West Indies after he had killed a seaman, Hewes befriended him."

Johnstone smiled briefly. "Even that story is wrong. Hewes found John Paul one morning at his shipyard with a note to him from a ship captain he knew. It told Hewes that the lad had accidentally killed a man on his ship. He advised him to get away and come to America. The man who really befriended the lonely John Paul was Wylie Jones of Halifax. It was because of him that John Paul added Jones to his name."

"A name he has set in history," commented de Braille.

Charles Johnson brought the war back into focus by asking de Braille: "Is de Grasse's French fleet in the Indies, sir?"

The Duc hesitated a moment, then said: "Sir, I have no recent intelligence about our fleet movements. They were cruising in the Indies the last I heard."

"I trust they have received orders to sail for this country soon," Johnson said. "We will need men now that Clinton is coming south."

Stephen answered: "I am sure we can count on the French fleet pursuing Admiral Rodney. I have that intelligence from a recent letter from my uncle Cabarrus."

"I had forgotten that the Spanish banker Cabarrus had befriended Benjamin Franklin," de' Medici said.

"Yes. He is very favorable to our ideals of liberty, as you have doubtless heard."

"This interests me," de' Medici said thoughtfully. "Here we sit in a small village in eastern North Carolina while the great world touches us through Admiral John Paul Jones, then through the great Spanish banker Cabarrus, then through our own Dr. Williamson, and William Hooper of Hillsborough."

"Do not forget the close friendship of Judge Iredell with George Washington."

The Duc de Braille nodded his powdered head. "Amazing! We might be dining in one of the great capitals of Europe—Paris or Madrid or Rome. Amazing, is it not?"

"Indeed, yes."

"This information must not go outside of this room," James Iredell said, "but I have heard that Lafayette is having great success around Williamsburg. He is by frequent forays pinning the British troops down. Soon they will be backed up against the York River. Then will come Washington's big move."

"But Washington is in New York!" Charles Johnson exclaimed.

"Not for long, not for long," Stephen Cabarrus said. Then he closed his lips tightly and refused to say another word.

Dr. Williamson added something. "I may have orders to move my field hospital up the canal into Virginia before long."

De' Medici looked from one to the other. "I think it is time for me to join my troop in Suffolk. All these things lead one to believe that we are nearing a battle."

"Please God you are right. I have had the feeling ever since Cornwallis and Tarleton were on their way to Virginia that the closing battle would be in that state in spite of the British keeping their main force in New York."

Johnson picked up his wine glass. "To an early finish of the war!"

As the dinner party broke up, Hooper said: "I am

leaving for Philadelphia in the morning. Can I give anyone a seat in my coach?"

De' Medici, who had been talking with Samuel Johnstone, turned quickly. "I'd be glad of accomodation. I must get to Williamsburg is possible."

"Will seven be too early for you?"

"I'll be at your door before seven. I can secure my mount to the back of your vehicle."

James Iredell walked to the gallery with the Duc de Braille. "I have news by a fisherman from the Outer Banks. The vessel *Free Eagle* from Bordeaux, Captain Meredith commanding, passed the Bar yesterday and should dock at Edenton tomorrow before nightfall."

The Duc's face lightened. "That is indeed good news. I am sure the Captain, an old friend of mine, will bring letters and papers for me, and perhaps something of interest to you, Judge Iredell. If so, I will give myself the pleasure of riding over to your house tomorrow evening."

"My wife and I are always honored by your company. News of the war effort would pleasure us."

Led by the slave Ebon carrying an ignited flambeau, the guests went down the brick walk to the landing, where their pirogue waited.

From the gallery to which she had withdrawn as the men were leaving the dining room, Marianne Cabarrus watched the moonlight shimmering on Pembroke Creek. The night was very still. The voices of the departing guests came distinctly over the water. Judge Iredell was speaking.

"I wish the Governor could find suitable places for these charming Frenchmen after they have come all the way to America to help us."

Johnstone answered: "He could if we had any troops in North Carolina. You know all our fighting men are either with Marion in the South or Washington in the North. We haven't a fighting man in the state. Somehow I have the feeling the war will soon be over, one way or another."

"Pray God you are right!" Marianne murmured.

II

A Ship from France

The news that a ship from Bordeaux was arriving before sunset spread with incredible speed among the six hundred inhabitants of Edenton.

It was of such importance to the women that the events of the morning faded away. What was the departure of a delegate to the Continental Congress in Philadelphia in comparison with the advent of a cargo of French goods, silks from Lyon, laces and knick-knacks? Even the loss of the fascinating dragoon. Captain de' Medici, seemed of no moment. The ladies of Edenton had grown accustomed to the French aristocrats Stephen Cabarrus was constantly entertaining and a trifle bored by titles. But a ship from France, that was different!

The hot August day and the discomfort of stinging yellow flies and gnats could not keep the people indoors when such a momentous occasion was about to occur. At the pier waited a group of women—Madam Horniblow, whose husband owned the tavern, Madam Penelope Barker, Mrs. Blair. So few ships, they were saying, had come in since Admiral Rodney's war vessels had patrolled the coast. The last one was at least a year ago. It brought a cargo of fine French furniture which Hewes and Smith had immediately sold to the large plantation owners in Bertie and in Halifax. Wylie Jones had brought a satinwood commode at the suggestion of

19

his guest, John Paul Jones. Adam Rutledge had secured two fine Aubusson carpets. Sam Johnstone and his cousin Charles had been rivals for the carpets until Rutledge stepped in and carried off the prize. Charles Johnson was greatly disappointed. He wanted the carpets as a gift to Elizabeth Earle, Parson Earle's daughter at Bandon. They were exactly the size to use in the two halls he planned to enlarge and redecorate, when they were married in the autumn.

The young girls—Penelope Blair, Hannah Iredell's niece, Mary Blount, and Mary Copeland from up-country—had gone to Dr. Armitage's Cupola House to watch for the ship through his telescope. Dr. Armitage was away in the Dismal, serving at Dr. Hugh Williamson's field hospital, but his wife had given them the keys to the little tower room, from which the whole broad sweep of Albermarle Sound could be seen beyond Edenton Bay. They would blow the hunter's horn at the first sight of a ship, and then the townsfolk would pour onto the dock to watch the ship anchor.

The houses along the waterfront and the Court House were crowded. The Collins' place facing directly on the water and the Pollacks' on the opposite side of the Green were packed with women who preferred comfortable chairs on the broad galleries to standing on the Green or on the dock. Besides a rocking chair, another advantage was cooling rum drinks the owners were serving their guests. What could be more delightful than viewing the cypress-lined shore of Tyrell against the red of the setting sun, with a glass of such nectar in one's hand?

The guests of the Samuel Johnstones, at Hayes, had the advantage. They would see the French ship before the townspeople could get a glimpse of her ensign floating in the stiff breeze of sunset. Among them were Stephen and Marianne Cabarrus and their French guests, along with the Iredell family. At the first glimpse of the vessel the Frenchmen planned to mount their horses, ferry across Queen Anne's Creek and be at the Edenton landing when the ship put in at the wharf.

The children, down at the point in the garden, were the first to sight the French ship. They ran screaming to the house, "Ship! Ship! The ship is coming!"

With every sail spread to catch the evening breeze, the *Free Eagle* came into sight.

"We will leave now, Mr. Johnstone," the Duc de Braille said. "We do not want to miss the docking."

Samuel Johnstone rose from his chair. "You have plenty of time. An hour at least before she turns the Dram Tree."

As they came to the front of the house, a rider on horseback was coming up the drive. "A letter for Judge Iredell from the Outer Banks."

Iredell took the letter from the messenger and broke the seal. "From brother Arthur," he said to his wife Hannah. "He tells me that the Baron and Baroness von Poellnitz and the Baron's two children are on the *Free Eagle*. He asks me to look after them. The Baron was the Chamberlain of Frederick the Great. His wife is a connection of ours."

Hannah Iredell, Samuel Johnstone's sister, was so much shorter than her husband that she had to rise on her toes to peer at the letter he held in his hand.

"Oh," she exclaimed, reading, "she is the Lady Anne Stuart, Lord Bute's daughter."

James Iredell silenced her with a look, but not in time. The rest of the company caught the name of the hated Minister of George III, who had imposed such iniquitous burdens on the colonies. Bute had fallen from power twenty years before, but his name could even now bring a frown to the brows of the older guests at the Johnstones'.

Their looks did not escape Judge Iredell. What should bring such a woman here, they seemed to say? Iredell himself was but a remote connection of the lady. The Edentonians had too much respect for the Judge, and too much common sense, to reproach him for family ties which were none of his making, but now these were about to be thrust in their very faces.

Samuel Johnstone remembered the letter from

Pierce Butler that Iredell had read at Stephen Cabarrus' dinner party. It had advocated a more tolerant attitude toward the Tories. Try as he would to prevent it, the thought kept coming into his mind that perhaps there was more to the unexpected arrival of this daughter of Lord Bute than was immediately apparent. Certainly it was strange that she should be coming to a land that had despised her father. Why had she not gone to New York, which was firmly occupied by the British?

Still, he reflected, James Iredell was his staunch friend and—at the moment—his guest. He could say nothing, only think. It was inconceivable that the lady would have politics different from her father's. It was quite conceivable that she should appear at this crucial period of the war for no good to the Americans fighting for independence.

The voice of the Duc de Braille put an end—mercifully, Johnstone thought—to these dark forebodings he had indulged in far too long.

"She was the famous—or infamous—Lady Percy," the Duc was saying to Raoul de Polignac. "You remember the notorious case in London when the Duke of Northumberland divorced her?"

"Sh! The Judge will hear you," his companion said warningly.

De Braille dropped his voice. "I do not want that, but can you imagine what will happen in this quiet village when that worldly beauty arrives?"

"She may have changed now that she is the Baroness von Poellnitz."

De Braille laughed. "Can the leopard change its spots? Leopardess, I should say."

Judge Iredell was hurrying his wife down the front steps. "Come, Hannah, we must make haste to greet the Baroness when she steps on the dock. We want to make her welcome to America."

"Your brother did not sound very enthusiastic about her," Hannah Iredell said. "He only said she was a beautiful woman used to adulation from men."

De Braille smiled cynically. "I wouldn't miss this for anything, Raoul. That woman will have the whole village by its ears before this week is out. Trouble follows her like a dark cloud wherever she goes."

Silently Samuel Johnstone agreed with him, as he followed James and Hannah Iredell to their chaise to bid them boodbye.

Hannah turned to her brother. "I don't think I shall like her," she said.

"It is not like you to prejudge a person, Hannah," Johnstone said for Iredell's sake, though the hypocrisy of the remark stung his Scotch conscience even as he spoke.

"We shall soon see," his sister said enigmatically. "We shall see."

By the time the Iredells arrived at the dock, the *Free Eagle* had anchored at the Dram Tree off the Point in Edenton Bay. A dozen small boats, manned by skillful Negro oarsmen, had clustered around the ship to take off the passengers. The Edentonians on the dock had already heard that James Iredell's beautiful kinswoman was among them, and were talking of their eagerness to see her.

The chaise stopped near where old, doddering Thomas Barker and his wife Penelope were standing. Barker had formerly been North Carolina's agent in London. He croaked to James Iredell that he had known Von Poellnitz when the Baron was Chamberlain to the King of Prussia. He and his wife wished to entertain the visitors in their home.

Penelope Barker was accustomed to having her own way in Edenton. "It would be a pity," she said, "to have royalty stay at Horniblow's tavern when we have ample room in our own house!"

James Iredell demurred. "The best suite at the tavern has already been engaged, Mrs. Barker. Besides, the visitors are not royal, only of the nobility. I have had a letter from England concerning them. It will be a large party. Besides the Baron and Baroness there will be the Baron's two boys, aged thirteen and fifteen, the Baroness' woman and the Baron's valet. Six in all."

Penelope Barker was slightly taken aback by the size of the party, but she recovered quickly. "We could manage by sending the servants out. You know, James, Mr. Barker is quite used to the habits of nobility. We could make them comfortable."

James Iredell smiled. "No doubt, no doubt, Mrs. Barker. But the Baroness' sister is the wife of my uncle, Lord Macartney, which makes us almost kin, doesn't it?"

"It is too bad that you and Hannah have such a small house or you could entertain them yourself."

James had no time to answer. The rowboat that held the Baron and Baroness had touched the dock. James hurried down the plankway to greet the visitors.

The blond Baron von Poellnitz hunched in front of the strong oarsman. In the stern, as erect as royalty, sat Lady Anne Stuart, Baroness von Poellnitz.

The Edentonians at the dock saw only her uncovered mass of red-gold hair, dressed in the latest London fashion, with a monstrous high pompadour brushed back from her broad forehead. Long curls lay over her ears and down the back of her neck. They did not notice the look of disdain that crossed her features, for it was gone in an instant. As the boat neared the dock they saw that her face had a pure classic look, with a long straight nose and arched brows plucked to a thin line. Her lips were curved and slightly sensuous. Her low square bodice of puce taffeta revealed the voluptuous curve of her breasts, only half concealed by her lace modesty. Her large hazel eyes darted here and there, from the small white houses of the little village to the watchers at the dock.

The Baron got to his feet in the bow of the boat. He was a tall Saxon, seemed much older than his wife, but aristocratic, too, in appearance, and he wore fashionable nankeen breeks and an embroidered coat with silver buttons. The Baron's lads were in the second rowboat with the servants. They were fine-looking children who favored their yellow-haired father.

"Look at the little darlings sitting with the servants," Hannah Iredell exclaimed. "I don't like that. They should be beside their father."

"Hush, Hannah. They will hear you."

"I don't care if they do!"

James Iredell pressed forward to the edge of the dock, but before he reached the landing place, the innkeeper Horniblow was at the boat, bowing deeply. "Baron, your carriage is waiting to take you to the tavern."

While the Baron was acknowledging Horniblow's courtesy, the Baroness arose with dignity. Extending her hand to her husband, she stepped from the boat. The Baron was too far away to reach her. Her foot missed the planking and plunged into the water. The Baron got to her just in time to prevent her from toppling backward into the boat.

"Damn you for a clumsy oaf!" she cried. Her voice was loud. The crowd at the dock looked from one to the other. The Baron's fair skin reddened perceptibly.

"I'm sorry," he murmured. "Let me assist you to the carriage."

Lady Anne put her hand lightly on the arm of the innkeeper. "You may show me to the carriage," she said.

She walked swiftly down the planked dock, her taffeta skirts billowing behind her. The Baron followed, repeating his apologies, leaving the children to get into the luggage wagon with the servants.

The tavern ordinary was crowded with merchants, drovers, yeomen and townsfolk when the Von Poellnitz family went through the hall on their way up the wide stair to the suite that had been engaged for them.

The Baroness stood in the middle of the drawing room and looked about her critically. But she could find no fault with the crisp white ruffled curtains or the gay chintz covering for the split-hickory chairs and settee, which had been made by the mountain folk. Braided grass rugs covered the floor, giving the room a cool summery look. A fresh breeze from the water added to the comfort of the room. Beyond was a balcony overlooking the Green and Albemarle Sound.

"I like this," Lady Anne said to the waiting innkeeper. "Please have my luggage put in my chamber, the Baron's in the opposite rooms."

"The children?" Horniblow asked.

"Let them sleep down the hall. They make too much noise for me when they wake in the morning. I want my woman Dawkins in my dressing room, the Baron's valet in his."

The Baron came into the room. "My dear, is everything to your satisfaction?"

Lady Anne had forgotten her ill temper. "I've just told Horniblow that the room is charming. Call my woman, Baron. I want a bath—hot. I haven't had a decent bath since I left the Islands."

There had been no time for James Iredell to welcome the guests to Edenton. He turned away. Hannah walked by his side without words. She could have said "I told you so," but she knew this was not the moment. She knew there would be plenty of time to express her views on Lady Anne.

At half after eight that evening James Iredell lighted his carrying lantern and walked the short distance to Horniblow's. He cut through the stable yard in the back court and came in at the side door. Two of the townsmen were playing backgammon, others were throwing darts. Everyone greeted Iredell with enthusiasm.

"What luck you have, James!" Charles Johnson said. "A beautiful woman sails into our midst and, behold, you are her kinsman! How do you do it?"

Iredell grinned. "I always told you the Macartneys are a lucky clan."

"But to extend so far . . ." Stephen Cabarrus said. "What is Lady Percy like?"

"She's no longer Lady Percy but the Baroness von Poellnitz."

"I know. But everyone calls her Lady Anne. I suppose she is a devout monarchist."

James Iredell shook his head. "I'm sure Baron von Poellnitz is deeply concerned about our American freedom. He wants to buy land and to live here. As his wife, Lady Anne, of course, thinks as he does."

Stephen Cabarrus smiled at Iredell. "I fancy the Baroness has a mind of her own, Jemmy."

Iredell did not answer. He made his way upstairs in the direction of the Baron's suite. Baron von Poellnitz answered the door himself. The remains of the evening meal were on the center table. Two small King Charles spaniels were lapping milk from a silver bowl on the floor.

James mentioned his name.

"Come in, sir," the Baron said. "I must beg you to excuse my costume—or, rather, my lack of one. I removed my coat because of the heat." He walked across the room, picked up his blue nankeen coat and slipped it on.

The two shook hands, "Please sit down, Judge Iredell. I apologize for not calling my wife. She has already retired. She is worn out by a long tiresome day."

Iredell explained that he merely wanted to pay his respects. He indicated his relationship to Lord Macartney.

"Yes?" the Baron said with interest. "I did not know. So, my wife's sister is your aunt by marriage. I am sure Lady Anne will be happy to know this."

Iredell thought that the Baroness was undoubtedly well aware of this fact, but he said nothing. Von Poellnitz asked a few questions about the farming around Edenton. Iredell gathered from his questions that agriculture was the Baron's real interest.

"I suggest you talk to Samuel Johnstone or Charles Johnson. They both have considerable plantations in Chowan County. They will answer you more sensibly than a mere lawyer who doesn't own a solitary plantation."

When James Iredell left, he was impressed by the Baron and his deep interest in the land. The Carolinians would like that. They were land lovers themselves. He had told the Baron he would introduce him to Adam Rutledge when Adam came back from Williamsburg, where he had gone on some secret war mission.

Hannah made no comment when James told her he had not met the Baroness, but she smiled a little secret smile. She well knew her James held women in high esteem, and beautiful women had an especial niche. She admitted to herself that Lady Anne was certainly beautiful.

Late the following afternoon, Iredell locked the door to his office and made his way along the short cut behind the tavern to his house on Church Street. He was weary from a hard day's work on legislative matters, and he wanted nothing so much as a hot cup of Hannah's fine China tea. When he walked across the long gallery before his house he heard women's voices. If he could have retreated he would have gone around the house to the kitchen, where he knew old Janie would be brewing tea for the servants.

But Hannah heard his step and came to the door. She was wearing a pale gray muslin bordered in rose, one of her better gowns. "Come in, James. You are just in time for tea," she said in her best company voice. "We have guests."

Sitting across the room on the yellow satin settee were the Baroness and her husband. The Baroness put her delicate china cup on the table and extended her slim hand for James Iredell to kiss, while the Baron rose to his feet. James performed the act as though he kissed ladies' hands every day, and turned to greet the Baron.

The Baroness engaged his attention. "I am all apologies, Mr. Iredell. I would have slipped on a negligee if I had known it was you calling last night." She smiled engagingly. "But I was exhausted by the trip. After my hot bath, the bed looked so inviting that I got into it at once."

"James was really disappointed," Hannah said.

"He has been interested in you and the Baron ever since he received his brother Arthur's letter."

The Baroness' mobile face clouded ever so slightly. "It is well not to break the home ties. Too many people do that. Does Arthur write to you often?"

"Quite often," Hannah answered. "Great long detailed letters sent though Holland with all the London and country gossip. Just now Arthur is in Bath. He writes amusingly about the people who are taking the waters."

Lady Anne shot a quick glance at Hannah. "I dare say. Bath is always filled with interesting people in the season."

She turned at once to James and began talking of her sister, Lord Macartney's wife. Hannah rang for fresh tea. A moment later Stephen Cabarrus with Marianne, the Duc de Braille and Raoul de Polignac came to the door.

Lady Anne's face brightened after the introductions. She devoted herself to the foreign visitors, speaking to them in elegant Parisian French. Young Raoul was enthralled with her beauty, her gaiety and the fact that he could speak with her in his native tongue instead of stumbling through a conversation in unfamiliar English. De Braille seated himself near Hannah and the Baron, and began to talk to the Baron about the countryside.

Hannah was in her element, dispensing hospitality. In her quiet way she saw that everyone was comfortable and well served—a dollop of rum for the men's tea, which Lady Anne took also; a slice of lime for the ladies or a bit of milk if they preferred. As she glanced about the room, she thought that even in London there could not have been better conversation. Lady Anne would have no cause for complaint at the back-country manners of Edenton.

Marianne Cabarrus, seeing young Raoul's expression of adoration, moved over and joined the conversation between him and Lady Anne. Lady Anne looked up in surprise. "Where did you learn to speak such perfect French, Mrs. Cabarrus?"

"In France, where I was born."

"Oh, I did not understand. I thought you were an American."

"So I am."

"And your husband?"

"He was born in Spain."

Raoul said: "Stephen is the nephew of the great Spanish banker Cabarrus, who befriended Benjamin Franklin."

"Really?" said Lady Anne in a flat voice.

Her tone produced a dead silence in the room. Even de Braille and the Baron stopped talking, as if infected by it.

Lady Anne held her teacup motionless at the level of her breast. She looked straight before her, her chin high, her head poised imperiously.

Unwillingly sensing his duty as a host, James Iredell made a lame attempt to ease the atmosphere. "Lady Anne is English," he said bluntly.

Hannah and Marianne continued to stare at the teacups in their laps.

"But she is married to a Prussian," Raoul faltered, realizing it was he who had inadvertently caused the gaffe. Then, gathering assurance, he added charmingly: "A lady takes on her husband's country when she marries. Is not that true, Madame Cabarrus?"

Lady Anne's eyes flickered toward him for an instant, as if she recognized his gallantry and might possibly be grateful for it.

Marianne Cabarrus was attempting to reply to Raoul, but Lady Anne cut her short:

"Indeed so," she said. "As a Prussian I could enter your colony without trouble." She gave a faintly disdainful emphasis to the word "colony."

The general embarrassment penetrated even to the Baron. "The devil you say, my dear! I had trouble indeed getting you in. If we had not come from a French port in a French ship, I doubt if I could have managed it."

"Perhaps it would have been as well if you hadn't," Lady Anne snapped.

Everyone began talking at once. Marianne rose to her feet. "Dear Hannah, we must be going to Pembroke. We are having an early supper tonight. Stephen is going over to Hayes for some kind of conference of the Edenton men. I believe some visitors have come down from the North with news of the war."

Lady Anne rose also. "Ah, the war! I had quite forgotten that there is a war. We are so far away from it here in the country."

"Not as far as you think," Stephen Cabarrus said seriously.

When the guests had gone, Hannah said, "Have you had news from Williamsburg, Jemmy?"

"A few rumors only. It is said that General Washington is near there with his troops. He made a forced march down from New York, and may surprise everyone by his next move. No one knows just what he will do, but one thing is certain, the British will be surprised."

Hannah threw her arms about her husband's neck. Tears glistened in her gray eyes. "Oh, Jemmy, Jemmy, I'm sure General Washington will defend us. I hope this war will soon be over—it's been so long and tragic, with brother killing brother, a civil war as terrible as in the days of Cromwell."

"I am afraid we will have some hard times yet," Iredell said, putting his arm about her.

Hannah drew back. "I hope Cornwallis is not coming, or that traitor, General Arnold."

"Not Cornwallis, my dear. He is pinned down on the peninsula."

"Or Tarleton or that terrible Craig coming up from Wilmington. I don't want to run to Bertie County the way the others did the last time the British came this way."

"You won't have to run. I promise you that Samuel Johnstone says we do no good to run. What he says, I believe."

"You do worship my brother, don't you, Jemmy?"

James Iredell nodded. "He is the wisest, most astute man in the colony of North Carolina."

Hannah kissed her husband lightly on the cheek. "That includes Caswell and Wylie Jones?"

Iredell nodded. "Caswell, Wylie Jones, Davies, Hooper, Williamson and all the others! Come, my dear, please see that I have an early dinner. I want to get over to Hayes before the others. I have some things to discuss with Sam."

Hannah held his arm to detain him a moment. "Sam may be the most important man in North Carolina, but I notice it is James Iredell he leans on for advice."

"Nonsense, that is wives' talk."

But Hannah saw that her husband was pleased at her praise.

After James had departed, she remembered that he had said nothing about Lady Anne. She thought, too, of Marianne and her expression when she saw Raoul sitting beside the Baroness, a look of bemusement on his transparent face. Marianne was knowledgeable, she did not intend to have her young inexperienced guest walk into the spider's web. Her action gave Hannah satisfaction. Now there would be two of them who did not trust the London beauty.

III

The Rising of a Tide

The war did not greatly disturb the little village of Edenton for it was no nearer the war itself than it had ever been. But North Carolina had suffered severe shocks. Torn by domestic troubles and the battle of Tories against Whigs—finance disorganized; her fields laid waste; houses destroyed by friends and foes; and her laws threatened. While the enemy was not on her soil her sons were fighting to the north and to the south. Yet the movements of the armies of each side caused apprehension on the one hand and hopefulness on the other. Some husbands had sent their womenfolk over Albermarle Sound to the safety and security of Windsor, in Bertie County, but most families remained intact, waiting eagerly for the arrival of aid from France.

The French! They were the unknown factor. Benjamin Franklin had worked hard as American Ambassador to persuade the French to take up the rebel cause in earnest. When the Spanish banker Cabarrus had listened to Franklin's pleas for help, the tide had turned, and many a Frenchman following the lead of Lafayette had sailed to America to fight for freedom in America.

The British general in the South, Lord Cornwallis, had moved out of Wilmington a month ago, in July. After his defeat—though the astute Cornwallis called it a victory—at Guilford Court House on March 15, 1781, he had had to retreat with his tattered, disrupted army to Wilmington, North Carolina, to restore the morale of his troops and whip them into a fighting force again. Now that Cornwallis was in Virginia, he could expect help from General Clinton, whose troops were in the North, around New York. In his heart, however, Lord Cornwallis had little hope for help from General Clinton. Clinton hated him personally, and more than once had intimated that Cornwallis had a soft spot in his heart for the Americans. Had he not stood on his feet before Parliament and pleaded the American cause in the matter of the Stamp Act? He and William Pitt had spoken for the colonies with vigorous voices. That was before Cornwallis had been ordered to America to take part in the fight of subduing the colonies.

Now if the French fleet could only arrive in time, they would be a mighty force against the land forces.

The rumors of the French fleet reached Edenton through Pierce Butler, who kept up a lively correspondence with James Iredell. He wrote from Philadelphia: "The last vessels from France bring accounts of twenty sails of the line and eight thousand troops that have sailed from France to the Islands."

Iredell pocketed the letter, and walked across the lane to Horniblow's tavern, where he knew he would find Sam Johnstone playing at backgammon with Stephen Cabarrus. He wanted to bring them the cheering tidings of the French fleet. Even if it were only at the West Indies it could be moved up the coast handily, a deterrent to the cruising British ships of the line that guarded the coast.

When Iredell entered the common room he discovered the powdered, bewigged heads of Johnstone and Cabarrus bent over a table in the far corner of the room, near a window that looked out on the Green. They did not notice his approach until he drew up a chair beside them. He waited in silence until Sam Johnstone took note of his presence.

"Ah, James, what information have you now? I

know by your air of suppressed excitement that you are the bearer of news. Is it good or bad?"

"Good, sir." He took the letter from the tail of his coat. "Here, sir, read what Pierce Butler has to say." Johnstone read aloud:

> We hear there has been an engagement in the West Indies between the Comte de Grasse and Sir Samuel Hood, in which de Grasse gained a considerable advantage, having sunk one eighty-four-gun ship, run one ashore and taken two frigates! One British ship of the line blew up. This account is from the French minister's secretary in Baltimore. It is also reputed that the French and Spanish fleets from Europe are arrived at the Cape and that they are going against Jamaica with 35,000 men. How this account got here, I do not know. The British cruisers and privateers are so vigilant that they have taken about every vessel that tried to come into Philadelphia. In three months there have not been six arrivals here.
>
> The Vermonters begin to be really troublesome. They have lately confined a sheriff belonging to the state of New York for doing his duty. They refuse to release him. A committee from Congress is now sitting on the affairs of Vermont. I am of the opinion that spirited measures will bring these gentry to their senses. Their conduct gives too much reason for suspecting some of them to be under the influence of British gold.

Johnstone handed the letter to Stephen Cabarrus with the remark that the North would do nothing to ease the situation between the North and the South. "Butler is right, British gold is finding its way into the pockets of some unworthy Congressmen."

Cabarrus fingered his checkers thoughtfully. The furrow between his eyes deepened. "I can't understand," he said, "a man who calls himself a man selling out his country for money."

"You are young, Stephen," Iredell said. "I would be the last to induce you to think differently, but gold has an untold fascination for some men—more than friends, more than reputation, more than honor itself, they crave gold."

Johnstone spoke solemnly. "The thing I don't like is this division in the colonies. The North aligned against the South. It will lead to continued bad feeling. That is not good. Our basic interests are the same. We are fighting for freedom, both North and South. England would like nothing better than to have us divided. They have a saying, 'Divide and rule.' We don't want that to happen."

James Iredell talked to his wife Hannah that night as they readied themselves for bed. The night was warm. The crickets chirping in the pecan trees foretold hot weather. They walked out on the upper balcony to look at the Sound over the treetops. The full moon rippled like silver on the still waters, making a long path from the shore, broken only by a floating log. The war seemed far away. Nothing seemed real. Even life itself was illusive. James put his arm about his wife's slender body.

"We two, Hannah, only we two in this magic world, we and our love."

She leaned against his shoulder. "Dear James, we have everything, each other and our happiness."

"I am almost afraid to speak of our good fortune," he said.

Hannah's arms tightened around James' shoulders. "Oh, Jemmy, I have you. I want to keep you close to me day and night. If only this war would end, this cruel, cruel war."

Hannah stayed long awake after she had climbed into their high bed, thinking of how James had been fascinated by the beauty of the English woman who had come to Edenton. A phrase from Pierce Butler's letter, which James had read to her, came suddenly into her mind—"British gold." James was too easy on the Tories. She thought of the terrible plight of their friends, the Hoopers.

When Hooper had gone to Wilmington he found that his wife and child had been expelled by the British commander there, Captain Craig, whose cruel order had given them no time to gather their things together. The British had carried off all their furniture. The whole place had been looted, feather beds slashed, one hundred valuable books of Hooper's library carried away; the few that were left behind, mutilated.

When Hooper finally found his wife she told him a harrowing story. When she first tried to leave Wilmington Mrs. Hooper secured a boat and a couple of men to row it, but the soldiers discovered her. Craig himself came down to the river and ordered her to leave the boat and come ashore. Several British officers present protested so violently in her favor that Craig was obliged to reverse his order and allow her men to row off, up the Cape Fear River.

When they were ten miles upriver, Mrs. Hooper ordered the boat to land. Weak as she was, she got out, accompanied by a ten-year-old colored boy. She found a farmer who let her have two horses and a wagon, and then she started on the long journey to Hillsborough through a hostile country. She got through, and Hooper walked seventy miles following her until he finally overtook her not far from their house in Hillsborough.

What, Hannah thought, if something like that were to happen to her!

With that Lady Anne—that *Baroness*—in the village, the British might descend upon them there in Edenton, lured by some fellow-villager who had been corrupted by the wicked Lady Anne's gold. Good heavens, it might even be her own James . . .

In terror she shook him awake. "James, what is that kinswoman of yours doing in Edenton?"

James mumbled sleepily, but not ill-naturedly. She repeated her question.

"She has come with her husband, of course," he said distinctly and a little testily now. "Would you have it otherwise?"

"I would have her far away, yes. She does not appear to me so loyal to her husband as to follow him across the ocean out of faithfulness alone."

"For what other reason then?"

Hannah sighed. "I wish I knew. I distrust her, Jemmy. I fear she may be a spy."

"The Baron would not countenance that. He is most loyal to our interests. Bésides, what could one woman do?"

"She is very beautiful, James."

"A spy must be more than beautiful."

"So you admit she is beautiful?"

James laughed. "Of course. But does that make her wicked?"

"Poor James, you are so straightforward yourself. You cannot see that not all others are like you."

James turned on his side. "I am a lawyer, my dear. I see before me every day the deviousness of us mortals. But I do not fear the Lady Anne."

"They are not all beautiful," Hannah said.

But James' regular breathing told her he had not heard her. She sighed, and murmured a prayer that her James would not be blinded by the Baroness' blandishments. Then she closed her eyes and turned to keep the moonlight from her face lest it enter her mind and cause her evil.

At Pembroke the Cabarrus family sat on the balcony watching the moon shimmering in the lazy waters of Pembroke Creek. The pocosin in John's Island was black against the sky, black and mysterious, spelling evil.

Marianne shivered as she watched the moon path break against the island. She said, "She is wicked, a wicked woman, Stephen."

He started at her words and said, "Who? Who is wicked, dear one?"

She turned her dark eyes on him. "Why, the Baroness von Poellnitz. Who else?"

Stephen brought his thoughts back from the war. He looked at his wife in complete surprise. "What are you talking about, my dear? I thought the Baroness beautiful and charming."

"Oh, you men. You see nothing but the surface. I tell you she is wicked, wicked. Did you not see now she affected poor Raoul? He was like a bird charmed by a viper. The woman is evil, I tell you. She will fascinate the poor young fellows of no experience. She would not try her blandishments on a man of the world like you, Stephen."

Stephen's eyes twinkled. "Not when I have you to guard me, my dear."

In Penelope MacLaine's bedroom at Cupola House the next morning the three Penelopes were holding an informal meeting. "The Three Pennys," some villagers called them, but Penelope MacLaine, the niece of Dr. Armitage, who was staying with her aunt while the good doctor was caring for the sick and wounded at Williamsburg Hospital, preferred the title of "The Night Watch." She and Penelope Blair, and Penelope Cabarrus, had come to Edenton, so they believed, for no other purpose than to protect the female members of the family if the males should go off to the war.

Of an age, they were different in character and looks. Penelope Cabarrus was dark, olive-skinned and of a sanguine temperament. Penelope Blair was as quiet as her mother, Hannah Iredell's sister, was lively. She was blond, blue-eyed, even in disposition and serene. Penelope MacLaine was a fiery redhead, impulsive, out-spoken, with a quick tongue and temper, tenacious and possessed of all the stubbornness of her Highland ancestors. Together they led the activities of the Edenton young people with a high hand. Half the youths of the village followed their lead.

The subject under discussion among them at the moment was not the progress of the war, but the ball which the French visitors were to give in the Panel Room of the Court House the following Friday night.

"I never heard of such a thing," Penny Blair said. "It is certainly not according to tradition for men to give a ball."

Penny MacLaine said: "All Frenchmen are a little crazy. But isn't Raoul the sweetest thing? So handsome! I am glad he doesn't powder his hair or wear a wig. His dark curls are beautiful."

"I think you have lost your head over him," Penny Blair said. "Are you going to the ball?"

In one breath both of the other girls said: "Of course we are. Aren't you?"

"My aunt says 'No,' but I haven't made up my mind. It's so strange to invite us. Why, they haven't even drunk yaupon with us. I don't think the ball is good manners."

Penny Cabarrus interrupted. "French etiquette is different. My Aunt Marianne says it is quite good style for strangers to give some form of entertainment. These Frenchmen are of the highest society in Paris. They are of the nobility. They couldn't be unmannerly if they wanted to be. You are being quite countrified, Pen."

Penny Blair pouted. "I am not. Edenton is famous for its fine entertaining of strangers. I think you are being quite snobbish, Penny. It's just because some of the men are at your aunt's house."

Penny MacLaine clapped her hands together sharply. "Girls, girls, no quarreling! Of course we are all going to the ball. Wild horses couldn't keep us away. The big problem is what are we going to wear."

Penny Blair gave way. "All right, what are you going to wear? I haven't a rag."

Penny Cabarrus said, "They have the most beautiful brocades at Smith and Hewes' store. They came in on the ship from France on Saturday. Uncle Stephen says I may have a bolt. He says the Frenchmen have such fine clothes he doesn't want us to look countrified."

The two other girls showed their enthusiasm. "Have they any peach-colored silk?" Penny Blair asked. "I'd love to have peach over pale yellow. It would be lovely over my new farthingale to hold it out."

"Of course you would plan something to go with your blond hair and put us all in the shade," Penny MacLaine cried. "I dare you to try to bedazzle Captain Raoul. He is mine, for I saw him first."

Penelope Cabarrus tapped on the top of the dressing table with an ivory comb. "Girls, girls, no quarreling! We must work together as a unit or else the other Edenton girls will capture these delightful French officers. Remember Mary Blount and Mary Copeland are pretty girls."

"Mary Blount is engaged to Andrew Davenport from across the Sound."

"No longer," Penny Cabarrus cried. "Mary told me last night that she never wished to speak to him again."

"They are always quarreling. What was it over this time?" Penny MacLaine asked.

"He tried to kiss her in the boat when they were out fishing."

The girls laughed. "I don't blame her. A boat is no place for kissing and hugging," Penny Blair said.

"No matter," Penny Cabarrus continued. "Mary is a charmer. We had better watch out for her. She will be dangerous if she has lost her lover. But have any of you seen the new woman at Horniblow's, the Baroness von Poellnitz? There is a real danger, for they say she is a beauty and attracts men like Circe."

The two girls were at once filled with gloom. "What chance has a girl against a beautiful married woman?"

"She's not only beautiful," Penny Cabarrus continued, "but she is a fashionable London hostess, and, most important of all, she is Lord Bute's daughter."

"What is Lord Bute's daughter doing in America?" Penny Blair exclaimed. "We are at war with England, doesn't she know?"

"But she is married to a German who is greatly interested in America."

"I wish these high-born, titled people would stay at home and keep their wives at home," snapped Penny Blair.

"Well, we will have to do the best we can." Penny Cabarrus spoke with decision. "Come, let's go to Smith and Hewes' store and look at the brocades and laces that came in on the French ship."

As they trooped down the narrow curved stair, Penny Blair had the last word. "It is all right for Captain Meredith to bring in satins and silks and laces from France, but I wish he would leave beautiful married women in their own countries."

In the common room at Horniblow's tavern other matters were being discussed. Dr. Williamson, who had arrived that morning from his hospital in the Dismal, was talking to Iredell, Cabarrus and Samuel Johnstone. Dr. Williamson was a big man, inclined to be blustery and, at times, rather domineering. As he addressed Iredell his voice was unnecessarily loud.

"The Articles of Confederation, I say this with reverence, are not infallible. Congress has reserved the powers of making treaties, and yet has not reserved any power over commerce. We borrow money and have not the means of paying sixpence. There is no measure, however wise or necessary, that may not be defeated by a single state, however small or wrong-headed. The clouds of public creditors, including the army, are gathering about us. The prospect thickens."

Williamson banged the table, jingling the glasses of rum.

"Belive me that I would rather take the field in any hospital military service I ever saw than face the difficulties we must meet in government in the next few months. At least, in my field hospital, I can do something to alleviate suffering. I have fervently desired peace. Whoever goes in the delegation I shall not envy his station. I shall wish him patience, diligence and a good deal of political knowledge.

The men around the table were silent. Iredell thought the doctor was at his best when he reviewed the affairs of government.

He said, "Pray God, they serve our country with the vigor and intelligence that you have.

Williamson glanced up. "Thank you, James, thank you."

They fell to talking then about the news from New Bern which Archibald MacLaine had brought on his arrival yesterday.

Iredell said: "I hear that a large Jamaican brought in a cargo of rum and of sugar. Half a ton of gunpowder was concealed in the hold. The ship has run the blockade into New Bern successfully."

"They say there were passengers from New York," Williamson said. He paused and looked over his shoulder, then waved to the tall man who stood in the doorway. "Here is Archibald MacLaine himself."

MacLaine joined them. After he had ordered a rum from the boy with the leathern apron he answered their questions.

"Yes, the Jamaican had passengers—officers who have been paroled and are bound for New York. Lord Charles Montague, his son Captain Montague, and four other officers. It is said they have written the Governor for permission to travel north, but no reply has come yet. I heard that General Greene treated them with all civility. They may travel by land or water to any British port on the continent or to Europe or the West Indies. I hope you will treat them as well when they arrive in Edenton as they were treated in New Bern. Lord Charles is a man of plain and easy manners."

He turned to Iredell. "James, Lord Charles told me he was well acquainted with your kin, Earl Macartney, and was anxious to meet you and your family."

"I shall be pleased to be of service to Lord Charles. Shall we engage rooms for the party here?"

"That has already been attended to," MacLaine said. "I talked with Horniblow last night. It seems he is pressed for good rooms. The best suite has been taken by the Baron von Poellnitz."

Johnstone, who had been sitting quietly, now spoke. "If I remember rightly, Lord Charles is a cousin of the Duke of Northumberland, the Baroness' former husband. I wonder if he will fancy seeing the Baroness."

The men looked at one another. Stephen Cabarrus said, "Ah, we have the makings of a stage play here in our little village!"

James Iredell was troubled. "Do you suppose Lord Charles will annoy that lovely lady on account of the relationship with her former husband?"

"Your brother did not inform you of the scandal, James? According to Thomas Barker, the divorce caused a great stir in London."

Iredell's face grew red. "Thomas Barker is an old gossip. He is envious because the Baron did not bring a letter to him."

"It wasn't the Baron's divorce I was talking about, but the Baroness'," Johnstone said. "Lady Percy, the English people still call her, though she has no right to the title. You might more honestly call her Lady Anne Stuart since she is Lord Bute's daughter."

Iredell looked suspiciously at Sam Johnstone. "You seem to know a great deal about these people."

Johnstone's stern face relaxed into a grim smile. "I have my sources, Jemmy. I have a good deal of knowledge of what goes on, both here in North Carolina and in London."

The party soon broke up. It was a worried James Iredell who walked across the Green to Cullen Pollock's house at the far end facing the curve of Edenton Bay. Perhaps Ann Pollock knew something about the case. She managed to know most of the gossip at home and abroad in spite of the war. But when he rang the Pollocks' bell the old slave, Eph, told him that his master and mistress had taken the pirogue across the Sound to their country house at Balgray.

Iredell continued home slowly, disturbed by what he had heard. Although Hannah had said nothing more about the Baroness von Poellnitz his instinct told him that he had better say nothing to her about the information he had learned from Samuel Johnstone. Sam was no gossip, he knew. There might be some truth in what he had hinted about the beautiful Lady Anne Stuart.

IV

The Frenchmen's Ball

The night of the much-talked-about ball given by the
visiting Frenchmen was one of soft beauty, a night for
romance. The young maids of the village dressed by
candlelight, their hearts beating rapidly in anticipation.
Each one of them thought in her heart that she might be
singled out by one of the fascinating young Frenchmen
for particular attentions. Failing that, there were young
lads of the village and the nearby plantations to draw
from. Everyone knew that a starry sky and soft music
turned men's minds and thoughts toward love—if not
serious love, then a stolen kiss or two when they walked
under the shadowy trees on the Green or along the verge
of the water.

Slave housemaids were called upon to lay out the
most alluring lawns and muslins and brocaded gowns,
ruffled underskirts, fine lace sleeve ruffles, satin shoes of
every color, laced with ribbons or buckled in silver or
rhinestones. Blond and brunnete locks were piled high,
with long curls falling over bare white shoulders. This
was an exciting time, equal to Christmas or Boxing Day.

The Cabarrus family coach driven by old Enoch in
the Cabarrus livery drew up before the Court House
promptly at ten o'clock. Already the streets beside the
Green were crowded with coaches, phaetons and chairs.
The Green itself was jammed with the commonalty, who

had come out of curiosity to watch the elite, to see what costumes the young women (and the old) wore, to comment on the satin and brocade coats of the men. The barber was anxious to see the effect of wigs and hair arrangements he had made; the tailor, to see that the coats he had sewed set well across the shoulders; the seamstress, to be proud of the result of her needlework.

"Ah, ah!" greeted the descent of the Cabarrus women from their coach. Madam Cabarrus was a favorite with the townsfolk for her gracious manner and her interest in people of less good fortune than she. Many a village family knew her kindness in gifts of food, or clothes or toys for children. Childless herself, she had a warm heart for the children for others. Penelope was well liked also for her gaiety and her natural manners. "No uppishness," a farm woman said, "no better-than-you manner in that young woman, God bless her."

"Her Uncle Stephen would not allow her to be high and mighty," said another. "He's a fair plain man himself. He always has a kind word for us folk."

The Cabarrus family walked up the stone steps that led to the Court House and the Panel Room above the main court room. Madam's violet taffeta, over a pale pink underskirt, created comment. "So French," one woman whispered, "so French."

"Why not?" her companion snapped. "Is she not French and does not her fine gown come from Paris?"

"But Julie, there's a war on. How can she get Paris clothes now?"

The woman laughed knowingly. "My Jamie says plenty of goods come in from France and Holland. Run the blockade, they do, at Charleston and on our own coast. But look at little Miss Penny. She's as gay as a spring bouquet in yellow and green. Minds me of a crocus or a daffodil."

The attention of the crowd was diverted as the Cabarrus party entered the broad Court House doors. Several young Frenchmen were arriving on foot from Horniblow's tavern, a scant hundred yards away. Their satin coats, white doeskin small clothes, silk stockings and high-heeled shoes were as gay as the costumes of the women.

"Godamighty!" a young craftsman said. "Look ye, look ye, how can the foreign men fight in battles with that fine raiment?"

"Zack, silly, they don't fight in such as those. They wear uniforms when they are soldiering."

"Praise be! I thought me that they couldn't go a-sloshing through the swamp dressed thataway."

Family after family arrived at the Court House steps. "There's Sam Johnstone and his lady. He's dressed almost as fancy as the Frenchmen. And look at his lady all in blue."

"There comes the Mulberry Hill Blounts dressed to the nines. Godamighty, Jim, our folks are right up with the Frenchies."

The Blairs and the Iredells arrived together, the ladies being sisters. The arrival of James Iredell brought cheers from the crowd. He was a prime favorite with the villagers. The Creecys were near the last to come, having to drive from Yeopim, where their plantation, Greenfield, was located on the Sound and the Yeopim River.

The last to ride up were two officers in uniform, one in a British uniform and one in blue and buff. A loud clapping of hands greeted them. "Who's that?" an old yeoman asked. "Who causes the people to clap their hands so loudly?"

A boy who had climbed on the Green called out, "It's Rutledge—Colonel Adam Rutledge, and a stranger."

The name swept over the crowd like a whirlwind. Adam Rutledge was here. What did it mean? The end of the war? The people knew that Rutledge of Rutledge Riding was stationed near Williamsburg. What was he doing at home?

As the tall, lean Adam walked up the steps, someone from the crowd called out. "Is the war over, Colonel?"

Adam turned away from his companion to face the

crowd. "No, I'm sorry to say, the war is not over yet."
He waved to the crowd and walked through the door
followed by his unknown companion.

The Panel Room was crowded with a company of
laughing, chattering women and elegantly dressed gentlemen. Chippendale chairs were ranged along the wall,
leaving the polished floor of the long room free for dancers. Before the two fireplaces on either side of the room
were long settees, occupied by some of the dowagers,
whose escorts stood beside them. At the far end of the
room three Negro men—a fiddler, a mandolin-player,
and a very old man with a little drum suspended from
his neck by a thong—were tuning up their instruments
for a minuet.

The Duc de Braille stood near the door to greet the
guests. The younger officers had already found partners
and were taking their places on the floor. The three Pennys had been chosen from the first group along with
Mary Blount. Just as old Elijah scraped a bow on his fid-
dle, the master of ceremonies at the door announced the
Baron and Baroness von Poellnitz. The buzz of conversation died away. Every eye was turned toward the visitors as the Duc de Braille led the Baroness to the dais at
the end of the room.

"He's seating her in the Governor's chair," was the
word that was whispered from one end of the room to
the other.

A suppressed "Ah" from the women folk gave a
reluctant acclaim to the Baroness. "She's a beauty. Look
at her gown! It must have cost fifty guineas! Look how
the men crowd around her! She has a great preference
for young men they say."

The Baroness wore a heavy white satin over a petticoat of ruffled lace. Lace across her bosom did not
hide the voluptuous curves. The pointed basque made
her figure look as slim as a girl's. Her hair was dressed
high in elaborate puffs. Two long curls fell over her
white shoulders. The whole elaborate headdress was
powdered white as snow and seemed to accent her large
hazel eyes. Rouge was high on her cheekbones, and two

black patches were posed on her cheek and chin at the curve of her scarlet lips.

"She looks like the portraits by Raeburn I saw in London," Marianne whispered to Hannah Iredell.

"I think she is the most beautiful woman I have ever seen," was Hannah's reluctant answer. "The most beautiful and the most deadly." Hannah spread her dove-gray taffeta skirt over her buckled shoes.

The music began and the dancers took position, toes pointed, hands held high. One-two-three-four-curtsy. One-two-three-four-curtsy.

Adam Rutledge, of Rutledge Riding, one of the greatest of the plantations on Albermarle Sound, stood in one corner of the Panel Room, surrounded by a group of Edenton men. Of all the inhabitants of the region Adam was perhaps the best known. Ever since his part in opposing Governor Tryon's quit rents, he had been regarded as a hero. Everyone knew how often he had risked his life on behalf of the colonists, how staunch a defender of the land and the landowners he had been, how sadness had tinged his personal life.

Knowing Adam had come from Williamsburg, his friends talked at once, bursting with eagerness to learn what he could report from the nearest seat of war. "What news did you bring?" "Is the war near an end?" "Has Washington taken New York?"

When he had answered their questions he introduced his companion Lord Charles Montague to James Iredell. "Lord Charles is here on parole with letters from General Greene."

Several of the men shook hands with the visitor American-fashion. Others bowed and looked dubious. Johnny Blount was cordial. "I think I met you in London a few years ago at the Kit Kat Club. I was visiting Sir William Hutchison at Woolsey."

Lord Charles smiled. "I remember perfectly. Everyone was eager to meet the young American who was a first-rate cricketer! We thought it quite amazing that an American could master the game."

Iredell waited impatiently while the two men

talked. When there was a lull in the conversation he said to Adam: "Come, I want to present you and Lord Charles to the Baron and Baroness von Poellnitz, our distinguished guests."

Adam started to follow Iredell, but Lord Charles said, "I have already met the Baroness," and turned to continue the conversation with Johnny Blount. Iredell remembered then what MacLaine had told him, that Lord Charles was a friend of the Duke of Northumberland. He devoutly hoped there would be no untoward incident to mar the Frenchmen's ball.

The Baroness von Poellnitz acknowledge the introduction of Adam Rutledge with a regal bending of her head. When she looked up at the tall blond man with quizzical blue eyes, her own deepened with quick interest. She extended a languid hand. Adam raised her hand and brushed it with his lips, amused by the inviting look in her eyes and the quick pressure of her fingers. Then he turned to the Baron.

"Sit beside me, Mr. Rutledge," the Baroness invited. "I am by way of being bored with no one to talk to."

Adam took a chair near her but off the dais. "I can't usurp the Governor's chair," he said smiling, "even to sit beside a beautiful woman."

She smiled at him through the lace of her fan. "I see that you are not a village man," she said. "You are too much of a flatterer. Have you spent much time in New York or Philadelphia?"

Adam ignored the implied compliment. "You are the flatterer, madam. I am a soldier not long from the field, with all of a soldier's lack of elegance."

James Iredell, who had remained standing near the Baron, broke in. "Colonel Rutledge has spent much time in London, Baroness. That was before the war."

"Oh, the war! A very stupid business. Since I have been in America I've begun to wonder if we Tories have not made a mistake in thinking we can subdue you Americans."

"A wise conclusion, Baroness." Adam rose. "I see they are about to form another minuet. I want to dance with your wife, James." He made a deep bow. "Adieu, Baroness. Perhaps you will honor me later.

Baroness von Poellnitz watched Rutledge make his way across the room. "Handsome as a god," she murmured. "Is he married?"

"His wife died some years ago," Iredell answered. "He is at present thinking of Mrs. Mary Warden. His friends would all be happy if he married her."

Lady Anne followed Rutledge with her eyes. "It would be too much to expect a man like to be long free from entanglements. Is the woman you mention here tonight?"

"No. At present she is in Williamsburg, helping at the Army hospital."

"But she will return?"

"That remains to be seen," Iredell said. "She has had tragedy in her life."

"Oh? I suppose she lost her husband in the war?"

Iredell caught the inflection in the beautiful woman's voice. It showed, he thought, too great an interest in the affairs of a person she had never heard of until a few moments ago. And perhaps too great an interest in the affairs of the colony, Adam Rutledge included. He hesitated to answer her.

"Poor soul!" Lady Anne said, as if to pursue the matter. "To be widowed so young! I gather she is yet young. But in your eyes she had a hero for a husband. That must be a consolation."

James Iredell felt her hazel eyes boring into him. He looked into them and found it hard to take his own away. What amazing eyes they were! Still incredibly soft and alluring, yet somehow steely and hypnotic. There was a cold glint in them now that he had not noticed before. Gad, they were eyes that could lure a man's very soul away and cast it into perdition.

He forced himself to look away. "William Warden," he said bluntly, "was hanged as a spy by our General Morgan after the battle of Guilford Court House last March."

He looked back at Lady Anne to see what effect

this solemn announcement of his might have on her. She had not moved. Even her eyelids did not stir. In the hazel eyes beneath them he glimpsed for an instant the glassy paralysis of terror.

Then she lowered her eyes to the fan she held in her lap, tapping it ever so gently against the white satin of her gown.

"I see," she said dully. Then, in a more spirited tone, and looking at Iredell again, her eyes softer, she added: "It is noble of her to work for the wounded."

"I believe it is doing her good," Iredell said. "Mary Warden is not one to permit herself the selfish luxury of grief."

"Then your Mr. Rutledge would be fortunate indeed in winning her." Lady Anne smiled as she added, "Such a woman deserves a better husband than her first."

"He would help her with her plantation. It is a beautiful one called Queen's Gift, on the Sound. She inherited it from her grandfather Roger Mainwairing, a planter of substance. He was exiled after his part in Monmouth's rebellion against Charles II."

"Rebellion seems to run in this colony of yours, Mr. Iredell," said Lady Anne. " 'Tis a grave fault, I hold. Suppose now that you should win this rebellion of yours, would you not in time rebel against the very principles you might have established?"

James Iredell looked at her quizzically. He had not suspected that she might be so quick-witted. He was unused to reasoning in women, particulalry beautiful women. The women of Edenton acted rather than thought, relying on intuition rather than logic, on traditional loyalties and inbred sense of duty rather than on strategy. He cleared his throat as he did when about to interpret a ruling from the bench.

"The law, madam," he said in deadly seriousness, "exists for the protection of the individual's rights and property. When those are violated or endangered, the individual is obliged to protest, even to deny the law that oppresses him."

"La, sir," Lady Anne laughed, "if that's the way you think, I vow you'd change the Ten Commandments."

Her sally brought sparkle to her eyes. There were dimples at the corners of her mouth that the tiny black patches emphasized. She had tossed her head slightly, causing the curls on her shoulder to vibrate provocatively.

Iredell felt his blood warm his cheeks. "I speak of the laws of men, not of God," he stammered.

"Yet men are always trying to improve on God. They waste their time. As Mr. Pope says, 'Whatever is, is right.' "

"Then since there now is what you call a rebellion, my Lady, is not that rebellion right?"

Iredell glanced at the Baroness to see how she might answer his retort, but found that she seemed not to have heard him. Her expression had changed. A look almost of fear was on her face as she stared across the room.

"Who is that man? The one talking to Colonel Rutledge? The one in the British uniform? I can't recognize him from this distance."

"But he said he knew you, Baroness. He is Lord Charles Montague."

Her face was white. "Montague," she whispered, "Montague! Lord Charles," she murmured, "Lord Charles here in Edenton." She rose hurriedly. "Please take me to the supper room, Mr. Iredell. I should like a glass of wine. I feel a little giddy."

In the supper room, Raoul de Polignac hurried over to speak to the Baroness. "Will you do me the honor to tread this minuet with me, my lady? The music is just starting. Don't say no. I shall be desolated if you do not honor me."

Lady Anne tapped the young man's shoulder with her fan. "I really can't dance, my dear Raoul," she said, with a dazzling smile. "I have the beginning of a migraine. Instead of dancing you may bring me a glass of your delightful French wine."

She seated herself in a corner of the supper room from which she could watch the Panel Room for Lord Charles Montague, whom she did not want to meet face to face. She accepted the wine and dismissed James Iredell with a nod. She drank hurriedly, watching all the while.

Presently she said, "Dear boy, I won't dance, but I will allow you to walk me to Horniblow's."

Without pausing she hurried the young Frenchman out of the room. At the head of the stairs she glanced back over her shoulder. "Come, be quick," she said sharply. "Give me your arm. I am terrified of steep stairs."

Without looking into the court room, where many people were seated, she hurried out of the wide door into the street. The night air was cool and sweet after the crowded ballroom.

"Ah, how delightful!" she said, tucking her hand under Raoul's arm. "I detest crowded rooms and a press of people close to me. This is pleasant."

They walked the short distance to Horniblow's and through the deserted common room to the Baroness' rooms upstairs. Her woman, Dawkins, rose from a chair, startled by their sudden appearance. "Your ladyship is home so early. Is there anything wrong?"

"Nothing at all, Dawkins. You may retire. I will not need you."

The woman curtsied and left.

"Come into my sitting room, Raoul. It is more comfortable. I want to get some lotion for my poor head."

They went into the next room, which was more feminine in décor. A chaise longue with pillows was near the windows that gave on the balcony.

"Sit down. I'll be back presently."

Lady Anne went into her bedroom and closed the door. After a time she returned. She had taken off her elaborate white satin gown and was attired in a soft silk negligee, a revealing garment of delicate pink, almost the color of bare flesh. In her hand she held a small bottle.

"Come, dear boy, and stroke my head. This is the only way I can ward off a heavy migraine." She stretched herself out on the chaise longue. "Take off that fine satin coat. It is so elegant I wouldn't want you to spill lavender water and ruin it."

She indicated a stiff chair beside the table that held the candelabra.

Anxious to be of service to the beautiful woman, Raoul did as he was told. He sat down beside Lady Anne.

"You have such wonderful strong hands," she said; "I am sure you can rub this headache away."

After dipping his fingers in the fragrant lotion, he began to stroke her temples. She lay full length on the couch, relaxed. Her robe fell aside, revealing her rounded limbs. The young man, embarrassed, tried to keep his eyes away from her beautiful body, but they returned to her against his will.

Her eyes were closed. "Now the back of my neck," she said after a time, turning to him. "Now in front. Follow down to my bosom." She was breathing more quickly as his fingers touched the division of her breasts. Raoul felt her excitement pass to him. What did she want, this beautiful woman?

Suddenly she threw her arms around his neck. "You are beautiful, my Raoul. Beautiful and strong and so male. You are as male, as strong, as I am female. Kiss me."

Slowly Raoul bent over her, until his lips touched hers. The bottle of scent fell to the floor, forgotten.

Her hands moved to the nape of his neck, pressing his mouth to hers, which stole open until her soft moist lips encircled his. He moved to kiss her eyes, closed under the violet-tinted lids that tasted of the fragrance of lavender. Then her hands were running through the hair at the back of his head, subtly stroking his scalp, sending delicious shivers down his spine and into his loins.

Gently she moved his head until their mouths met once more.

At last she released him, but he could not tear himself away. He covered her neck and bosom with quick, passionate kisses.

"Lie beside me," she whispered. "I need a lover like you. I want the full strength of your love. I am hungry for love, my beautiful boy."

Anticipation of this moment had driven Raoul insane with passion. He heard her moan, felt her bite through the lawn of his shirt into the flesh of his shoulder, but the sharp stab of her teeth only increased his voluptuousness. A shimmering veil of oblivion seemed to descend on them and enwrap them.

Later, as Raoul made his way down the stairs and into the street, his blood was still running high, pounding against his temples. His last act at parting from Lady Anne was to press a lock of her hair against his lips. He was amazed at his own prowess. He felt no melancholy.

Yet a disturbing thought crowded into his mind. Such a lovemaker as Lady Anne must be the graduate of experience. What other men had she loved? How many?

The thought caused him swift, aching pain. How many?

To return to the crowded ballroom would have sickened him. He needed the cool, sweet air from the sound. He walked to the creek where the boats were waiting to row the Cabarruses back to the plantation. Gradually his heart ceased its throbbing.

V

Rutledge Riding

Adam Rutledge with his friend, Captain Cosmo de' Medici, sat on the gallery of his plantation home, Rutledge Riding.

The sun was low on the confluence of Albemarle Sound and the winding yellow Roanoke River. From their position on the side gallery they looked out on the broad fields of the island that formed the plantation. The corn was in tassel. The cotton bolls were beginning to show white. In the bean fields, twenty-five or thirty Negro women were picking beans and dropping them in baskets. They were working in a group, singing as they advanced down the rows, singing a song brought from their home in Nyasaland:

> *Mike pa nandolo, ndri-opa*
> *Chimpembu, Ku-nde-dic*
>
> The bean pods rattle,
> I fear the rhinoceros
> Lest he eat me.

The two men listened to the rhythm of the Bean Song, each with a glass of San Juan rum in his hand. Cosmo said, "Why do the Negroes stay so close together as they work?"

Adam lighted a pipe of tobacco before he answered. "It is an African custom based on the fear of danger from the jungle." He called to his body servant. "Come here, Herk. Why do the women work so close together in the fields, chopping or picking beans?"

The gigantic Zulu man answered, "The Bwana knows. Women fearful creatures. They band together for company. Protect themselves against lion, leopard or rhino, as song say."

"But we have no wild animals here," Adam said.

"Bwana, old custom he die hard. People carry old ways from old home to new. Work same, all time work same."

"What do you mean by that?" Cosmo asked.

"Our land, man works. Woman's have day work. Man till fields, make land ready for to plant. Woman do chopping and carry in crops. Man he hunt. Bring home meat, but woman she lean over cooking fires and make ready food. Woman carry food to men who eat. When man through eating mealies, woman sit and eat. Same in old and new."

"By Jove, that is true. I had never thought about it. The men till the earth but the women cultivate the growing plants. It is a native ritual transferred from the jungle, just as the song they were singing belongs to their old life."

De' Medici said, "Curious, very curious. Do you understand your people, Rutledge?"

Adam laughed. "I do not. Here I live surrounded by native Africans. They know all about me and what I do and where I go. Perhaps they even know what I think. But I know nothing at all about them. Nothing at all."

De' Medici's dark eyes followed the tall muscular figure of Herk, walking as easily and as lightly as some jungle animal.

Adam read his thoughts. "Herk is a Zulu, the son of a paramount chief in his own land. Now he controls all the natives on my plantation. Even here they acknowledge his kingship without question.

"A great help to you, Rutledge."

"Yes, a great help. On the other hand I, too, acknowledge his kingship. I do not ask any menial tasks of him."

A house boy brought fresh drinks. The two men sat watching the sun go down on the rough waters of the Roanoke. The quiet of evening fell upon them. After a time the dressing bell rang. Adam unlimbered his long legs and got to his feet. "We have quiet and peace here on the river. Have you noticed that we haven't mentioned the war for an hour or more?"

Cosmo pushed back his chair and removed his feet from the gallery railing. "War is far away here, very far away, but not too far. Sitting here looking at the river brings thoughts to me of my imprisonment and the losing battle we fought at Lenud's Ferry last year near Charleston."

"I never heard the right of that," Adam said, "only that you and the dragoons were captured and in prison for a year at Hadrell's Point opposite Charleston."

Cosmo's expression changed to one of serious thought. "I was prisoner of the British for the best part of the year. Paroled, of course, as all the ranking officers were. My regret is that it was so unnecessary. The colonel would not listen. He had the idea that the swamps on both sides of the Santee River were our protection. Several of us warned him that although the swamp was almost impassable on the north side of the river, we did not know what the land was on the south. It was swamp all right, but there was hard ground there in the thicket of trees. That was our undoing. Tarleton was waiting for us there. His men attacked as soon as men and horses were unloaded from the ferry. He couldn't have chosen a better time or place. We were intent on getting the horses off."

He paused for a moment to light a pipe. "You can imagine what it was. Horses and men—intent on disembarking—when he opened fire. 'Never underestimate your enemy' is an old military axiom." Cosmo paused again, remembering. "Tarleton is an astute general, Adam. Astute, bold and relentless."

"What is he like really? We hear such tales of him. 'Butcher Tarleton' is the kindest name he's been given."

Cosmo smiled. "War tales you know. It is to his advantage to be feared. As his prisoner I was well treated. He had been often in Florence. He knew my family. He told me once when we were dining at Hadrell's Point that he regretted finding me in the trap he had set for the dragoons. I think he spoke the truth."

Adam said, "How did you bear up under such conditions of confinement?"

Cosmo laughed. "The conditions were ideal, Adam. We were in a beautiful and comfortable private home on the banks of the Ashley River. Across from us were the fortifications of Charleston, Castle Pinckney, Fort Sumter and Fort Moultrie. Just beyond was Sullivan's Island and the open waterway to the Atlantic."

"Did you never think of getting away?"

Cosmo raised his heavy dark eyebrows. He said simply, "I had given my word. I was paroled, you know."

Adam walked to the edge of the gallery and sat down on the rail. "I know, but what I don't know were the conditions of the parole."

"I was forbidden to cross the river into Charleston. Otherwise I could travel for six miles in any direction."

"What good was that? Was there any place to go except down the river to the ocean?"

"You would be surprised," Cosmo said. "There were interesting places in the district they called 'Hungry Neck.' We were on a high bank. In the middle of the river was a sand bar. The ships used the channel on the opposite side of the bar. On our side the fishing and crabbing boats came. They used the seines to drag the river. We went out to help them or we crabbed with a net."

Adam asked the question which he knew would bring back sad memories: "I've never known just what you lost at Lenud's Ferry. How many men and horses?"

Cosmo rose and walked up and down the long gallery. Finally he stopped in front of Adam. "It was a debacle—a horrible debacle. Our men behaved well, but they were in the midst of maddened, frightened horses. Their arms were either in cases on the saddles or still on the ferry. My God, I never saw such confusion! The colonel was on deck, shouting orders no one could hear. The men who were in the saddles were driven into the swamp and bogged down. The British had us in a trap, and the jaws of the trap were sprung before we were aware. Adam, we were over forty miles above Charleston. The colonel could not be convinced that we were in danger at that distance. For green men—boys really— our company was heroic. We lost thirty-six men and two officers, killed. They took seven officers and sixty men prisoners and all the horses."

He paused in his pacing. "Tarleton lost two men." His voice was full of scorn. "Two men only. I shot one of them with my pistol." His face was sad. "The only man I have killed in this war so far. I think I shall never forget the sixth of May 1780."

There was silence. Adam found no words and de' Medici was deep in recollections. Adam did not venture to break the long silence.

After a time Cosmo said, "There were some pleasant aspects to my confinement. Within the six-mile limit of my parole was Snee Farm. It was there that two famous South Carolinians were imprisoned, General Moultrie and the Charlestonian planter Pinckney." He laughed with a gay boyish laugh that lightened his dark Italian features and brought a glint of humor to his large dark eyes. "Many a game of hazard I have played with these two gentlemen. Diced and swum in the lake and stayed overnight at the fine old farm house. A lovely spot set in a grove of live-oaks with Spanish moss drooping from the great trees. A driveway of live-oaks led to the farm, a beautiful entrance, almost the finest I have seen in America."

Adam asked about General Moultrie. "It is said that Lord Charles Montague wrote to him, offering him many honors and much money if he would betray his country."

"That is true. I have heard the general refer to the circumstances many times and the pleasure he had in composing his spirited reply. I can't imagine how Lord Charles could have had so little discrimination. Moultrie is a man of noble character. That he would have betrayed his country was unthinkable. He often said, 'I am no Benedict Arnold.'"

Cosmo sat down again. "But here I have brought war to this quiet spot. Pardon me, my friend. When I think of that useless battle at the ferry and long year that I was paroled I lose all sense of proportion."

"I can well understand," Adam said, "but the dressing bell will ring the second time soon. Perhaps you will want to go to your room."

When they were at supper Captain de' Medici brought up the purpose of his visit, which was to consult Adam about recruiting. He planned to bring his company up to full strength and to buy horses.

Adam said, "I think I can help you. I have three young tenant farmers here who are eager to get into the army. I'll send for them so that you may interview them in the morning."

"Can they ride? You know I want only horsemen."

Adam smiled. "Born in the saddle. Don't you know that all Carolinians are horsemen?"

"Do they have horses?"

"I suppose so. If they haven't, I'll mount them myself. I have plenty. Herk drove all of our horses into the swamp when we thought the British were coming this way, but they didn't come. Cornwallis took the middle road from Wilmington and entered Virginia at Suffolk."

The men had finished dinner and were drinking their port when Dr. Armitage, the beloved doctor of the Edenton folk, rode up the drive. Herk took his horse to the stable himself, to show his respect for the doctor.

The doctor accepted a glass of port. "This is perfect, Adam," he said. "To rest my old bones in an easy chair, glass in hand, and with two friends to listen to my complaints, is something to cheer the soul. I've had so many nights on a damp camp bed, in the Great Dismal, with red bugs itching me and outsized mosquitoes buzzing my ears, I'm ready to appreciate civilized living again."

Adam asked, "It's been pretty bad, Doctor? But I understand you've been doing great work in your hospital."

"You've been talking to Williamson. You'd think there wasn't a hospital in the army to match ours. It's all right for him. He's off in Williamsburg half the time. Besides, when he's at the hospital he is busy trying to work out the reason the soldiers have chills and fever. Me, I just accept the fact that they have the chills every autumn and let it go at that."

Cosmo leaned forward in his chair. "The reason people have the bone breaker—has he a theory? If he did discover the reason he would be blessed by the whole world." He turned to Adam, his dark eyes alight. "You know in Italy we have chills and fever too. It is a menace in the late summer and autumn. I hope he discovers a cure."

Dr. Armitage lighted a clay pipe. "I'm more interested in treating my patients than in why they get sick. I'm not a scientist like Dr. Williamson. I cure their aches and pains when I can. I don't go any further."

Adam smiled. "You're pretty good at that. I'll vouch for you. Remember last year when I had that bout?"

"Do I? I thought I was going to lose you before I could break the fever. As it was, I really think it was Herk's witchcraft that did the work!"

"I was half out of my head," Adam recalled, "but I realized that Herk was making strange incantations and holding some evil-smelling things under my nose. Then I went to sleep."

"And when you awakened the fever had left you, Adam. As I said, I believe it was Herk who cured you."

The doctor turned to de' Medici. "You've been in

the thick of the armies about Williamsburg. Do you believe we are nearing the end of the war?"

De' Medici hesitated. "I'm not sure, of course, but
I have on good authority that General Washington will
send help to Virginia. If the French fleet under de
Grasse comes to the Chesapeake, then Cornwallis will
be on his own. I feel sorry for that general. He is an excellent officer, but General Clinton will never back him
up, even at the risk of losing the war. Clinton won't listen to Cornwallis' plea for men or ships."

Adam Rutledge spoke. "That's the best news I
have heard since the beginning of the war in Virginia.
With Washington, Lafayette and de Grasse we really
have a chance of victory. I am glad to hear you say that
about Cornwallis. I've always felt that he has been shab-
bily treated by the high command."

Dr. Armitage said, "Well, we'll all be back near the
camp at Yorktown before the week is out. Then we will
know what is going on."

Herk stood in the doorway. "Bwana, strangers on
horseback come up the avenue."

Adam glanced out the window. "It's almost dark.
Light a lantern and bring the visitors in."

He went to the veranda to greet his guests. He recognized the Baron von Poellnitz, followed by a groom.
Adam walked down the steps to greet the Baron.

"I am all apologies, Mr. Rutledge," the Baron said.
"We lost our way coming home after a trip to Tyrell
County to look at land. Some of your people showed us
the way to Rutledge Riding. I am afraid I must beg for
shelter for the night."

"You are more than welcome at Rutledge Riding,
Baron, if you can put up with bachelor fare."

An hour later, the Baron, well fed, with a glass of
port in his hand, began to question Adam on matters
pertaining to the plantation. Dr. Armitage excused himself. "I suppose I have my usual room, Adam?"

"Yes. Take a candle from the table in the hall to
light you. I think the house boys have gone to the quarters line."

"Never fear, I know my way. Gentlemen. good night. I leave you to discussions of soils and fertilizers." He left the room amid laughter.

The Baron said, "This is harvest time, is it not, Mr. Rutledge?"

"Yes, beans, peas and corn. Next week we begin tobacco, and next month we pick cotton and peanuts."

"Peanuts—I know nothing of peanuts. What soil do they require? I don't think I know how they grow. I am very interested. In my own country I write articles for the agricultural journals."

They launched into talk of soil and crops. Cosmo left them, got his candle from the table in the hall and went to bed. His departure was scarcely noticed. As he went into the hall he heard Adam Rutledge say: "You cannot take from the soil, deplete it, without giving something in return. That is the trouble in a new land. You take and take, giving nothing back. At present there is plenty, but in time the land will grow thin. It will not yield its abundance. It is the same with our forests. We take and take, cut our trees, but we do not re-seed. We will overwork our land and chop down our forests."

Von Poellnitz said, "You are the first person I have met in America who is looking ahead. Your land is so rich now that you do not see an end to its riches. Being a European, I know what you say is true. You must put back into the soil. Why do they not see that?"

The talk veered to machinery for harvesting. The Baron rather diffidently admitted that he was working on a threshing mill that would allow a man and a boy to thresh seventy bushels of wheat a day. Unquestionably Baron von Poellnitz was a man of scientific taste and training. His idea was that his machine could be manufactured at the low price of £12 and that one machine would serve a whole township by being used by various planters.

The tall clock struck one. The Baron got quickly to his feet. "I am sorry, sir. As my wife says, I am without sense when I talk of agriculture. She will not allow me to speak of land in her hearing." He smiled an engaging boyish smile. "I am like a boy out of school when I find a man who thinks as I do about the problems of the earth we live on. Sir, I cannot tell you what this talk has meant to me." The Baron took up his candle and lighted it. "Thank you again, Mr. Rutledge, for a very profitable evening."

Adam went to his bedroom. Sleep was not easily won. He was thinking of the problems of this fine gentleman. He would have plenty before he got the acreage he wanted. The men of the Albemarle bought land; they did not sell land. In that, they showed their kinship with their forebears, the men of Devon and Cornwall.

He thought of the Baron's wife. A few rumors about her had come to his ears. He must ask Cosmo de' Medici what he knew. Cosmo had been in England more recently than he had. In the back of his mind there was something about the scandalous divorce of the Duke of Northumberland and Lady Anne. From the short time he had seen the Baroness he got the impression that she was a woman to whom men were necessary.

Breakfast at Rutledge Riding was a slow process. It was always served from the hunt board, English-fashion. The guest helped himself from a variety of covered silver dishes: ham and pork chops, hominy with gravy, eggs, and, instead of strong China tea, a good substitute made of yaupon leaves. The doctor and Cosmo were already at the table when Adam came in from his early-morning ride to the tobacco fields. In answer to Dr. Armitage's question, he said, "They will finish pulling tobacco today. I shall be glad to know that it will be in the sheds before I leave for Williamsburg."

"When will that be?" asked the doctor.

"In a day or two at the latest."

"Too late," Dr. Armitage said sadly. "I should have liked to go with you. I must go today. We are setting up a field hospital."

Cosmo de' Medici said: "Perhaps I shall have my

quota of men by then. I should like to go with you, Adam, if I may." He turned to the doctor. "I am eager to be back with my company. I . . ."

Dr. Armitage interrupted him. "Do not tell me. I do not like to carry weighty secrets. I've enough troubles curing the agues and mending the broken bones without having to watch my tongue about military matters." He rose from the table. "My thanks, as always, Adam. Goodbye to you both."

The doctor had no sooner left than the Baron came into the dining room.

"Again I must impose upon you for your advice," he said to Adam. "My wife and I must visit New York within a month. I have a deal of business to do in that city. My man of business, Sayre, is already looking out for a suitable house for us. Meanwhile I should put my two boys in school. Can you tell me of a good one?"

Cosmo de' Medici excused himself. "I shall talk to the men you promised me, Adam. Shall I see you again, Baron?"

"I want to cross on the noon ferry from Mackey's," the Baron said. "At any rate, may I count on both of you for dinner tonight?"

After Captain de' Medici had left, Adam Rutledge returned to the Baron's question about a school for his sons.

"I would suggest Parson Earle's school at Bandon," Adam said. "The Parson is a man of sound learning, and his daughter, Miss Ann, is an excellent teacher. You will find the Parson to your taste. His is an Irish guardsman turned clergyman, and has the best qualities of both. His place is named after his old home at Bandon in Ireland. He is a lusty, open-hearted man with a fine laugh. He loves his people—all people, in fact. He has done much for the country folk, teaching them how to fish commercially so that they can have the benefits of the spring run of herring in the river. He has taught them to ride to hounds also, for he is a mighty huntsman. He teaches the boys mathematics, Latin and Greek, leaving the other studies in the hands of his daughter Ann. His younger daughter Elizabeth is married to Charles Johnson, a Scot, who sits in the colonial assembly."

The Baron thanked Rutledge. "I hope your Parson Earle can find room for my boys," he said. "I have been a widower, like you, sir, and know how dreary a man's life can be without a mate. A man, no matter what his age, needs the companionship of a woman to temper his natural savagery."

Adam nodded, thinking of how rude and rough his own life had become since the death of his invalid wife Sara. Mary Warden, whom he had truly loved and who had cared for David, his son by the slave girl Aziza, he saw infrequently now. When the war was over . . . ? He, too, was sick of the war. He longed for the peace and the constructiveness of his old life at Rutledge Riding, so different from the destructive turmoil of the war. And he longed for the presence of a woman he could love and who would love him. Almost unconsciously he thought of the Baroness von Poellnitz, whose beauty had impressed him in the brief moments he had seen her at the Frenchmen's ball.

"You are blessed with such a wife as yours, Baron," he said. "I venture to hope that soon you may have a more permanent home among us, in which your boys may have the privilege of their new mother's influence."

Baron von Poellnitz stared at his plate. "The Baroness is unused to children," he said almost sadly. He finished his tea. "I must be off, sir. My thanks to you for all your generous help and hospitality. Until tonight, then."

Cosmo de' Medici returned to the plantation house as the Baron was riding off down the avenue.

"A charming man," Adam said, "but a little sad." After a pause he added, "Tell me what you know about his wife."

"How do you know I know anything about her?"

"Because you looked as if you had a secret."

Cosmo laughed. "You are too observing, Adam. You will have to wait until I go back to Pembroke later this morning. I have a complete report on the divorce case which was sent to me from London before the war. But you will have to swear secrecy. I wouldn't have Jemmy Iredell learn about it. The Baroness' sister married his uncle, Lord Macartney. That almost makes him kin, doesn't it?"

Adam laughed. "I would certainly claim kin to the Baroness if I were in like case, but I swear secrecy." He caught up his sword which lay on the library table. He raised its hilt upward in front of him. "On my Knight's Oath," he said.

VI

The Baron Entertains

When the Baron reached his suite of rooms at Horniblow's tavern he found no one to greet him but his wife's maid Dawkins.

"Her Ladyship has gone riding, sir," Dawkins told him. "She did not expect you before nightfall."

He went down the hall to his sons' room, and hearing no sound from within it, opened the door without knocking. At first glance the room seemed empty. Then he noticed that the bed curtains were drawn, and presently from behind them came a giggle—a woman's giggle. The Baron strode across the room and flung the curtains apart.

On the bed sprawled a girl he recognized as one of the tavern maids. The laces of her bodice were unloosened, and her skirt was above her waist, exposing her shapely bare legs. Athwart her, his face buried in the girl's bosom, was his elder son Hans.

Seizing the boy by the shoulders, the Baron wrenched him free and in the same gesture flung him across the room. Then he reached for the girl. But she had already sprung up, and before the Baron could catch her, she had leapt for the door and dashed through it.

The Baron slammed the door shut and bolted it. Then he turned to his fifteen-year-old son.

"A fine thing for you to do indeed!" he said sternly, trying to keep his voice in control. "Wenching with a servant girl! And you the son of a baron!"

Tousled though he was from his amorous adventure, the boy stood tall and straight, facing his father with bright blue eyes made brighter with the excitement of the moment. His normally rosy cheeks were scarlet, the only sign of embarrassment—or was it anger? The Baron was calm enough to consider that alternative. The boy was indeed his son, and the son of his ancestors, too proud to grovel. In spite of himself the Baron felt proud of Hans.

"You are a fool," he said to the boy. "If that girl talks, she can ruin our reputation in this village."

"She will not talk, Father."

"Little do you know about such women. It would be worth her while to talk."

"I have already made it worth her while not to," Hans said. "I gave her a gold piece."

"That was even more foolish. Besides, it is whoring. That I will not have."

Still the boy did not flinch. If anything, his blue eyes burned brighter. He ran his hands through his mussed blond hair and continued to face his father.

"Have you nothing more to say?" the Baron asked. When the boy made no answer, the Baron added: "Where did you get such ideas? I thought I had trained you to respect womanhood, no matter of what class."

"I am no longer a child, sir," Hans said. "At least, so I have been told."

"And who has told you that?"

The boy set his lips firmly. The Baron realized he would get no answer from him. He admired his son's discretion. He became aware that he needed no confession. Who else could have talked to his boy that way but his own wife?

A pang of conscience smote the Baron like a sword-thrust. He himself had lusted after the Lady Anne as this boy had a serving wench. Even knowing her past, he had brought her into his home. How stupid he had been to think she might be a mother to his boys! That, as he had painfully reflected before now, had been merely a feeble rationalization of his own desire. However much he might have deluded himself, he had not succeeded in fooling this intelligent son of his —if, indeed, anyone else. He found himself unable to reprimand Hans further.

Instead he walked to the window seat and motioned Hans to sit beside him. He put his arm around the boy's shoulder, noticing how firm it was and how it had thickened and rounded since last he had embraced his son. The boy's hands had grown too; the muscles showed along their backs, now covered with soft blond hairs, and the fingers had lengthened and strengthened, their nails broad and smoothed.

"Such things come of boredom," he said gently. "A child you are indeed no longer. But not yet a man. You do not yet understand responsibilities. You are not ready to assume them. I was talking this morning to Mr. Rutledge about a school for you and Eitel. You will be happier there, with plenty of work and diversion to occupy your mind."

Hans made a face. "What! Another school, Father? This will make ten schools we have attended."

Von Poellnitz smiled. "I wager this one is different from all the others. It is a small, simple country school."

"No military?" Hans asked.

"No military."

Below in the courtyard the Baron saw his younger son Eitel emerge from the stable. He called to the boy to come up to the room at once. Like his brother, Eitel was blond, blue-eyed and rosy-cheeked.

While they waited for him, the Baron patted Hans' shoulder. "I should prefer you not to discuss your adventure with Eitel. In another year, perhaps . . ."

Hans looked at his father as if to say he had had no intention whatever of doing so.

"Phew!" the Baron exclaimed as Eitel entered the room. "Where have you been? In a manure pile?"

"I was helping the groom," the boy said. "I must

learn to care for my horse. He was teaching me to rub him down and water and feed him."

"Good," said the Baron. "If you do not know yourself how to do those things, you cannot direct others or be able to tell when they are properly done."

"We're going to be sent to another school, Eitel," his brother said.

Eitel's face fell, then brightened as a new idea occurred to him. "Can I take my horse, Father?"

"We shall see," said the Baron. "Now, go and wash the stench of the stable from you. You know the Baroness cannot abide that odor."

The Baron caught the look that passed between his sons. Rather than embarrass them—and possibly himself—by inquiring what it meant, he rose to leave.

"We expect guests for dinner. When I send for you to greet them, I wish you clean and neatly dressed." He left the room.

He had hardly closed the door behind him when he heard Eitel say gleefully: "Won't *she* be glad to get rid of us! And I to be rid of her, the she-devil!"

"Shh!" his brother said. "Don't let Father hear you. He dotes on her. But he'll find out her antics some day—and then . . ."

Sorely troubled, the Baron walked back to the drawing room of his suite. At times like these he wondered why he had ever married the Lady Anne Stuart. Yet he knew in his heart that he was still under her spell. One side of him stood off and criticized her, the other came running whenever she lifted her slim hand to call him. Why? He did not know. Once when he was visiting her father, Lord Bute, she had put her arms about him and pressed her red mouth to his. From then on he had no other thought but his joy in loving her. She had the power to give him complete ectasy and complete forgetfulness of anything but his love for her.

He bathed, and changed into the clothes he would wear to receive his guests. The Baroness had not returned by the time he came back into the drawing room. Annoyed that there would now be no time to speak with her before Adam Rutledge and Cosmo de' Medici arrived, he took up an agricultural journal and tried to read it. But other thoughts kept coming into his mind and distracting him.

His mind kept drifting back to his first wife, the mother of his boys. She had been utterly different from Lady Anne, a short, rather dumpy, unimaginative woman, the younger daughter of a petty German prince. He had loved her, yes, but without excitement. By the time she died they had been married long enough for him to understand that she bored him, and that he was then mature enough to need and, yes, to merit a woman more stimulating in every way. He had searched for such a one for a long time. Lady Anne was the first he had found who was available and who answered his requirements. No, he could not be truly sorry he had married her. If she vexed him, if he suspected her loyalty, well, that was what he had asked for. There was precious little excitement in living with a woman whose every thought and feeling were transparent. And yet . . .

He flung the journal to the floor in exasperation. At that moment the door of the suite opened, and in came his wife, closely followed by Raoul de Polignac.

"Bruno," she trilled, tripping across the room to kiss him. "I'm glad you are home at last. Where did you spend the night?"

She was wearing a madras riding habit with a small hat from which a green plume curled down across her cheek.

"With Mr. Adam Rutledge," the Baron said, rising. "I have asked him to dinner, and also Captain de' Medici."

"How delightful!" exclaimed Lady Anne. "I was much taken with Mr. Rutledge at the Ball. And I have invited Raoul, who has taken me on a long, beautiful ride along the shore."

The Baron crossed the room to Raoul. "You are welcome, indeed," he said.

Lady Anne excused herself to change. The two

men sat over a glass of port, trying desperately to make conversation.

After the first few lapses in their exchanges, the Baron had come to the firm conclusion that Raoul was a nincompoop without any notion of a purpose in life except to make himself agreeable to women. Like all the French, he thought. He had seen plenty of them at the Court of Frederick the Great, and had deplored their influence on his enigmatic monarch. Finally, in desperation, he picked up the agricultural journal from the floor and began expounding to Raoul the theory of one of its articles.

Raoul, in his turn, thought Baron von Poellnitz as boring a man as it had ever been his misfortune to be confined with. His mind wandered to the activity of the tavern servants who were laying the table in one end of the drawing room. Likely as not, he thought, this crude Baron would serve beer with the dinner; his mouth was watering for a full-bodied French wine. It occurred to him that the man would be vulgar enough to challenge him if he were to discover that his wife and Raoul had been intimate. The more Raoul thought of her, the more he longed to be in her boudoir with her now.

At last Lady Anne returned, wearing a simple gown of green lawn. Her unpowdered hair was simply arranged. She seemed to bring a breeze of cool air into the room, which Raoul thought had grown intolerably close.

But there was no time for her to revive him further with the charm of her presence, the intoxication of her nearness. Almost at once the other guests were announced.

Lady Anne seated Adam Rutledge on her right and Raoul on her left, with de' Medici between Raoul and the Baron.

At least, Raoul thought, I am not next to that tedious husband of hers, but why is she paying so much attention to Rutledge?

Adam Rutledge was talking of the victory at Cowpens, which he considered North Carolina's own victory, for the elite of her army had been there with General Dan Morgan.

"I think," he said, "when we have finished the war and we begin to evaluate, we will find that the battle of Cowpens, which opened this year's campaign, was the real turning point of the Revolution. Think of what happened. Southern valor over three times the number of trained regulars—a greater victory than Bennington, perhaps. A victory largely of militia over tried troops. A battle that upset Colonel Tarleton's calculations and that was a step toward sending Lord Cornwallis out of the Carolinas into Virginia."

De' Medici nodded his agreement. "It must have been a source of great satisfaction to General Greene as well as to General Morgan. South Carolina will soon be shed of British troops, and the seige of Charleston will be a minor event to the coming seige of Cornwallis in Yorktown."

De' Medici continued: "I am glad that the French are playing such a major role in this part of the war. General Lafayette has had his troops augmented by new troops from France. Count d'Estaing has taken three ships of the line, three frigates and twenty sail of transport ships from Sir Samuel Hood's squadron—a great blow to British prestige. This news I had in a letter that came this morning."

Raoul tried to acknowledge the compliment to his countrymen, but he was interrupted by Adam Rutledge, who said: "Splendid. We will win yet. The man I want to see captured is that traitor, Arnold, who has been swashbuckling through Virginia. I would like to see him dangling from a tree or a yardarm."

"You really despise him, don't you, Mr. Rutledge?" said the Baroness.

"I do. I hate a craven who sells his country for gold. When I heard he was on a ship bound for Edenton it was all I could do to keep from sailing over and destroying him with these bare hands."

Lady Anne laughed at Adam's vehemence. "It is good that he got away."

"Between darkness and dawn, they tell me. A fitting exit for a snake in the grass."

Quite by accident Adam Rutledge felt the Baroness' knee touching his. He murmured, "I'm sorry," and moved a little, but a short time later the accident occurred again. He gave her a quizzical look. Her fixed smile did not change, but the pressure of her leg increased. This time he did not move but allowed the furtive caress to continue until the length of her leg from her knee to her foot was pressing against him. The sensation was not unpleasant. Adam wondered how far she would go if the occasion were more propitious.

The Baron von Poellnitz was talking to Cosmo de' Medici.

Adam glanced across the table. Raoul's eyes were fixed on Lady Anne with a hungry expression that changed quickly when he encountered Adam's glance. Adam thought: Ah, here is an undercurrent! I wonder if the woman is toying with this young Frenchman.

Raoul was trying frantically to win some attention to himself. "I fear," he said, "the Baron and Baroness are frightfully bored by all this talk about American affairs."

Adam turned to Lady Anne. There was laughter in his eyes. "I believe you find interest in everything, Lady Anne."

"Especially in America where the men are so handsome and so vital."

"You flatter us, dear lady. We are not used to compliments. Our women are likely to take us for granted."

"How stupid of them!" she answered, allowing her hand to drop on his arm possessively. Adam's handsome face took on a look of pleasure. She leaned forward so that her low-cut dress displayed her ample charms.

The other men rose and moved to the far end of the room, but Lady Anne restrained Adam Rutledge from following them. He sat, looking at her penetratingly.

"Why do you stare at me like that?" she asked, her

voice low. "You have the look of an eagle ready to fall on its prey and devour it."

"Would you not be a toothsome morsel?"

"I do not like your tone, sir!"

"Why not? Am I not looking at you? You are a beautiful woman. Is it not the province of men to look at and covet beautiful women?"

"But you, sir, are not coveting me. You look as though you loathed me." Her voice sank lower. She moved her hands back and forth restlessly.

Adam laughed. "How could a man loathe a beautiful woman?" He leaned back in his chair surveying her with his unreadable eyes.

"I know when a man likes me!"

"Madam, your trouble is that you have been playing with boys—not men. You like to dominate. You can't win *men* that way, even with all your charms."

"Ah, so you do think me charming?" She leaned forward, her face eager.

"Of course. But also very youthful and naïve. You must have only praise—from a young, inexperienced man like Raoul."

She was startled. "How did you know?"

"Can you imagine you can hide by looking the other way—or rubbing my knee? One has only to look at the jealousy in the man's face to be positive."

"He is a fool," she said angrily, "a fool to show his feelings so plainly that anyone can read."

"Not anyone, Lady Anne. Only a man who has had experience."

Lady Anne was silent. She looked at Adam, her eyes glowing. "Why can't you like me, Adam Rutledge? I could give you everything, everything a man like you wants. You attract me strangely."

"Only because I am not taken in by your blandishments. I've met women like you before. Remember, I have spent some time in London."

Lady Anne was silent, a look of defeat on her mobile face. "You do not like me," she repeated sullenly.

Adam thought she needed a lesson. Why should not he be the one to withstand her charm? He began to relish the situation.

He started to talk about her husband, how much he had in common with the Baron in their interest in agriculture, and about his inventions. "I have read his piece in the *Virginia Agricultural Journal*. I think it very fine, indeed. We planters know the way to plant and grow crops, but the Baron knows the theories of planting and fertilization."

Lady Anne pounded the table with her clenched fist. "I don't want to hear any more about land and crops and fertilizer. That's all he knows or has any interest in. He wallows in fertilizer—wallows."

Her face was suffused with anger. Tears gathered in her eyes. Adam was undisturbed by her motion which he was sure was turned on and off as she chose. He looked at her, a glint of laughter in his blue eyes, his tall, lean frame lounging in the chair.

Seeing that she was making no impression, she stopped weeping as quickly as she had begun. "You are a devil," she pouted, "a very devil."

Adam laughed aloud. "That's better. Anger is a better weapon than tears. Tears do not become you."

She sat up, interested. "What is my type, Mr. Rutledge? Please tell me."

"It's simple. You are an egoist. You have a diabolical urge to hurt. You like to see people suffer—men or women, it makes no difference to you. Yet, you are beautiful and sharp-witted, and you have a power over men which you like to use for your pleasure. All in all, you are quite wicked, Lady Anne."

"Ah, so I am beautiful! That is something. Pray, may I ask how you know so much about me?"

"It is no secret. I read the London papers and Lord Charles Montague talked to me about you at the Frenchmen's ball."

A look of anger disfigured her perfect features. "Ah, Lord Charles Montague. He is a cousin of the family. He never liked me. I tell you I was bored. You

can't imagine how I was bored. Northumberland had
put me out in the woods in a hunting lodge 'way off
from everyone. The Duke was in America with the
army in New York and there was nobody—nobody."
Tears were near the surface again.

Adam took a handkerchief from his sleeve and
handed it to her. "There, there!" he said as though he
were comforting a child. "It's all over now. You've all of
Edenton at your feet."

"But I haven't, Adam Rutledge. What is wrong
with you? Have you a loving wife or are you a woman
hater?"

"My wife has been dead for several years."

Lady Anne's tears ceased to flow. "Then there is
hope for me?"

"I'm afraid not," Adam said. He got to his feet,
pulled at his fob and glanced at his watch. "I have a
long ride before me."

He made his farewells to the Baron. The two other
guests also rose to go.

"Come back to Pembroke with us," Cosmo de
Medici said. "Stephen Cabarrus will be glad to put you
up. Then I can give you the papers I promised."

The Baron offered to go with them to the courtyard to see them properly mounted, and off. Adam ma-
neuvered so that the three men preceded him out the
door.

When they had passed into the hall, he paused before Lady Anne. Bending over her, he lifted her chin
and planted a firm kiss on her red mouth.

"In case you thought that I had no experience in
these matters," he said.

He picked up his tricorn and walked out of the
room. She heard him go down the hall whistling "Drink
to me only with thine eyes."

For a moment she was shaking with rage. Suddenly
she smiled. Aloud she said: "I must see something more
of Mr. Adam Rutledge. He is a man to set the pulses
tingling."

VII

Bandon Plantation

Baron von Poellnitz waited impatiently the next morning at breakfast for his wife to appear. The waiting did not improve his humor. When he had gone to Lady Anne's room the night before, she told him firmly that she would not have him with her. When he protested that he merely wished to talk with her, she complained that she had been tired from her long ride and that his guests had tired her more. She had pushed him out of the room and slammed and locked the door behind him.

Bruno von Poellnitz had, he was confident, been an indulgent husband. He had shown his wife every consideration he could. Even this present trip to America he had embarked upon, planning to settle in the new land, partially, at least, was to provide her with a new environment, in which the past was not so likely continually to be thrown up to her. He was not to be imposed upon. The morning was growing late, and he had plenty to do that day.

He rang for Dawkins, her maid.

"Is her ladyship ill?"

"She has not called me yet, sir."

"Then go and tell her I wish her to join me."

Presently the Baroness appeared and took her place opposite her husband at the table without speaking. She was wearing a pale blue negligee. Her hair, un-rolled, lay in waves down her neck, held loosely by a blue riband. She looked at him with a kind of charming insolence which implied a challenge as to why she had been summoned, and at the same time an acquiescence to his request.

"I have a long ride today . . ." the Baron started.

"So I am to be left alone again? Really, Bruno, this is unfair. In this isolated spot I am as lonely and bored as I was on old Northumberland's place with no one for company but my goody-goody sister and her squalling brat." She poured herself a cup of tea and sipped at it sullenly.

The Baron felt disquieted, and already somewhat defeated. She had sworn to him that it was solely her lo-neliness in the grim Northumberland castle on the moors that had driven her into the adulterous act which had led to her being divorced, no concupiscence on her part, only a need for companionship and love, and that it would never happen again.

"I am sure the ladies of Edenton and of the planta-tions would welcome a call from you," he said.

"Faugh!" the Baroness exclaimed, setting down her cup with an angry clatter, "they bore me worse. They are like middle-class Englishwomen. They put on a childish masquerade in which they impersonate Chast-ity and Fidelity and all the other impossible virtues, and believe the sham a passport to Heaven."

The Baron looked at her in shocked surprise. "I do not care for such talk," he said loudly. "I do not wish my sons exposed to such cynical attitudes."

"Your sons!" she said scornfully. "I am not to be a nursemaid in your household."

"Nor have you ever been, my dear," said the Bar-on with no little tone of irony. "As a matter of fact, I go today to investigate a school for them at Bandon."

"And high time," she snapped. "They are becom-ing unbearable. Dawkins tells me they ask her all sorts of indecent questions. They even want to hang around

the barns when they hear a cow is about to drop a calf."
Lady Anne's laugh rang out. "Already they are farmers
and peasants!"

The Baron's skin took on a fiery blush. "I see nothing to laugh at," he said. "Why did you not instruct
them better?"

"I did!" Lady Anne pushed her chair back from
the table and stretched her arms above her head. "As
well I should have. Hans is fifteen, an inquiring age.
When I was fifteen I had my first lessons." She laughed.
"A handsome young groom it was. I used to meet him
in the stable in the tack room. He was very timid at first,
but later he grew quite bold."

The Baron glared at her.

She laughed. "I love you when you look like that,
Bruno. I assure you it was only innocent play. The
groom—I forget his name—never attacked me, just
played a little. It made me feel very excited. I begged
him to go further, but he would not. He was afraid of
me, I think. Afraid I would tell. I wouldn't have. I liked
the idea of a guilty secret too much. I remember him
now. He was a handsome blond youth with hair as yellow as corn and blue eyes—much your complexion, my
dear." She laughed again.

The Baron struck the table with the palms of his
hands, almost upsetting it. He got to his feet and strode
around to tower above his wife.

"This is indecent," he roared. "You are a . . ."

In a flash she was on her feet, her eyes blazing. "I
will not be called names," she said, her voice deep and
menacing with the anger she was holding in reserve.
"You are a fool, sir, to try to abuse me. I have no use
for the romantic notions you have sucked from that idiot
Rousseau—nature, the simple life, the purity of children, the nobility of this ridiculous war the Americans
are fighting for an infantile conception of freedom. 'The
pursuit of happiness,' they call it! If they had any experience with the world, instead of being back-country
peasants, they would know the only happiness is being a
full human being in the world as they find it. Like all

Germans you have some moonstruck dream that you can reform the world and its people in some glorious pattern. Pooh! Man was born to sin, and sin he shall—and woman too, God knows, though for myself I call it no sin to be as I was made."

The Baron found himself cowering under her taunts. Never before had he seen her defend her willfulness with philosophical arguments. He could not answer them. His own speculations had convinced him that the Devil could not be out-reasoned, only subdued by Faith. Were her temptations merely a test of his own beliefs? Only if he did not yield to them. And yield he felt himself doing. Surely he had desired her with everything that was male about him. Desired her now, passionately, even at the moment she was flaunting him insultingly. He could not resist her. Impulsively he grabbed her to him and kissed her deeply.

"You are like a goddess," he murmured. "You flash fire that terrifies me and makes me adore you. I am unworthy of you."

He felt her relax in his embrace. Her hands moved to behind his head, pressing his mouth closer to her own. Without removing his lips from hers, his strong arms swept her up. He carried her into her bedroom, kicking the door shut behind him.

Far later in the day than he had intended, the Baron hurried down the stairs from his suite, crossed the tavern's common room, and went out the side door into the brick courtyard. He ordered his bay mare, mounted, rode down Broad Street to the fork, and turned into the Virginia road. It was sixteen miles to Bandon Plantation on the Chowan River, where Parson Daniel Earle had his school for boys. He could, with good fortune, get there by dinner time.

It was one o'clock when Baron von Poellnitz turned into the drive between the pines leading to Parson Earle's home. Bandon he found to be a clapboard house, long and narrow, with two one-story wings at each end. Painted white with green shutters, it looked just what it was, a comfortable country-style dwelling. What saved it from mediocrity was that it was set in a grove of great oaks and pines from which hung long gray streamers of Spanish moss. The wide curving Chowan River beyond added to the beauty of the setting, for it was more than a mile wide—a quiet river that, according to Hakluyt's *English Voyages and Navigations,* had been the stream which carried Governor Ralph Lane's ship on a voyage of discovery in 1584. In that far-off time this was the country of the Chonoke, and a skirmish with the Indians was fought with the English settlers on the beach at the foot of the high banks.

On one side of the house were the dependencies: a milk house and a smoke house and a larger building which the Baron took to be the kitchen from the number of small Negroes playing in front of it and the Negro men going back and forth between it and the house, carrying covered silver dishes. He had evidently arrived at the time of noonday dinner. The sun was high in the heavens, and the sky brightly blue, without the cumulus clouds which were wont to drift in on the Bermuda high in mid-summer.

He was of a mind to ride to the river to give the family time to finish their meal when he saw a house boy in a white coat coming down the brick walk to the upping block to take his horse.

"Master says step right in, sir, and join him."

The Baron dismounted and dusted off his breeches with his riding crop. At the entrance to the house a tall Negro held the door open for him to pass into the wide hall.

"Rest your hat, sir. The master is at table. I will show you the way."

The Baron had time only to glimpse a long drawing room beyond a cross hall before the man led him into the large dining room at the left.

Parson Earle, whom he had not met before, greeted him. "I had your note, Baron. I shall be happy to show you our school. But first led me introduce my daughter, Elizabeth, and her husband, Charles Johnson."

The Baron accepted Parson Earle's invitation to take a seat at the table and have a glass of wine. The Parson was a strong, hearty-looking man with bold features. His clubbed hair was unpowdered. He wore a hunter-green riding coat with brass buttons and tan leather breeks above his high riding boots. There was a fine air of geniality about the Parson that made the Baron like him on sight. Charles Johnson, he knew, was a member of the Assembly and a man of means.

Johnson had been talking about the incident of the row galleys, when the British Loyalists from the coast had brought in ships and captured Smith's and Littlejohn's schooners on the Sound a month earlier. He explained this briefly to the Baron.

"You see, sir," Johnson said, "I have just returned from an extraordinary session of the Assembly, called to deal with the problem of the Tories in our colony."

"The incident," explained the Parson, "was the greatest excitement Edenton has had during the war. The whole of the town wanted to go in search of the British galley which had retreated to the coast after having plundered Smith's schooner." He turned to his daughter. "Elizabeth, my dear, will you ask Ann what she did with the letter Robert Smith sent me from Eden House when he heard that his vessel had been taken by the Tory pirates."

Presently Mrs. Johnson returned with her old sister, whom she introduced to Baron von Poellnitz. Miss Ann was a woman in her late twenties, not beautiful, but with a charming manner. She resembled her father somewhat but with more refinement of features.

The Baron rose to greet her. "May I ask what you do in the school? I have heard you are of great assistance to your father."

Anne Earle's voice was soft, yet he thought it carried authority. "I teach reading, writing and spelling," she said. Then she added with a little laugh: "And manners."

She handed a letter to her father.

"I want to read this," said the Parson, "because it is characteristic of Smith . . ."

> 'Mrs. Dawson must have written you of the ill news of the day. I am just going over to town to know the worst. They have given me a pretty little switching but it might have been worse. They have ruined poor Littlejohn and would have left me nothing if they had not taken fright. Many of my papers are destroyed, all my clothes, bed, table and other linens squandered. Indeed, they must have done me more damage than I can name, but it is useless for me to repine if even the rest should follow. I have serious doubts that those pirates may go up to Cashy River. They went up as far as Stumpy Reach for my vessel and must have had a pilot on board.
>
> Robert Smith'

The Baron asked: "Who is this Robert Smith and what is this schooner that he lost?"

Johnson answered. "He is a merchant here, the partner of the late Joseph Hewes, the signer of the Declaration of Independence from Edenton."

"He is an amusing fellow from his letter. I should like to meet him."

"I am sure you will, Baron. You will find that he is at Horniblow's every day for his meals and in the common room for backgammon."

"What happened? Did anyone go after the pirate row galley?" the Baron asked.

"Indeed, yes," Johnson answered. "Four boats, under the command of Captain Gale, Captain Bateman, Captain Allison and Captain Finch. Altogether they had about fifty men. They were joined by Johnstone's canoe, Pollock's barge and Caswell's barge. They had a swivel besides muskets. Mr. Smith kept up his gaiety through the whole affair. I think he was more regretful of his seven barrels of rum than his merchandise and his papers."

Ann broke into the conversation. "Father, I am sure the Baron must be frightfully bored by all this talk about Edenton affairs."

The Baron laughed. "I am not in the least bored, madam. The little sidelights of war are most interesting."

Parson Earle said: "May I ask just one question? Were Mr. Smith's and Mr. Littlejohn's schooners recovered?"

"Yes," Charles Johnson said, "but that was after the pirates had abandoned them and most of the contents been stolen."

As soon as he could, the Baron turned the conversation to the plantation. He found that the Parson had a thousand or more acres, running from the river to the Virginia Road, three miles to the east. His main crops were corn, tobacco, and pigs.

The Parson said with a laugh, "We fare not too badly for a clergyman of the Established Church, but if you want to know about plantations, Charles is the one to consult. He owns more land around here than I do. He farms it himself while I depend on a good overlooker."

Charles Johnson smiled a little. "Don't let the Parson put you off, sir. It was he that taught the people around here to fish commercially. Fishing on the Chowan is a money crop. The herring run in the spring is a fine source of income to the small farmers who live in the district. Smoked herring is a year-round food for the table. Pickled herring is just as important. We will have to show you the fish house on the river before you leave."

The Baron complimented the Rhine wine and accepted a second glass before they rose from the table. With a murmured word about a class Ann Earle slipped away. The Parson led the Baron von Poellnitz into his study across the hall in the wing beyond the library. They got down to business.

"I want only the best, sir," the Baron said. "That is my first precept in life—only the best."

"You are an idealist, Baron," the Parson replied, sucking on his pipe. "But I think we can come close to satisfying you."

"I should like to have my sons trained in good manners, American style. I find many customs here are not the same as abroad. I want them to be familiar with good manners in any place they go."

"I understand. My daughter is adept in such matters. Now, would you like to go over to our little school? There will be a class in progress, but perhaps that will be good."

The two men went out the side door and down the gallery steps and walked across the short stretch of lawn to the schoolhouse in the garden.

Before they reached the open door, a droning sound like the buzzing of bees reached them. It was the spelling class singing out the words. The Baron smiled. "Sir, this pleases me. Your Miss Ann uses the old method of teaching spelling. That is good. Good!"

They walked into the room. Fourteen boys were standing in a row, their eyes on the windows looking out toward the river. In a short time they would take their books and go down to the cave near the spring and do their studying in its cool interior. The Baron studied the boys. They were of all complexions—blond, brunette, two redheads. They were dressed in cambric ruffled shirts and knee breeks of soft leather, with woolen stockings and buckled shoes. They all had their hair clubbed and tied with black riband bows. In spite of the similarity of their clothes they were not alike in looks: some solemn, some merry-eyed, some ready to burst into laughter, others merely curious. They were all sons of planters who lived in North Carolina or Virginia near the border. Young gentlemen, the Baron thought, suitable companions for his sons.

He asked Parson Earle about fencing. "Two lessons a week," he answered. "Sometimes I teach them, sometimes Mr. Johnson. My son-in-law is a famous fencer. He has studied in Edinburgh, in London and France. If I may say so, the lads prefer his teaching to mine. I teach them only the rudiments, while Charles takes the more advanced."

The Baron said, "My boys have been moved around so much, they have not had a real home. I would like them to be your special care. I see that Miss Ann is a kind person. I hesitate to say it, but my wife is impatient with children. She does not understand them. I would like to leave them here for a year, if you will take them. I am willing to pay extra for extra care."

Parson Earle said, "We will be glad to have them if they like the place. Bring them out so that they can see for themselves how the boys do. They sleep in the dormitory above the school. They eat at the house in a room of their own with Miss Ann to watch their manners. Come, I will take you to the dormitory."

They mounted the outside stairs to a room above the schoolroom. It was the same size, but the roof sloped. There were fourteen slat beds made up neatly, a locker for clothes beside each bed, and a small washstand with copper bowls and ewers. An earthenware chamber pot was under each bed. There was a fireplace at the end, a duplicate of the one in the schoolroom. The small windows looked out into a pine forest.

The Baron thought of the castle in Prussia where the children had spent their young lives—a depressing thought thrust quickly aside.

"Excellent, excellent! It reminds me of my young days in the military school in Coblentz. I like it immensely, sir."

"Let us go to my study and talk about the monetary affairs."

In the Parson's study they came to an agreement, the Baron paying for a year's tuition with something over for extras, such as horses to ride, fencing and boxing lessons.

The Parson said, "This is the midsummer session. We have a young man who tutors at Princeton in the summertime to help my daughter in the autumn. He teaches all the sports, including swimming and boating, leads the boys on walks in the woods for their botany, and instructs them in choral singing. You will find they have a well-rounded education, Baron. I think you will be pleased with the results."

The Baron rose. "I will fetch them out tomorrow. I forgot to say they have a servant."

"White or black?" the Parson asked.

"White."

The Parson pursed up his lips. "That poses a question, Baron. The other boys have Negroes. Perhaps it would be better if I assign one of my young slaves as their body servant. I have a good, well-trained boy who will do the work."

The Baron took some banknotes from his pocket. "How much extra?"

The Parson hesitated a moment. "Three English pounds will be enough, Baron."

As the Baron mounted the upping block he noticed for the first time the whitewashed cabins along a lane to his right. A number of small children were playing in the sand. Two or three Negro women were bending over washtubs or open fires where great iron kettles hung. In the fields, slaves were working with tobacco plants, stripping the long leaves. Others packed the leaves carefully on small low sleds, dragged by a mule. He had seen enough of tobacco culture to know that the tobacco was being hauled to the barns for smoking and curing. He thought, as he mounted his mare, that tomorrow, when he brought the boys out, he would talk to Parson Earle about plantation work.

It was too late in the day for him to reach Edenton before nightfall. He was still unfamiliar enough about the roads to wish to travel after dark. It would be a good occasion, he thought, to stop at Pembroke. Stephen Cabarrus had offered to show him over the plantation.

To his surprise he found the Baroness there.

"I took your advice, my dear," she said sweetly. "I availed myself of Madam Cabarrus' kind invitation to visit her. She has been showing me the portraits in her lovely drawing room."

Marianne Cabarrus said: "Of course you will remain for dinner. Your other friends are here—Mr. Rutledge and Captain de' Medici and Count de Polignac." She called to Penelope. "This is my husband's niece, who now makes her home with us."

Lady Anne urged her husband to stay. "I came in the coach," she said. "The man knows the way. You will not have to ride home alone in the dark."

At dinner the Baroness sat between Stephen Cabarrus and Cosmo de' Medici. Across from here were Penelope Cabarrus, next to Raoul. The Baron and Adam Rutledge flanked Marianne Cabarrus.

Try as she would, Lady Anne could get little conversation out of Cosmo de' Medici. She talked spiritedly in French with Stephen Cabarrus, yet keeping her eyes on Raoul. Penelope, she noticed, kept trying to divert Raoul, but he kept looking across the table at the Baroness and joining in the conversation to the point that he almost ignored the young girl.

When Marianne gave the signal, the ladies arose and passed into the drawing room for coffee, as old Samuel was setting the brandy decanter on the table for the men.

"You have made a charming room," the Baroness said to Marianne. "But you Frenchwomen have a talent that way. You must be happy to have this delightful little maid with you. She is so fresh and blooming! Aren't you afraid your handsome husband will cast his eyes on her?"

Marianne could not avoid showing her surprise. "Stephen?" she exclaimed.

Lady Anne laughed. "Yes, Stephen. Your bold, handsome Stephen. I am sure he has been a great heartbreaker. Women love his vital, virile type. I do myself. Frenchmen always interest me and so do Italians, like de' Medici. Is he your lover?"

For a moment Marianne was silent, too stunned by

Lady Anne's question to reply. "Certainly not!" she said at length.

Lady Anne shrugged. "Don't be so indignant. I just wondered. With your husband gone away so often . . ."

"You seem to forget that I am a married woman." There was anger in Marianne's voice.

Lady Anne laughed a high, brittle laugh. "La, madam, you sound like an Englishwoman. I would never have known you were French!"

"Married women are not loose women in this country."

Lady Anne said, "Too bad. You miss a good deal." She put her coffee cup on a small tripod table. "But we must be on our way. Penny, run tell my husband to call our coach." She left the drawing room, her taffeta skirts rustling.

Marianne watched the von Poellnitz' coach drive off, a queer expression on her face. "That woman is a devil," she said half aloud, not realizing that Penny was near enough to hear.

Penny was watching the departing coach, a look of admiration on her young face. "But she is ravishing, completely ravishing!"

Marianne looked after Penny as she left the room. Perhaps it would be better if I protected Penny instead of Raoul, she said to herself.

VIII

A Defeat and a Triumph

Adam Rutledge woke early. For a moment he did not know where he was until he heard noises in the courtyard and recognized that he was in his room at Horniblow's. He had a headache and his mouth tasted as though he had eaten bitter fruit. Then he remembered the late game of cards with Cosmo de' Medici, Jasper Charleton and Meredith Bunch. Plenty of wine had been drunk, and at last Horniblow had come forth and opened a new cask of Jamaica rum that had been smuggled in through the Outer Banks.

He reached to the table beside his slat bed for the papers de' Medici had given him. Propping himself against his pillows, he strained to read them. They proved to be a bulky report on the divorce of the Baroness from the British peer who had been her first husband.

. . . in the year 1764 the Rt. Hon. Hugh Baron Percy, son and heir apparent of his Grace, the most noble Hugh, Duke of Northumberland, made his courtship and addresses in the way of marriage to the Right Hon. Anne Baroness Percy, then the Honorable Anne Stuart, commonly called Lady Anne Stuart, daughter of the Right Honorable John,

Earl of Bute, who was, at that time, spinster, of the age of seventeen years; that on the 2nd of July, 1764, in pursuance of a special license the said Hugh, Baron Percy, and said Anne, now Baroness Percy, were with the consent of said John, Earl of Bute, lawfully joined together in holy matrimony, according to the rites and ceremonies of the Church of England in the dwelling house of the Earl of Bute, in South Ardley St., by the Most Reverend Father in God, George, Lord Archbishop of Armagh, Primate of all Ireland, and were by his pronouncement made lawful husband and wife, in the presence of credible witnesses. That the said Lord and Lady Percy afterward cohabited together, at bed and board, and consummated their marriage by carnal copulation. By the later end of 1766, while Lord Percy was Colonel of His Majesty's Fifth Regiment in North America, Lady Percy, accompanied by her sister, Lady Augusta (wife of Drew Corbett, Esq., sublieutenant in the 2nd Troop of Horse Grenadiers) and a young child of hers went to a house Lady Percy had taken at Ash Park in the County of South Hampton (the same having been a hunting seat of the late Lord Craven). The Lodge was in a very retired situation in the middle of a wood not far from South Hampton.

About the middle of July 1777, Lady Percy with Lady Augusta Corbett and her child went to South Hampton for the season; Lady Percy took a house large enough to house her sister and child, herself and their servants.

It was at this time that Lady Percy met a personable young man who lived next door with his mother and sister, Mr. William Bird. It was this same young man that caused the trouble that led to the divorce courts and a great scandal that rocked all England. The court allowed that Lady Percy was and is a very loose woman of lustful and wicked dispostion and during the time she resided at Ash Park and South Hampton, and afterward when she resided at Brompton Row in the parish of Kensington, she secretly, without the knowledge of her husband, Hugh, Baron Percy, kept company with William Bird, Esq., with whom she committed the foul crime of adultery . . .

Adam laid the papers aside. Why should a beautiful, intelligent woman—and Lady Anne was both—have so far forgotten her honor to conduct herself in such an outrageous manner? He got up and walked about the room, more disturbed than he cared to acknowledge. There were more pages that he had not read—the whole sordid story told step by step by witnesses, servants who had seen and heard, and who, no doubt, were eager to tell horrifying tales about their betters. Were they their betters?

His body servant Herk came into the room.

"Pour my bath, Herk." He wanted nothing so much as to wash away the fetid taint of the divorce court.

Herk said: "Bath laid, Bwana. Behind screen."

Adam stepped into a long tin tub. He lay down in it and rolled over a couple of times. The icy water stung him to action. He leaped out onto the rug. "No need to put ice water in the tub, Herk!"

"Master need quick soaking after night at cards and drink."

Adam knew that Herk was right, but he resented being told. Suddenly he laughed.

"Better Bwana laugh than wear scowling face."

Adam laughed again. "You are quite right, Herk. I think it was that last tot of rum that did the work."

"Bwana remember time in Jamaica when rum was bad for his stomach?"

"I do indeed," Adam said, remembering the evening when he had tried to out-drink the captain of a British ship of the line. "I do indeed. What time is it, Herk?"

"Bwana, little clock say almost ten, sir."

Adam dressed quickly. He wanted to get out into the open air, to walk through the pine forest and allow the clean scent of the trees to dispel from his nostrils the foul stench of the scandal he had read.

As he walked, a charitable thought occurred to him. It was possible that Lady Anne had repented, and was planning a new life with her new husband here in America. He liked the Baron. How had that idealistic German happened to meet such a notorious woman? Why had he married her?

The more his thoughts tended in that direction, the less charitable they became. She must somehow have tricked the Baron into marriage. He was sure in his heart that she would cause as much mischief as she could, no matter who was hurt. She was a woman who relished disturbance, loved to be in the midst of turmoil.

He wondered whether her kinsman James Iredell knew of the scandal. In a sense, Iredell had introduced her and the Baron to the village, and thus might be thought to have sponsored her. Surely, Judge Iredell would not have done so if he had known. His wife Hannah would be horrified. He resolved that it was only loyalty for him to let them know that he himself—and at least one other—knew.

Turning, he quickened his pace back to the village.

Hannah Iredell was in her garden when Adam approached her house. "Jemmy has gone to his office," she told him. "He's behind with his work on the western circuit. Court sits in Hillsborough next week, and that means always a full docket."

"I can talk to you just as well," Adam said.

"Then come in for a cup of tea. Though it's only yaupon, it's hot, and a good muffin helps."

Adam looked at his watch. "I cannot stay, much as I should like to. We can talk, perhaps better, in the garden."

"Such a sorry garden," Hannah said. "Next year I think I'll have a box garden, nothing else."

Adam smiled. "I have more to distress you with than that, my dear Hannah." He summarized the contents of the report he had read earlier that morning. "I believed you and Jemmy should know," he concluded.

Hannah's sensitive face was sad. "Oh, Adam, I'm glad you told me. Of course, we should know. And it's better coming from you than by cheap gossip—as surely it would in time." Her face brightened. "But we can't throw stones. Remember what our blessed Saviour said, 'He who is without sin among you, let him cast the first stone.' We must remember that."

Adam smiled. "I can't imagine any sin that you have committed, Hannah."

She smiled. "You don't know me, Adam. I have a fiery temper—and I think I have been a little jealous. Jealousy is a sin, you know."

Adam kissed her hand. "If we were all like you, Hannah, there would be nothing but goodness in the world—no horrible wars, no armies opposite to each other waiting to kill, no ships with loaded guns on their decks."

He turned and went down the steps to walk to Horniblow's. At noon he was to meet de' Medici and they would start their journey to Williamsburg.

Around eleven was the time that the men of the town, the merchants, the lawyers, and the doctor came to the tavern for a drink and a game of backgammon. The countrymen, who rose at five, wanted something more substantial, so they ate a second breakfast of bacon and eggs, sausage, broiled herring with grits and ale.

As Adam entered the tavern, Nancy Ann Horniblow walked briskly down the hall. She was a pretty, fair-haired woman with candid blue eyes and a quiet dignity, and was younger than her husband by a dozen years. She had been a great help to him in making the tavern an integral part of the village of Edenton, especially since the war, for it had been her suggestion that Horniblow collect the news items of the war and disseminate them in his tavern. This answered two purposes: to give out the information for which the village was so eager, and to make his tavern the common meeting ground for the prominent men of the town.

Adam stopped her. "I know you can keep a secret, Mrs. Horniblow. Will you keep one for me?"

"Of course, sir. I promise."

"Then wait here a moment."

Adam went to his room and picked up the report Cosmo de' Medici had given him. When he returned, Nancy Ann Horniblow was where he had left her.

"Take this at once, if you please, to Mrs. Iredell. No one must know."

"I understand, sir," she said gravely.

Raoul de Polignac was sitting at a window that gave on the courtyard, watching for the hostler to saddle Lady Anne's horse. He had called for her early. Then, after an hour in her sitting room, waiting for her to change, he had grown impatient and had come downstairs for a mug of ale.

When Cosmo de' Medici and Adam Rutledge saw him, after they had ordered a meal, they picked up their glasses and joined him.

"What are you doing here at this hour?" Cosmo said. "I thought you were going across the Sound today."

"That trip to Pollock's has been postponed. I'm going for a ride with the Baroness presently."

De' Medici laughed. "You are finding out that waiting around for beautiful ladies consumes a lot of a man's time."

"But it's worth it," Raoul said.

The bar boy came with more ale, and both men lifted their glasses.

"To beautiful, but dilatory ladies!" Adam said. "May we all maintain patience!"

Horniblow came in from the common room, having seen to the serving of this late breakfast, and to preparations for the early dinner.

They began to talk about the news that had just come of Wake Court House by messenger.

"Governor Burke has been captured by the British. They are taking him to Wilmington to put him in prison." Adam gave out the news. "I've just heard from Hillsborough that the whole state is up in arms about it."

De' Medici said, "Fancy the boldness of capturing the state's Chief Executive."

"Boldness! I call it insolence," Adam said heatedly. "If I had not been going to Williamsburg I would surely have joined one of these groups. I am outraged."

Raoul asked, "How did this happen, sir?"

Adam said, "This is the story I had from Jasper Charleton last night after you had retired, Cosmo. A large body of Tories, about four hundred, under Governor Tryon's favorite, Colonel Fanning, with a companion named McNeil, came into Hillsborough and surprised the small guard the Governor had, and captured him. They were so elated over their success that they went wild, looting and plundering, until two in the afternoon. They released all the prisoners in the jail, entered houses, stole silver, even to shoe buckles of the inhabitants, and left about an hour later. Colonel Little, who was a prisoner on parole, was hacked and cut by Fanning himself in the most cruel manner."

Adam paused in his narration to light a pipe. "I always despised Fanning. He was a despicable character, a liar, always intriguing. Yet he completely fooled Governor Tryon, astute man that he is."

Raoul, who had followed the story closely, said, "What did they do with the Governor, sir?"

"Took him to Wilmington, then by boat to Charleston, where they have him on James Island as a prisoner of state. General Leslie is in command at Charleston. I fear for our Governor under his hands."

"It is very disquieting," Raoul said, "for a state to lose its Governor in times like these."

Adam looked at him. "Disquieting? It is a tragedy!"

Horniblow, the innkeeper, had been in South Carolina. He had tales about the Eutaw Springs engagement that they had not heard before. The North Carolina Brigade was on the right of the battle, the Virginians on the left and the Marylanders in the center. When they advanced into action Summer's Brigade was the first in the engagement, then the Virginians kept up a heavy fire and were ordered to charge with bayonets. The English forces broke in that quarter. The North Carolinians and the Marylanders pressed the charge. The whole enemy retreated with great precipitation, the army passing through their camp to a farm a small distance away. Here the enemy possessed themselves of a strong brick house in a position of opposition.

General Greene did not think it wise to attack them for their position was advantageous, but retired to his farm encampment. The enemy had seven hundred killed and wounded and five hundred twenty-seven made prisoners—sixteen captains and subalterns.

"We lost," Horniblow said, "five hundred killed and wounded and seventy-two captured. General Greene had the feeling that it was a real victory although it was the bloodiest battle of the war. The British and the Loyalists are in a low frame of mind now. Some thought that General Greene could have closed the war if he had been more belligerent—but perhaps not."

But Raoul was not listening. With a muttered apology he rose and made his way through the room and out the door to the courtyard. Adam looked out of the window. Lady Anne, dressed for riding in her madras habit, was walking across the coutyard toward the stable, where a groom was saddling her horse. He smiled to himself—up to her old tricks, with a handsome young man in attendance. He felt sorry for the lad.

De' Medici was also looking out the window. "I worry a little for Raoul. He is a fine, sensitive young man of real promise, but what can one do? Perhaps it can be set down as experience."

"Pretty strong experience I say, and not too healthy," Adam replied. "But we had best be starting. It is almost forty miles to Suffolk, and a dusty road."

They went out to the courtyard for their horses. Lady Anne was mounting her horse from the upping block. She turned when she saw Adam. A brilliant smile came to her lips. "Ah, what luck! Come ride with us, Mr. Rutledge."

"My apologies, Baroness, but we are off for the north and will be riding fast toward Suffolk."

She said eagerly, "We could ride up the Virginia Road as well as any direction."

Raoul was disturbed. "I thought we were going to the Creecy Plantation. I sent word we would be there for dinner." He showed his disappointment in his face.

"I am afraid we will be riding too fast for pleasure, Baroness. We must deprive ourselves of your charming company." Adam grinned as he looked at her, a boyish, impish grin.

Lady Anne's face flushed. "I am sure you will find Captain de' Medici more agreeable company. You can talk of war."

"And not of love?" Adam replied.

She spurred her horse viciously and rode off toward the east gate, Raoul following.

De' Medici laughed, his large brown eyes sparkling. "Weren't you a little rough, Rutledge?"

Adam shook his head. "Roughness is something new to her. She doesn't know whether she likes it or not, but she is inclined to come back for more."

They trotted off, and when they came to the end of Broad Street, turned into Virginia Road.

"I don't know why I have taken it upon myself to punish the woman," Adam Rutledge said. "Perhaps it is because I think her husband such a fine man."

De' Medici laughed aloud. "I never knew before that you were the defendant of injured and abused husbands."

"I'm not, usually. But a feeling of pleasure comes

over me when I say something rude to the woman. That is the way she affects me."

De' Medici was thoughtful. "I wish Raoul had a similar approach. I am afraid he is in for some sadness before she finishes with him. When will that be?"

"As soon as another handsome young man appears. Variety is what she needs to whet the appetite—infinite variety."

The next afternoon the three Pennys sat drinking yaupon tea in Mrs. Armitage's drawing room at Cupola House, their wide-opened eyes fixed on the Baroness von Poellnitz in wondering admiration.

The Baroness was dressed London-fashion in a puce muslin with a wide billowing skirt trimmed to the waist with small ruffles of pleated lace. Her pointed bodice was of dark brown taffeta laced with a brown twisted cord. She had on a natural-straw Milan hat, faced with rose taffeta, a garden of pink and red roses. Her satin slippers were brown, laced with brown ribands, and she carried a small reticule of the same color.

They watched with fascination as she took a gold and porcelain snuff box from the bag, abstracted a pinch, applied it to her patrician nose and sneezed delicately into a large cambric handkerchief. Her long, slim, white fingers covered with rings, moved gracefully; in truth, every motion of her slender body was studied and full of grace. Her well-modulated voice was studied. Although the girls listened with the closest attention, each one was feeling that her own movements were awkward and her voice uncultivated.

The Baroness, pleased at the attention, was talking about society in London. "My dear young ladies, you must go to London as soon as this stupid war is over. You must take your bow in society. You will never get anywhere unless you have attended one of the Queen's soirées, nor will you ever make a suitable marriage unless you have appeared at Court. If you come over next year, I will present you myself."

Penny Cabarrus said, "But your ladyship, wouldn't that be very expensive?"

The Baroness' tinkling laugh rang out. "How amusing—you the grandniece of the great Paris banker, Cabarrus, concerning yourself with money."

Penny MacLaine said, "Madam, is it true that young noblemen can be bought for husbands in London —that is, if the girl has enough money?"

Lady Anne shook her finger at Penny. "Tut, tut! You've been listening to tales. Our young men are not quite so bad as that. I confess that many of the most attractive are rather impecunious, but they are really not on the auction block. Young girls have really no place in society, always a chaperone at your side. You must be a married woman to enjoy life and have a lover. Why, la me, every married woman I know has a lover or two! That is what makes life gay and bearable."

The girls cast horrified glances at one another. Lady Anne laughed. "Are you shocked? Don't be so countrified. Everyone knows that married women have the utmost freedom. Why, when I was only nineteen and married to the Duke of Northumberland I had the gayest, handsomest young lover!"

"Oh!" Penny Cabarrus exclaimed. "Whatever did your husband say?"

"Nothing at all. He was in America with the army. He would never have known if it hadn't been that he had a spy among my house servants. That's what led to my divorce from the Duke."

Mrs. Armitage, who had been out of the room, returned at that moment, and with a glance of warning at the shocked girls, Lady Anne began talking about other things.

After the Baroness had driven away in her coach to make a call on Mrs. Johnstone at Hayes, the girls went up to the cupola.

"Did you ever hear anything like that in your whole life?" Penny Blair asked.

"Never. But then I've never seen a woman like the

Baroness before. I wonder if all beautiful women are as loose about men?"

"I don't know, but all the men in Edenton are at her feet right now. I hope she doesn't turn her charms on Raoul," Penny Cabarrus said. "What chance would I have?"

"I've heard that Frenchmen are the worst. They all have mistresses—little milliners or seamstresses, never a woman of their own class. But in London it is the other way, it seems, from what she says."

Penny MacLaine said, "I think she was just boasting. Three country girls like us are good sport for her— to shock, I mean."

"Maybe you are right. She may have wanted to shock and disturb us. I intend to find out."

"How can you do that?"

"I don't know, but there must be a way."

There was a long silence. Then Penny Cabarrus said, "It must be exciting to be married and have a lover —awfully exciting. Maybe it might be exciting to have a lover without being married."

"Pen! What are you saying?" her two friends exclaimed at once.

"I don't know, but she puts thoughts into my head. I don't believe she is a nice woman even if she is a Baroness and has been a Duchess."

Penny Blair said, "I think she is horrible, even though she is a beauty."

The girls took up the telescope and began to search the water of Albemarle Sound for a sail, but they saw nothing larger than a fisherman's pirogue.

As the sun was sinking behind the pine trees on the Tyrell shore, the girls tripped down the narrow steps of the curved stairway. They bade Mrs. Armitage good night and left messages for the doctor, and went their several ways, thinking of the things that Lady Anne had said. At first they were shocked—then wondering. Perhaps it would not be too bad to be married and take a lover.

Penny Cabarrus was so silent at supper that Marianne noticed her abstaction. "A penny for your thoughts, my dear."

The girl came back from her dream world with a start. She looked up at Raoul's laughing eyes. "I am sorry," she said. "I was thinking of something."

"But, of course, mademoiselle," Raoul said. "You were thinking deeply from the look on your face, very deeply and not too happily."

A blush came to the girl's cheek. "I am sorry," she repeated. "I was thinking of something the Baroness said."

Marianne saw the quick change of expression on Raoul's face. Something of fear showed in his eyes. Or was it wonder?

Stephen signaled Samuel to fill his wine glass. "What's this? What's this? Has the Baroness been filling your little ears with her London talk?"

"Not about London, sir. About men."

Raoul tipped over his wine glass. The Burgundy made a red stream on the white linen of the tablecloth.

"Oh, madam! I am so sorry. I have ruined the cloth."

"Think nothing of it, lad. It has happened before."

The interruption put an end to talk about the Baroness. They all left the table and walked out on the gallery. A half moon was throwing shadows along the length of the pocosin. Chimney swallows were darting across the housetop and beside the river. It was a quiet night along Pembroke Creek and the wide Sound beyond.

"Would you like to go out on the creek, mademoiselle?" Raoul said. "It is a beautiful night."

Marianne said, "Run up and get a wrap, Penny. The nights are cool on the water in August."

Penny hurried down the broad hall and mounted the stairs, pleased that Raoul had invited her, but determined not to show her pleasure. She must take things calmly, like a society lady, and veil her real feelings behind a mask of indifference. She would use the Baroness as a model. Much as she disapproved of her conduct, she found her exciting—very exciting.

Guided by Raoul's strong hand, Penny stepped lightly from the dock to the pirogue. She took her position in the stern, spreading her wide muslin skirts about her. Her little feet in bright red shoes were straight in front. She reminded Raoul of a little doll. She was not really pretty, but her dark hair, her greenish eyes and her white skin gave her a certain distinction. Like all Frenchwomen she had a certain chic that lent an interest the American girls lacked.

He wondered as he bent his broad back to the oars just why he had so impulsively asked her to join him on the river. He was already regretting the invitation. Young girls bored him. He had no conversation when he was alone with them. They giggled or simpered or looked at him with wide soulful eyes. But Penny Cabarrus was different. She had more poise than the other girls he had met in Edenton. Was that because she was a Frenchwoman? She did not seem to expect him to entertain her. That was good.

He could imagine he was out on the water with Lady Anne this romantic night. He fell to thinking of her lying full length unclothed on the sofa, as unashamed as if she enjoyed displaying her naked body. Surely she was the most beautiful woman in the world, a Venus with arms to enfold him and carry him to Paradise.

A cool, quiet voice broke in on his dreams. "Do you think we might row over to John's Island? I long to see it by moonlight—the moss hanging from the trees, the cypresses thrusting their knees out of the black water."

He thought, "The girl has imagination. Perhaps I should get to know her better. He turned the boat and headed for the island.

John's Island was all that Penny had imagined. The pocosin came down to the banks. A little stream made its way among the grotesque cypresses into the darkness of the swamp. The moon shadows filtered through their heavy crowns and made curious streams of light on the black water. A few strokes of the oars and they were in a different world, a primeval world of twisted trees and dripping Spanish moss.

Raoul secured the oars in the locks and sat at Penelope's feet, looking up at her. In the faint moonlight she seemed more mature. He moved forward and put his head against her knees. The night enfolded them in its magic. He lifted her hand to his lips, a firm but tender little hand that smelled of lavender, a pungent clean smell, he thought, unlike the cloying perfume that clung to Lady Anne. He felt tender toward her as he stroked her hand. She touched his cheek gently with her slim fingers. Her nearness was causing him to tremble. Presently she leaned forward and pressed her lips tightly to his in a timid kiss. A moment later he turned and clasped her in his arms, murmuring endearing words in her ear. She kissed him again, now with rising passion.

He broke away from her embrace. "No," he murmured. "No."

She did not answer. She seemed to have withdrawn. All at the once the night had changed. The magic beauty had retreated. The pocosin was grotesque, not beautiful.

"I will row you home," he said. "I am sorry I forgot myself for a moment."

The boat floated out of the deep swamp into the open water. The half moon was bright above them. Glancing at her, he saw her eyes were filled with tears.

"I am sorry," he said. "I did not intend to disturb you."

She spoke at last. "It is all so beautiful, a beautiful enchanted world that I can never forget."

Raoul thought: It was not I whom she kissed so ardently. It was her dream world, a young girl's dream world, her first step into maturity.

Marianne had more time to give to Penny after Stephen had gone to Wake County Court House to attend the legislature. She worried a little at the girl's abstraction, her inattention and lack of interest in affairs of the household. She thought Penny acted like a girl in love, but with whom?

It occured to her that it might be Raoul. Perhaps Penelope was not such a child after all. Marianne regretted that the Duc de Braille had departed to join the French contingent under the Marquis de Lafayette at Williamsburg. She could have talked to him. Now she must watch her niece more closely. She did not want her to be hurt, as she surely must be if she fell in love with Raoul, whom Marianne considered too sophisticated for Penelope. Still, they did not seem to be interested in each other. The only times they were together were when they occasionally went out on the creek in the pirogue. Surely no harm in that.

But as soon as Stephen Cabarrus returned, she brought up the subject.

"It's curious that you mention it, my dear," Stephen said. "I stopped at Horniblow's to catch up on the news, and walked a distance afterward with James Iredell. He spoke to me—quite reluctantly—about Raoul.

"Hannah is worried about him. He spends so much time with Lady Anne. They ride out in the country together almost every day while the Baron is down country looking for land to buy. She thinks it is unhealthy for him to become so involved. The landlord of the Red Lion told James that he had seen them together walking through the woods back of his inn when they had left their horses in his stables. He thought it a strange proceeding and so do I."

"Any way you look at it, it is a delicate situation," Marianne said.

Stephen asked where Raoul was then. Marianne told him he had ridden over to Bertie County, to the Pollocks', with Lady Anne.

"An all-day trip," she said. "They went alone. You know how Dishon runs his ferry. If you are not there on the instant, he pulls out. Suppose they are late? What happens? Don't you suppose her husband will worry?"

"I suspect her husband is accustomed to her comings and goings. At the moment he has just returned from New Bern."

Penny came in at that moment and the subject was dropped. After supper, when they were sitting on the gallery, Penny brought up the subject of Raoul. "Aunt, do you think Raoul is in love with the Baroness?"

Marianne looked at the girl, who had never seemed to her so young and defenseless. I am afraid she has heartbreak in store for her! Marianne thought. What chance has an innocent young girl against a woman like Lady Anne, surrounded by the mystery of London life?

"My dear, I'm sure I don't know," Marianne said. "Raoul has never spoken to me about the Baroness. Perhaps he is infatuated. It is not unusual for a young man to be swept off his feet by an older woman."

"They say the Baroness has a preference for young men."

"My dear child, if you pay attention to everything the village gossips say . . ."

"I don't. Only when they talk about Raoul. It hurts me in my heart."

"Dear child," Marianne said, "I pity you. If Raoul fell in love with any girl here in America, and his father learned of it, your charming young Frenchman would be dragged home forthwith."

Penny rose, her eyes flashing. "And perhaps with that girl as his wife. We women have a thing to say about that sometimes, don't we, Aunt?"

She left the room so abruptly Marianne was sure she was going to cry. Marianne started to follow her, then quickly changed her mind. The child was becoming a woman, she thought, let her learn as a woman does. After all, I was only sixteen . . .

Raoul came in the following morning. He was filled with excuses. They had missed the ferry and stayed the night at Avoca with the Capeharts. The Baroness had been very disturbed, for her husband was expected back home after a trip south, and she would not be home to greet him. He had not seen the Baron, for he had come directly back to Pembroke.

Marianne and Stephen listened to his excuses without comment. After a time Stephen said: "It is not necessary for you to explain your goings and comings to me, Raoul, but I will say that in this country it is not considered quite the thing to go about too much with a married woman."

Raoul flared, his face red. "That is just like a country village of plebian people. Lady Anne is accustomed to the latitude a married woman has in London."

Stephen smiled at his vehemence. "I am not your father, Raoul, only your host who is interested in your good. I am only suggesting that you might compromise the lady, staying out all night.

Raoul left the room without answering, and went directly to his bedroom.

Penny joined them a moment later. Marianne knew from her white and stricken face that she had heard Stephen's words of admonition.

Poor child, Marianne thought. She hasn't a chance against that woman.

A few hours later, when Raoul came down to dinner, he looked rested, and was his old gay self again. Penny ate little. She kept glancing at Raoul from time to time, but she said nothing.

Stephen talked about the war and the news he had heard in town about the battle at Eutaw Springs. Raoul's face clouded. "I wish I could get into the army. That's what I came here for. I wanted to fight for liberty. We in France think it is the most wonderful thing that has ever been done by any country. To fight for men's rights, to be free! That is why the Marquis came here and all we Frenchmen followed him. Now I have to stay around until I get permission from my guardian."

"I know how you feel, Raoul," Stephen said, "but the Duc de Braille said he would let you know. Word may come from him any day now."

Raoul's face changed. "If I don't hear soon I'll go to Williamsburg whether he wants me to or not. I'm a man and I know my mind."

After dinner Penny went out to the gallery. The heat of the day had broken with the evening breeze off the sound. Presently Raoul joined her.

"Would you like to go out on the river, Penny? It will be cool now."

Penny got to her feet. "Indeed, yes. I should love to go. I am tired of myself."

Raoul helped Penny into the boat and took up the oars. Without any words he rowed straight for the pocosin on John's Island. It was almost two weeks since they had been there.

Now, under the late moon, the heavy woods took on a different aspect. The hanging moss that festooned the cypress trees was almost black. It appeared more mysterious than ever before.

When they reached the little lake in the center of the pocosin, Raoul said: "I've heard a little tale about this spot. It seems that some years ago a beautiful woman, a pirate, was killed in here by one of her own men."

"Her lover perhaps?" Penny asked. There was a breathless eagerness in her voice. Raoul rested his oars and turned to her. She was leaning forward, her eyes shining, her face avid.

"Her lover?" she repeated, dwelling on the word. "Tell me, Raoul, tell me the story."

Raoul laughed. "Ah, you are interested, aren't you?"

"Certainly I am interested. I like strange love stories."

"Well, I'll have to disappoint you. That's all I know."

Her face showed her disappointment. "You don't even know her name or who her lover was?"

"I don't even know her name. I am afraid, my romantic young woman, that it wasn't a lover. It was one of her guilty pirate companions who killed her to get her share of the jewels she had stolen from Queen Caroline. He drove a dagger into her back and threw her into the black juniper water."

"How disappointing! This is a spot for romance, not murder and sudden death."

He moved to the seat opposite her. "If you must have romance, my dear, may I offer myself?"

She pouted. "Now you are teasing me."

"Never. I am in deadly earnest. Did anyone ever tell you that you are beautiful? Beautiful and bewitching and beguiling?"

"No. Tell me." She leaned forward.

He caught her hand and raised it to his lips. "You are. When you grow up you will make men's hearts turn to water."

She drew back, her face cold and withdrawn. "I am grown up now. Quite grown up."

He laughed, his fingers on her arm caressing the cool skin. "Adorable child," he whispered. "Adorable child."

Suddenly she leaned forward. With her hand under his chin she pressed her lips to his, a hard, passionate kiss. Then she leaned back. "Is that the kiss of a child, monsieur?"

Raoul's hand tightened on her arm. "God no! It is a woman's kiss to stir a man's blood."

He had moved to the seat beside her. He put his arm about her slim waist and drew her to him. She did not resist as he put his lips to hers in a long kiss that set his blood beating in his veins. He held her close until she broke away.

"That is enough," she said quietly.

He drew back abruptly. "You are a little devil."

She laughed teasingly. "Not really? You pay me a great compliment, monsieur. Come, let us go ashore. I like the slow swaying of the hanging moss. It adds beauty to the trees."

They walked along the bank to a mossy knoll. She sat down and pulled off her shoes and stockings. "I want to put my feet into the cool black water."

"You are a child," he laughed.

"One minute you accuse me of being a devil. The next moment you have me a child. What am I sir, tell me?"

"I don't know. An elf, a dryad, a witch."

Penny laughed, throwing her head back. Her heavy hair tumbled over her white shoulders. She raised her slim arms to confine it.

"Let it lie. It is like molten copper against your white skin."

She leaned back against a tree trunk. "You are a poet," she said.

"You would make a poet out of any man."

Penny made no answer. She lifted her slim hand to her lips as though she were stifling a yawn.

Raoul got to his feet. "Perhaps we had better go," he said in a strained voice. "I don't want to bore you."

Penny saw that she might have imitated Lady Anne a little too closely. "Please, not for a moment. It is so beautiful here. I do not want to lose such beauty. It happens so seldom."

The young Frenchman dropped back on the turf. "If you wish," he said. His voice was sulky.

"Here we are a thousand miles from anybody or anything. Only the forest and the moon."

He took up her hand again. "Only the forest and the moon and us."

"And us." She laid her hand lightly over his. He felt the blood pound in his body. He moved a little away from her.

"Don't go so far away. I think I am chilling. Please draw my wrap about me."

Raoul put his arms about her. "I can think of a better way to keep you warm."

He kissed her soft mouth. For a moment she resisted him, then threw her arms about his neck. She was at once a warm vital creature in his arms. She kissed with such passion that she sent his senses reeling. He pulled back and got to his feet. He held out his hands and pulled her to her feet. "We had better go home," he said in a strangled voice.

She made no protest but followed him to the boat and took her place without words. Her heart was singing. "He loves me, he loves me. He is afraid of me!"

IX

The Hurricane

If Lady Anne missed Raoul de Polignac's frequent visits during the next few days, she gave no sign of it. The Baron von Poellnitz had returned from New Bern, bringing with him his man of business, Stephen Sayre.

Sayre was no stranger to the Baroness. She had known him in London, where for over a year he had been her lover. Sayre was as tall as the Baron, but much heavier, being built like a wrestler, with strong arms and neck and heavy features. He was no beauty, but, as she frequently said to herself, and sometimes to others, "A woman is a fool to choose a lover for his face instead of his figure. A husband you must see in the daylight, and it would be dreadful to face an ogre over the breakfast table. But who needs a lamp for love?"

It was a pleasure for her to see him again—with one exception. He was the one man in the world of whom she was slightly afraid, and she had not done what he had told her to do. That was to ingratiate—Sayre's ironic word—herself with the men of Edenton so as to discover the movements of the troops in the South and forward the information to him in New York, where he would sell it to General Clinton.

Sayre was always in need of money. Since the Baron kept too close an eye on his accounts for Sayre to be able to truly swindle him, he had found the Baroness' indiscretions a good means to get from her own allowance enough to keep him provided with the elegant clothes he craved and to help him out of tight spots at the gambling tables.

From the time Sayre had been a student at Princeton, he had been known for his love of fine dress. His elegant brocaded waist-coats, his lace neck scarves, his highly polished silver shoe-buckles had been a matter of comment among the young men at Princeton, and later in London and in New York, where he was now living. They soon attracted attention in Edenton also.

The first time he could be alone with Lady Anne, Sayre reproached her with her delinquency.

"I've had the devil's own time making out," he said. "Only one letter from you, and that about things that had already happened and were well known in New York long before we had your warmed-over accounts."

"I have exerted all my charms," the Baroness said coquettishly as she leaned against him, "and sometimes not without success."

"Of that there is no possible doubt," Sayre said. "But with whom, and with what result other than to gratify your vanity—and your lust?"

"Don't be unkind, Stephen. You know better than that."

"And you know better than to trifle with me. Whom have you approached?"

She told him of Raoul de Polignac and Adam Rutledge. "The rest," she added, "are caged in marriage. They'd as soon look at another woman than their wives as to trust you at dice—if they but knew your ways. Adam Rutledge is like the corrupt who have put on incorruption. He fancies himself a saint."

"A saint with a cloven hoof," Sayre said. "I daresay you've heard of his bastard by some Arab slave girl. You must work with the young Frenchman. He'll soon be called to the army. What we need most to know is the movements of the French and their damned fleet."

"I might make you jealous, Stephen."

"That's easily cured." He slapped his pockets.

"Hear that? Not even a tinkle. Not the jingle I love to hear, like the song of angels. Come, woman, I feel lucky."

The Baroness went to her boudoir and extracted her jewel casket from a drawer in her dressing table. From the compartment beneath its false bottom, she drew a netted purse, one of several she kept concealed there, through the mesh of which shone the gold of guineas.

Holding it behind her back, she approached Sayre, lifting her face to his. "A forfeit," she demanded.

Sayre laughed sardonically. He put his arms around her, drew her to him and kissed her lustily, meanwhile disentangling the purse from her fingers and slipping it into his pocket.

"Now see," he said, at last releasing her, "if your little French lad can match that."

Laughing sardonically again, Sayre went down to the common room of the tavern.

It was late afternoon, the time when many of the Edenton men gathered there for gaming and a tankard of ale before going to their homes for supper. Sayre had already made the acquaintance of some, and had been careful to lose at backgammon to them. They liked his hearty, jovial manner, quite in contrast to the dignified and reserved deportment of the much older Baron.

This afternoon he deliberately lost again at backgammon, heavily.

"My friends," he said, "I have no luck at your game. Will you try mine?"

He brought out his own dice box. The men could not refuse. Sayre ordered ale for all those who would play with him.

At first he lost consistently. Then, all that changed, and the pile of shillings by his place grew. It was late before the game broke up, and by then Stephen Sayre was the richer by several pounds.

He ordered ale all around again. "Tomorrow night, gentlemen, I shall let you take this away from me," he said. "I thank you all for a splendid game."

The next morning was the fifth in succession that Raoul had not called for Lady Anne to go riding. Now that Stephen Sayre had admonished her to pry war news from Raoul, she was perturbed at his absence.

Dressed for riding as usual in her madras habit, she sat nervously awaiting his knock at the door of the suite. What could have happened? More important, what should she do? She considered paying a visit to the Cabarruses at Pembroke. No, there was no reason to think she would see him there, and she could hardly ask for him. A note? That could be too easily intercepted. She could scarcely linger about the streets of Edenton in the chance that she might accidentally encounter him. "Oh, fie!" she said aloud.

The bell of St. Paul's church tolled eleven times. At that hour, she remembered, the men would be gathering in the common room for a late breakfast and to hear the war news. Raoul often was there.

Lady Anne hurried down to the courtyard. A quick glance through the common room window as she passed told her Raoul was indeed there.

Old Zeb, the slave hostler, had had her horse saddled and ready for an hour. He led the animal to the upping block for her to mount.

"Mistress late this morning," he said. "Better not ride now. Hurricane coming soon. Ol' Zeb, he smell it in the air. The debbil he ride in the wind a-lashin' he tail mighty fierce."

Lady Anne's mind was not on the old slave. She put only her toe into the stirrup. Then as she prepared to hoist herself into the saddle, she slipped her toe out and gently sank to the ground.

"Oh!" she moaned. "I am hurt." She let her voice grow weak. "Go . . . common room . . . Monsieur de Polignac." She closed her eyes and let her head loll against the block.

After a moment she raised her lids enough to see Zeb hobbling as fast as he could into the tavern.

By the time he reappeared with Raoul she was on her feet, dusting her madras riding skirt with the crop.

"How good of you, Raoul," she said, smiling as effectively as she knew how. "No, I find I'm not hurt at all. But since you're here, won't you ride with me?" She laid her hand on his arm. "Zeb here thinks there may be a storm, so I don't wish to go alone. But I need exercise —and so does my horse."

Raoul blushed. He had seen her riding before with the man he understood to be the Baron's man of affairs —a coarse, ugly creature, Raoul thought him. Yet Lady Anne had appeared so friendly, almost intimate, with him that Raoul had been furiously jealous. Now that he could scarcely refuse her, he found his firm resolutions to see her no more melting into thin air. She was so beautiful she made his blood tingle. Beside her pretty little Penny Cabarrus was—pretty little Penny. *Mon Dieu,* he thought, can't a man have two loves? Already he had found pretty little Penny growing possessive.

"I should be charmed," he said with a little bow. "Zeb, bring my horse."

Zeb did as he was told, but he shook his white head as he held the horses. "Hurricane will come," he croaked.

"I've never been in a hurricane," the Baroness said lightly. "I should think it poetic. I should feel like Lear in the midnight tempest." She laughed gaily. "Oh, it would be fun—like being in a real play."

"It's the baddest wind you ever see, mistress. Every tree, every bush lay right down flat on the ground when he comes. The cornfield he will fall on he face and bury hisself in the ground. Better stay in close to town, mistress. When you hear roaring like great waves, come riding home fast—for he sure will get you."

Lady Anne laughed again as she mounted from the upping block. "I'll come when the wind blows hard," she said as she took the reins, and galloped out of the courtyard with Raoul close behind her.

The sky was leaden with dark clouds scudding across. The wind was from the southeast, a smart, steady blow. When she rode out of the village she could see that the horizon was a strange green-yellow color.

Slowing her horse to a walk, she turned to Raoul. "It looks dangerous," he said. "We had best ride back."

Lady Anne tossed her head defiantly. Her eyes were flashing. "Not I," she said tauntingly, and dug her spurs into her horse's flanks.

Ahead of her she saw a turning, a little road that led through the woods to a small eminence from which one got a lovely vista of the Sound through the sycamores. She reined her horse in just enough to veer into it. A glance over her shoulder told her Raoul had had no choice but to follow her. The countryside had lost the lush green beauty of summer. It was too early for the glorious colors of autumn. But it had charm—wild asters and goldenrod bloomed by the ditches. Queen Anne's lace was gone and the leaves of the dogwoods along the edge of the forest were turning red.

As soon as they reached the clearing on the hilltop she pulled her horse up sharply and leaped to the ground. The wind had already risen noticeably. It whipped her skirt about her limbs. She tore off her little hat and faced the wind, letting it whip her hair in fiery golden streamers behind her. She flung out her arms like wings.

She could see the enraptured fascination in Raoul's face as he stood a bit before her. "How glorious it would be to make love," she exclaimed in a dithyrambic voice, "with a hurricane roaring overhead!"

Raoul's eyes were shining. His lips were parted in eagerness. In spite of the wind she could hear his feverish breath. In another moment she was in his arms, almost strangling in the intensity of his embrace.

"My goddess!" he murmured.

They lay in ecstasy, forgetting everything but their passion, until they could bear no more, then settled into a soft embrace.

"My darling," Lady Anne whispered, "I have missed you sorely."

"And I you. I have been a fool."

"Do you love me still?"

"Always. Always!"

"But for days you did not."

"I was a fool," he said.

"Is there another?"

"No longer," he murmured.

"But you will go away to war soon."

"Very soon," he sighed.

"Where will you go?"

"To Yorktown. The French are gathering to help General Washington besiege Cornwallis there."

"Will there be fighting?"

"I think not," he said. "If our fleet arrives in time, Cornwallis will be trapped."

"Who told you this?"

"My guardian, the Duc de Braille. He is there already."

A gust of wind tore across the hill, sweeping a great branch from a sycamore before it. The horses whinnied in terror. Raoul leaped to his feet and ran to them, reaching them just in time to keep them from tearing loose. They reared in fright, but he held them tight and gradually calmed them.

"Come," he shouted to Lady Anne. "We must seek shelter at once."

They galloped toward Edenton, the wind behind them impelling them so that they felt as if they were flying. Leaves and branches swept over and past them.

"I love this storm," Lady Anne shouted. "It exhilarates me to feel its power."

When they rode into the stableyard behind the tavern, objects were being hurled through the air with the rising force of the wind—boxes, buckets and trash of all kinds. Raoul took her arm to guide her across the courtyard to the side door that opened into the common room. As they turned the corner they heard a great crash as the swinging sign of the inn banged down on the cobbles of the street.

Horniblow came running out of the door and surveyed the twisted mass of iron.

"There you go, you old devil sign of the King's

Arms Inn. I've been meaning to take you down ever since I bought the place. Now I'm saved the trouble. I'll have a new one with 'Horniblow's Tavern' on it." Seeing Lady Anne and Raoul, he pointed to the fallen sign. "I'm well rid of that just as we Americans will be shed of old King George ere long." He turned and walked into the house.

The common room was crowded with Edenton men, gaming, drinking, talking in little groups or looking out of the open door. The windows were shuttered with heavy oak held in place with strong bars. A fire roared in the great brick fireplace.

Horniblow came in from the kitchen way as the Baroness and Raoul entered the room. With him were two slaves carrying buckets of water.

"Douse the fire," he ordered. "There is danger from fire in a hurricane." He turned to the company. "Gentlemen, I fear you will have cold fare at your meals today. I've had the cook draw the fires in the kitchen. Plenty of cold fowl, ham and beef, though. You won't starve."

Sayre rose from his dice game and came to meet Lady Anne. Seeing Raoul with her, he rolled his eyes just enough in his direction for her to sense the question he left unspoken. She dropped her chin in a slight nod by way of answer.

"Go on up to your rooms, madam," Sayre said deferentially. "The Baron is there waiting for you anxiously. He doesn't relish company as I do." He turned to Raoul. "But you, sir," he said in his most jovial voice, "since you are trapped here, will you not join us in a game?" He took Raoul's arm and led him to the table where the other dicers were waiting Sayre's return.

Lady Anne turned slowly to mount the stairs but cast a reluctant glance over her shoulder. "Go along," Sayre whispered. "This is a man's refuge."

"You will come to our rooms?"

"Perhaps. That depends on the kind of game your friend plays." He winked maliciously.

When Lady Anne got to her sitting room her husband had closed and barred the windows and was pacing up and down the floor. As he saw her, his face cleared. "My dear, where have you been? I have been anxious for you. They tell me that a hurricane is blowing and may be here at any time."

"Everybody has been telling me that all morning," she snapped. "What of it? Some rain, some wind, and it's over."

"It will damage the crops. The corn will be flattened to the ground. That will be tragic for the planters."

"Why do you worry? You have no growing corn."

The Baron stared at her. "I think about my friends, the planters," he said, his voice cold.

Lady Anne passed into her bedroom to change her habit. Her woman was sitting in the middle of the room, looking terrified.

"If you would get up and do your work," Lady Anne said, "you wouldn't have time to worry. Now get out the garnet taffeta with the blue overskirt. If we are to be blown away, I want to be properly dressed."

Dawkins shook her head and went to the wardrobe, stuffed with Lady Anne's gowns, lifted out the garnet taffeta and laid it on the bed. From the chest of drawers she took satin slippers with blue lacings, and a Mechlin modesty to fill in the gown at the bosom. She pulled and tugged at her lady's stays until her waist was only two hands' span, and her snow-white bosom was pushed up so that the division line was plainly visible.

Dressed, Lady Anne viewed herself in the mirror and arranged her curls to fall over her shoulders. At last, satisfied, she added a beaded reticule, put a kerchief in it and after anointing the corners of her mouth and the lobes of her ears from a bottle of French scent, she felt ready for the public.

When she came into the sitting room she found the Baron still pacing the floor and waiting for her to join him at dinner.

"What have we to eat?" she asked.

"Pork, cold ham and black-eyed peas with a pudding of cornmeal molasses for a sweet."

She made a little face. "The same today, yesterday and forever—black-eyed peas."

"What matter, when they are so good?"

Lady Anne picked at the food. "Poor cheer," she said petulantly. "In a storm like this I want excitement. I am going down to the common room to throw some dice or have a game of loo—if I can find a partner."

"My dear, you cannot. Only men frequent the common room. Women never go there."

Lady Anne moved toward the door. "Then I will be the first. Are you coming with me?"

The Baron followed her. "I suppose I must, to sanction your appearance."

"Don't if you don't approve. I am quite capable of going alone."

There was a break in the noise of talk when Lady Anne entered the room from the stairway, and a gasp of surprise—or was it admiration—at the picture she made.

Raoul de Polignac, seated near the door, sprang to his feet and hurried toward Lady Anne, but Stephen Sayre was before him to offer his arm and lead her to a table.

The men turned back to their cards, their dice or their backgammon. Lady Anne's clear voice broke the stillness. "I hope I have not offended the local custom in coming down to this room, sacred to you gentlemen, to wait out the hurricane."

The protests were loud and earnest.

"Where do ladies go if not to the common room?" she asked.

"There is a ladies' parlor," a man answered.

"Occupied only by women? How dull!"

Laughter followed, but Lady Anne paid no mind. She was delving into her recticule for some guineas, which she threw on the table with a careless gesture. "Who has the dice?"

Sayre cast them on the table. "I warn you I feel lucky. I venture I will soon pocket your gold, my lady."

The Baron sat down at the table, but refused to play. "I do not know the game. I will stake my wife."

The others at the table were Charles Johnson and a planter from the county. "First cast, your ladyship," Sayre said, putting the dice box in her hand. "Cast and good luck to you!"

Above the noise in the room sounded the rattle of the dice or the slap of cards. Outside, the wind was roaring. Gusts shook the shutters and carried debris down King Street. Men from the county worried about getting home. Horniblow came in and out of the room looking at doors and windows to see that they were secure.

"Barometer still falling," he announced. "I've never seen it so low in the storm area. The wind gusts must be one hundred and twenty-five miles an hour. You can't even hear the cannon booming for the wind's roar."

"Cannon?" the Baron said.

"They set off the cannon on the Green when a hurricane is coming, to warn the people. Usually two shots. Just now it was four. I've never heard four shots before in all the years I've been here."

Men got up and went to the door. The sky was a sickly yellow. The air was thick with leaves and small branches. Trees large and small were bending double with the force of the gale.

A man burst into the room as though he had been shot from the cannon. He was soaked to the skin. "The mill has gone. Flat to the ground. The roof is resting on the waters of the Sound."

"Too bad for Copeland," someone said. "It is filled with cotton. It will break him."

Robert Smith came in from the courtyard. "I want shelter. I can't stand to stay at my store and watch the roof sail off. My merchandise will be ruined if that happens."

"Don't be pessimistic, Robert. Perhaps she will hold—the roof, I mean."

Smith pulled up a chair beside Lady Anne. "With your ladyship's permission may I try my fortune in this game?"

Lady Anne liked the witty, forthright merchant. She smiled her permission. "Mayhap you will bring me luck, sir. I'm fast losing my guineas."

"Unlucky at cards, lucky in love," he quoted. "Isn't it better to be lucky in love? I am sure I think so."

Sayre said, "Why not be lucky at both?"

Lady Anne's laugh ripped out. "How wise you are, Mr. Sayre! I will be like that. Lucky in cards and lucky in love also."

She cast the dice. They came up double nines. She raked in the money on the table.

Charles Johnson said, "I'm at the end of my cash."

"No matter, sir," Sayre protested. "Your note will do. Play until the storm hits."

"I'm too nervous, gentlemen. My wife planned to have a young Negro drive her to Suffolk in the chariot. I do not know whether she is on the road or at home." He walked to the door and looked out into the street.

Horniblow went up to him. "I hope you won't try to ride to Bandon until the storm abates, sir. Bandon is in the direct path of the gale."

The Baron got to his feet. He seized Horniblow by the arm. There was such tension in his grasp that the innkeeper winced.

"How do you know?" the Baron demanded.

"The storm will follow the river if it keeps to its course."

From the gaming table came a peal of Lady Anne's laughter. "Aha!" she shouted triumphantly. "Nines again!"

The Baron turned to Charles Johnson. "I will ride with you, sir. If my boys are in danger, I must be with them." To Horniblow he said: "Order my horse."

"We must go," Charles Johnson said. "My father-in-law and Miss Anne will be alone there, with the boys to take care of. The negroes will be too scared to be of any help."

The Baron turned back to the gaming table. Lady Anne held the dice box in her hand, shaking it, her face showing only her intense excitement.

"Anne . . ."

At the moment he spoke, she cast the dice. But his voice had so startled her that they merely dribbled from the box. She looked in disgust at the twos that had come up.

"Bruno," she said sharply, "you have spoiled my throw." Then seeing the sudden anger in his face she said querulously: "Well, what is it now?"

Without replying, the Baron strode to the door. Charles Johnson had already gone out. Baron von Poellnitz shot open the door. The wind dashed it past him. It banged against the wall with a sound like an explosion, and the wind swept into the room. It required the strength of two men to force the door shut behind the Baron.

The hours passed with no surcease in the winds. Horniblow's servants set up tables and brought in food and drink.

"The ale is on the house," he announced. "Drink hearty and forget the wind."

But it was impossible to forget the wind, which kept howling down the street, shaking the tavern with its gusts and banging the shutters. Men left off their gaming and wandered about the room, looking out from time to time to watch the progress of the storm.

"Since no one will play longer," Lady Anne announced, "let us have some other diversion." Her eyes lit on a battered spinet against the wall in the far corner of the room. "Stephen," she commanded, "give us a tune."

Sayre went to the instrument and banged out a sprightly Scottish air. Some of the men, recognizing it, began singing the words of the marching song of the Stuart uprising of '45.

"Louder," Lady Anne called. "Now, everyone!" She herself led them in the chorus.

They sang it twice. Then Sayre changed to a jig.

Lady Anne picked up her skirt and began to dance. She called to Raoul to join her.

Immediately he got up and stood before her. Together they tapped their toes and heels to the lively tune which Sayre sang in a rousing baritone.

> Ye'll hear of the chieftains of old,
> Those sons of valor and worth,
> But Charles' favorite clan was
> MacDonald, the pride of the North.
> Oh, hie to the Highlands, my laddie,
> Be welcomed by hearts warm and true,
> For there's where ye'll see, my ain laddie,
> The tartans and bonnets of blue.

There were half a dozen Scots in the room. They joined in the chorus of the old Highland tune, banging their tankards on the tables in time with the rhythm. Suddenly the dance was interrupted, as the full force of the storm swept down upon the village. The rain fell in sheets. The roar of the wind was so great that it drowned out the singing.

Lady Anne left Raoul and ran to Sayre. She buried her head against his chest, her hands over her ears to shut out the howling wind. Sayre put his arm about her and pulled her to a settle by the fireplace. They sat close together, as though they could protect each other from the wind's fury. Fear showed on every face; even the most valiant men cowered before the storm. For a full hour the winds blew in gusts so strong that they seemed to shake the very earth under them. Then the roar of the storm died away. It was followed by an eerie stillness.

"The eye of the storm is passing," Horniblow told them. "Watch out for the backlash. It will blow tenfold the speed of the fleetest stallion."

But they would not heed him. Some of the men darted out of the door and ran down the village street, intent on reaching their homes. Those who lived nearby made it. Others, finding their way wholly impeded by the litter of limbs and branches and great trees blown over the street, rushed back to the protection of the inn.

The backlash was more severe than the early hurricane. The massive front door of the tavern blew open. Men dashed to lean against it to hold it in place, for the heavy board that formed the lock had been splintered like a match block. Candles on the table were blown out, and the room was in darkness, the shutters having long before been closed and fastened.

Horniblow shouted to the men to move the heavy tables against the door that six men could not keep shut. Finally by piling table upon table they managed to erect a barricade that held. The company sat in the almost airless darkness, silent and still, until the backlash passed and the deluge ceased. Finally the innkeeper ordered a window opened. There was light in the sky, a deep strip of blood red along the horizon across the South.

"The storm has passed," Horniblow cried. "Thank God, my inn still stands!"

In the stable yard the wind had blown all boxes and bales of hay against the barn. The horses were stamping and neighing in terror. King Street was a shambles. No houses were down, but many roofs were gone. Ships at the docks had been blown from their moorings. The waters of the Sound tossed with waves like the ocean, the water a muddy yellow.

A cardinal flew past the open window and lighted on the branches of a sycamore tree. Near by a mocker began his song. The storm had passed.

X

The Wake of the Storm

When Lady Anne awoke the next morning, the wind was still at almost gale force, but the sky was clear and the sun was bright. Too bright, she thought, as she put her hand to her head. A stab of pain shot from temple to temple.

She recalled that after the village men had all left the common room once the storm passed, she had sat alone there with Stephen Sayre over a bottle of Horniblow's Maderia. Raoul had lingered (hoping for what?), but she had sent him home on the pretext that she was exhausted and must go soon to bed.

Lady Anne was not at all happy over the way the evening had ended. Incidents returned to her with depressing clarity, and did nothing to alleviate the throbbing in her head or the ache in her arms from nerves springing back into super-tautness after being relaxed from the wine she had drunk. The Baron obviously had been furious with her. She shut her eyes in an attempt to blot out the image of his cold, hard expression of—she hated to admit it—possibly justified wrath.

Fool though she thought him, Lady Anne was not so sure of herself as to be entirely free from the nagging anxiety that her husband might have a stronger will than her own. "I should have married an Englishman," she

132

said almost aloud, "not a German. One never knows about a foreigner."

If the Baron were to learn of her affair with Raoul (that simpleton!) or, worse, with Sayre, he might quite probably divorce her. After all, he would have the precedent of the Duke of Northumberland. (Why had it twice befallen her to be married to old bores who left her by herself when she ached for love and had so much to give?) She could not do without the Baron—for many reasons.

The immediate one was that she needed more money. Except for the cache of guineas in the bottom of her jewel casket, she was far beyond her liberal allowance. And the hidden store was dwindling. Sayre had even pocketed her winnings at dice the previous evening. Sayre always wanted money. He said it was for "spy work," but she wondered now whether he did not use what she gave him to pay his gambling debts. Or perhaps he was keeping a woman, or several women, in New York. Just two days ago he had charged her three pounds for a trip to Suffolk in Virginia, to post a letter to Sir Henry Clinton in New York. "To be sure that the Edentonians did not discover letters to that source," was the excuse he had given her.

Damn Sayre! She recalled that as she had grown tipsy she had teased him about her affection for Raoul. But he had only been cross with her, even surly.

"You must be more discreet," he had said. "You asked too many questions about the destination of the Edenton troop. I saw Charles Johnson looking at you strangely."

"Stephen, I do declare you're jealous." She had laughed. "You know I don't care for anyone but you."

Sayre's voice had been gruff. "You don't care for anyone but yourself." His grasp on her arm tightened.

She passed her hand through his hair. He threw his arm about her shoulder. The knot at the base of her neck gave way and her heavy red-gold hair tumbled down her back.

"How can you say such things to me, Stephen? You know it is you I love."

He touched his lips to hers. "How can I be sure?" he said under his breath. He pressed her slim body against his with passionate force.

"Have a care, Stephen," she whispered, "someone may see us."

He released her reluctantly. "You are a witch, a devil. You don't care for anyone else in the world but yourself."

Lady Anne laughed. "And why not? A woman must look to her future."

He kissed her again. "How did a woman like you ever induce Bruno to marry you?"

She laughed. "It was not I at all. It was my father, Lord Bute, who arranged the marriage. My family was only too glad to make such an advantageous marriage for the black sheep. Besides, the Baron is a rich man. Very rich."

A door opened and closed in the upper hall. A man, a stranger, came down the stairs. He looked at them as he passed with a muttered "Pardon me," and went into the courtyard. Lady Anne gathered up her skirts, preparing to mount the stairs.

Sayre held on to her arm. "Wait, there is something else I want to say to you. People in Edenton can easily suspect you since they know that you are Lord Bute's daughter."

Lady Anne laughed again. "Still worrying, Sayre? The Edenton people know only what I tell them—that I *love* America. The Baron is heart and soul in his belief in their cause and wants to buy land. Besides, am I not a connection of their beloved James Iredell?"

She mounted one step, looking down at him. "In spite of your being an extraordinarily exciting bedfellow, there are limits to what you can say to me."

Sayre had given her a dark look of anger.

Well, she must placate the Baron when he came home. She stretched her arms over her head. She was broad awake. She thought she might as well get out of bed; some hot tea might make her feel better. She rang the bell for Dawkins.

Dawkins answered Lady Anne's ring. For a moment she stood looking down at Lady Anne stretched out on the bed, her body showing through her thin night-rail. "What time is it?" Lady Anne asked.

"Almost eleven o'clock," the serving woman answered, disapproval on her face.

"You can't imagine anyone staying in bed so late, can you, Dawkins?"

"No, madam," the woman answered shortly.

"Well, don't stand there looking. Get me some clothes."

Mumbling something, Dawkins went into the dressing room. Lady Anne called her back.

"You are impudent. I'm tired of your evil looks. I won't have angry people about me, do you hear?"

"Yes, madam."

"You have no cause for ill-temper, woman."

"I am worried about the Baron, madam. He has not returned from his ride in that terrible storm." Dawkins hesitated. "The Baron is a very fine gentleman."

"Do you mean that you think that I am not a lady, or have you forgotten that I am a Stuart?"

"No, madam. I have not forgotten."

Her answer angered Lady Anne. She snatched a clothes brush from the dressing table and threw it at her tire-woman. It struck her on the forehead. She put her hand to her face and ran from the room.

Lady Anne stood looking at the closed door. It crossed her mind briefly that first her husband, then Sayre, and now her woman had left her in anger. "Why is it that everyone is so annoying today?" she thought. "They take the joy out of a pleasant day."

It was almost evening when the Baron returned. His face was drawn with the fatigue of emotion, and his usually ruddy cheeks pale with physical exhaustion. He sank into a chair with a sigh.

Lady Anne bent over and kissed his forehead, but

he did not respond except to say: "Call my man to pull off my boots."

She went to the bell pull obediently. "What is the matter, Bruno?"

"Eitel is injured," he said hollowly.

"Oh!" Lady Anne exclaimed. "Is it serious?"

She paused by the buffet and poured a glass of brandy, which she brought to the Baron. He waved it aside. Sensing she might be going to have a more difficult time than she had anticipated, she swallowed the brandy herself.

The Baron's valet came and removed his master's boots, helped him off with his coat and unfastened his stock. After the Baron had dismissed him, Lady Anne said: "Will you not tell me about it?"

The Baron sighed as if it might be an effort beyond his capacities. His voice had the tonelessness of fatigue.

"There is a cave in the river bank. The boys had been going there to escape the heat. They went there during the storm. They heard a noise of earth sliding. The ground gave away and fell upon them. All got out except Eitel and a boy named Brooks Conner."

Lady Anne's hand fluttered. "Will they . . . ?"

"Eitel will live. He is badly bruised, but he will recover. The other boy was suffocated."

The Baroness sat down opposite him. Death meant little to her; it had never come close to her. If she thought about it at all, it was with a calm detachment. It would come to her, she believed, only when she desired it—when she would be very old, and withered, and tired of the life she now loved.

They sat in silence for several moments. Then the Baron said: "The boy was buried at once. There was not enough ice to keep his young body. The schoolboys sang very sweetly."

When Lady Anne looked at him, she saw his blue eyes dim.

" 'Death,' " he quoted from a Greek play, " 'takes those he loves—the young. The beautiful and the brave, and those who have lived out their life span.' "

The Baroness laid her hand on his knee. "Bruno, you are being sentimental. After all, it was not your son."

All at once he seemed to rouse himself. The color rushed back into his cheeks menacingly. The life returned to his eyes.

"It might have been," he almost shouted. "Had it been, I could not have forgiven you."

She looked at him in astonishment. "How am I to blame?"

"Because you would not be a mother to my sons. That is why I put them into the school. And to get them away from your wicked influence."

Oh God, Lady Anne thought, what does he know? She found her hands trembling so, she had to clasp them in her lap. Everything was going terribly awry. Her confusion rose until she could feel it smarting in her throat, choking her. She swallowed hard, trying to force it down. The effort made her eyes water. If she could only cry, she prayed. It had been years since she had wept. The burning constriction in her throat grew worse. Suddenly she felt the tears come again.

Her hands flew to her face. She tried to speak, but the only sound she could produce was a strangled sob.

Then, as from a different world, she heard her husband's voice. "Forgive me, my dear. I did not mean to be so harsh."

Dimly she perceived that she was saved. Saved! He had fallen into her all too unconsciously laid trap. The advantage now was hers. She lowered her hands and blinked the tears out till they coursed down her face.

"Why do you reproach me, Bruno?" she moaned. "What have I done to deserve such abuse? You mean a great deal to me. Why have you ceased to love me?"

The Baron reached for her hand and stroked it gently until she appeared to have recovered her control. Then he rose and put his arm about her.

"I shall never cease to love you," he said.

"Then take me away from this hateful place."

"We will go very soon," he said. "Sayre is conclud-
ing the purchase of the land I have found for sale. It is
not so much as I wanted, but it will do for a start."

Gracious in victory, she, too, rose. She put her
arms about him and lifted her mouth to his.

"My dear," she said. "I know you must be very
tired. Bathe and go to bed. I myself will bring you supper."

Lady Anne listened to the Baron's snores for a full
half hour before she deemed it safe to summon his valet.

"Go down into the common room," she instructed
him, "and tell Mr. Sayre I wish to see him."

A few minutes later there was a discreet rapping at
the door of the drawing room of the suite. Lady Anne
recognized the rhythm of the signal she had agreed upon
with Stephen Sayre for their previous clandestine ren-
dezvous.

"You are playing with fire," Sayre whispered after
she had admitted him and he had embraced her warmly.

"Nonsense!" she said aloud. "He is sound asleep,
snoring and snuffling like the stupid pig he is."

"I don't mean that alone," Sayre said. "Your behavior in the common room last night has become the
talk of the village. Who is this James Iredell?"

Lady Anne told him. "Why do you ask?" she concluded.

"He has just come back from some circuit court or
other. When he heard about your dancing, he was angry. 'What else could be expected of a woman with such
a past!' he said. How could he have known—everything?"

"People in isolated villages like this make it their
chief business to know everything, especially when it is
to the detriment of someone else," Lady Anne remarked. "It's the only way they can protect themselves
from gossip about their own cavortings."

"Well," Sayre said, "you are under suspicion, as a
loose woman and as a spy. It is rumored that you insti-

gated the attack of some Tory pirates on two merchants' ships. Did you?"

Vaguely she remembered a mild flirtation with the bachelor Robert Smith, whose store she patronized so much that she now had a long overdue bill there. His ship was one of those which had been captured by Loyalists on the coast. He had told her it would soon be in with a cargo of new goods he was sure would please her. She had written the information to a party Sayre had instructed her to inform of such movements in colonial shipping.

"Smith could never have found out," she cried. "He is merely jealous. A spinsterish old bachelor!"

"So you had an affair with him, too?"

"You are ridiculous," she exclaimed. "Even if I had, how else did you expect me to carry out your orders?"

"The real trouble is," Sayre said, "that Benedict Arnold is marching into Virginia. He is succeeding General Leslie. There is trouble on the Banks. Vessels cannot get out. Two row galleys are between here and the Bay, and the Edentonians are afraid they will come into the Sound and attack the town. The villagers hate Arnold, even Horniblow, who bonded his ship when he brought it into Edenton before his defection.

"The Bay is already infested with pirates," Sayre went on. "If Arnold came up the Sound, the town would be directly under the guns of the marauders. When Charles Johnson, the one who I told you looked at you so suspciously the other night, heard this, he said significantly: 'There are too many friends of the British hereabouts. We must watch out for the Tories, and get them out of here.' He looked directly at me."

Lady Anne listened intently to what he had said. The thought crossed her mind that Sayre had some ulterior motive in telling her this. He knew such reports bored her. There was, she knew, no honor among spies. Sayre might not think twice about betraying her.

"Well," she said. "I have been in no communication with Benedict Arnold."

"Nor did I say you had," he retorted, looking her in the eyes.

With a flash of insight the truth came to her. "But you have!" she cried in a panic. "Stephen, what are you doing to me?"

He laughed sardonically. "Only trying to protect you, you captivating witch." He came toward her, an evil gleam in his eyes.

"Stephen, no!"

He took her in his arms and pressed his body close to hers, holding her too tightly for her to struggle. Then he planted his mouth on hers, bending her head back with the force of his own.

"Never fear," he breathed into her ear. "You are too beautiful, and too useful to me, for me to let you come to harm. Tomorrow, or the next day, I will close the purchase of your husband's land. You must be ready to leave at once. You will go via Williamsburg, and when you are there, you must contrive to see Adam Rutledge." He laughed again. "You would have liked him in your bed, wouldn't you? Well, you shall have another chance at enticing him. But tonight it will be I. I swear I need no enticements."

XI

Off to the Wars

At Pembroke, the work of clearing away the debris left by the hurricane, and of repairing the damage it had caused, for several days consumed all the time of the men on the plantation, slaves and masters alike. Raoul de Polignac helped Stephen Cabarrus direct the overseers. They left the house early in the morning, and did not return till late afternoon. After their exertions they were so tired that they went to their rooms directly after supper.

Having Raoul so near and yet so unobtainable made Penelope Cabarrus restless. She knew he had been with Lady Anne again on the day of the hurricane. The gossip that they had been riding together and had returned to Horniblow's just before the storm really broke had percolated to Pembroke. So had the story of Lady Anne's scandalous behavior in the common room of the tavern.

Penny had had no opportunity to question Raoul about that day. The thought that she might have won him away from the wicked Baroness only to lose him to her again immediately, kept her from sleeping. Late at night she would get up and light her lamp. To take her mind from her anxiety, she would pore over the old copies of the *Town and Country* magazine that had reached Pembroke before the blockade began and that she had

141

stored for convenience in her bedroom. The gossip, though old, was still fascinating enough to divert her.

One item caught her eyes:

> " 'Oh, my dear lady, what a dish-clout you have made of me!' said the Duke of N—— of the lady recently divorced by him.
>
> "It is said that the lady in question has made other 'dishclouts' of a collection of men. Her followers include military and naval officers, physicians, lawyers and even divines; coronets have bowed at her shrine, baronets and squires also.
>
> "She says that her former husband. the heir to a dukedom, is not a man after her heart, but she has found many others. It is said that her husband overheard her making an assignation at Almack's with a certain Mr. F——."

Penny dropped the magazine. The Duke of N——? It must mean the Duke of Northumberland. The "lady in question" could be no other than the present Baroness von Poellnitz. Penny was utterly astonished.

Feverishly she turned the pages of other issues of *Town and Country,* searching for more revealing items about her rival. In one she found an article entitled "Memoirs of the Successful Gallant and the Paphian Votary." Then she found an item about the Presbyterian minister, Dr. Calder, who was the Duke of Northumberland's spy, and his reports of Lady Anne's infidelities with William Bird. After that, an item written by Mrs. Thrale about the great lady who had taken lodgings in Brompton, who never went downstairs but was seen through an upper window wearing a riding habit. It was rumored that she had had a child by Bird. Someone asked the sprightly Mrs. Thrale, "What was it?" "Half Bird and Half Beast," the witty lady replied.

The next morning Penny showed her midnight discoveries to her aunt.

"I believe you are right," Marianne Cabarrus said. "It does mean Lady Anne—Stuart, Percy, Von Poellnitz, whatever." She read on. " 'It is said that the husband once banished her to Sunning Hill in the care of two old ladies. It is said that she has lost her stomach since she has been in seclusion.' "

Marianne laid the magazines down. "So that's the kind of gossip spread about her in London! No wonder she wanted to come to live in America." For a moment she looked at Penny without truly seeing her. "My dear," she said at length, "I think Raoul should see this. Perhaps it would open his eyes."

That night when Raoul rode in from the fields Penny was waiting for him with the open magazine. She handed it to him. "Here is something about the Baroness." She thrust the magazine into his hands and ran up the stairs to her room.

Raoul was not in the best of humors. The work on the plantation, which he owed to his host, Stephen Cabarrus, was not according to his taste or his tradition. Furthermore, it had kept him from Edenton—from the company at Horniblow's, in a sense his only contact with the world, and especially from Lady Anne. Ever since their reconciliation—or perhaps, since they had never quarreled with each other, reunion was the better word—he had seen more and more clearly that he had been foolish to think he preferred the fresh virginity of Penelope Cabarrus to the expertise of a mature and sophisticated woman like the Baroness von Poellnitz. On that day of the hurricane she had certainly indicated that she was fond of him, and that he could satisfy her. Her reaction to him had swelled his self-confidence. He, too, was a person of the world now. Why should he be more than casually interested in a mere girl like Penelope Cabarrus?

The thought that Lady Anne, during his enforced absence, would be seeing more and more of that Stephen Sayre also troubled him. Sayre he cordially disliked. Sayre was not a gentleman. Sayre treated him like a child. Yet the Baroness seemed to like him. When he

himself had ventured to suggest that Lady Anne was de-
meaning herself by showing Sayre such favor, she had
loftily replied that she must be polite to her husband's
man of business. Raoul had accepted that explanation
unquestioningly, but, now that he had not seen her, or
seen her with Sayre, he had grown insanely jealous of
anyone to whom she paid the slightest attention. She had
not sent Raoul away. That was indication enough that
he was still her cavilier, her cicisbeo, her favorite, her
troubadour, her lover—whatever the name for it was.
She knew enough, surely, of the etiquette of courtly
love to respect his position.

In his room he read the piece in *Town and Country*. There was no question but that it referred to Lady
Anne. When he finished he threw the magazine across
the room in anger. Instead of condemning Lady Anne
he was angry with Penny for drawing the old scandal to
his attention.

He went down the hall and knocked at her door.
When she opened it, he began to scold her. "You have
no business to gloat over such a scurrilous piece, much
less show it to me. I don't believe a word of it. Do you
hear, not a word of it! A beautiful woman is always
open to attack by envious people. Lady Anne is a noble
woman. If I had a chance I'd call that fellow out and
run my sword through his heart."

Penny shrank back, frightened by his violence.

"You are too young to know what you are doing,
but why did you show that magazine to me?" He thrust it
into her hand, then turned quickly and stamped down
the stairs.

For a long time after Raoul had stormed out of her
room, Penny leaned against the door, weeping. She
could not forgive him, or forgive herself for having
thought he loved her. His kisses had meant nothing. He
had been only playing with her. She felt utterly humiliat-
ed. All her charm, all her schemes had failed.

When she heard the bell for supper, she knew she
could not face Raoul. Stealing down the back stairs, she
went out through the pantry, murmuring to Promicy as

she passed that she was going for a walk. She ran down to the boat landing, unfastened the little boat, and rowed out toward the pocosin.

Twilight fell quietly on the water. The soft coo of birds seeking their nesting places in the reeds at the verge of the water, a fish breaking, and the call of the whistling crane were the only sounds in the stillness of the September evening.

She turned the boat skillfully into the narrow stream that penetrated the deep pocosin to the little island she and Raoul had found. The cypress knees rising from the black waters took on a new look tonight. The drooping Spanish moss became unreal and brought terror to her in her loneliness.

Already she missed Raoul, missed the comfort of his strong arms about her, the thrill of his mouth against hers. She put her hands before her face. Tears streamed from her eyes. How could he? How could he have made love to her when it was Lady Anne who held his heart? She thought of every time he had been with her here in this little sanctuary. She thought of the joy of his kisses. She remembered now that he had never said that he loved her. The thought that he might have been laughing at her filled her with horror.

How stupid she had been! A man did not have to be in love with a girl to kiss her. A man kissed many girls. But she—she had taken kisses to mean love.

His few words had brought her dream world smashing about her. He had never loved her. He had spent a few idle hours amusing himself—hours when he could not be with Lady Anne.

She got out of the boat and walked up and down the bank, trying to accustom herself to reality. The pocosin darkened. The night birds called softly. Still she lingered, knowing that she must conquer herself. She must get used to the heartrending fact that Raoul did not love her.

No, she suddenly decided, that she would not do. She felt rising in her the strength of her Huguenot forebears, people who rose above danger and failure, who never gave way to adversity. Perhaps, indeed, she had allowed herself to be fooled. Perhaps she had been the victim of her own romantic imagination.

But had she? Why had her aunt advised her to show those horrid articles to Raoul? Penelope remembered the strange way in which Marianne had looked at her when she had told her to do it. She remembered also that Marianne had said Raoul's father would snatch him home if he were to learn that his son was in love with an American girl. Marianne was protecting Raoul!

She could not blame her aunt, much as she would have liked to. Marianne had responsibilities to her guest. Penny could see how embarrassing it might be for her aunt if Raoul were to fall in love with her niece in the circumstances.

Still there was plenty she could yet do. Raoul would be leaving any day now. Once he was out from under Marianne's roof, her aunt could not be expected to assume further responsibility for him. If he were to go to Williamsburg. . . . There was Dr. Williamson's army hospital there, where Mary Warden was nursing. And Dr. Armitage was setting up a field hospital. . . .

Restored, and full of ideas, Penny went back to the boat, turned it into the creek and pulled for the plantation landing. Her course was easy; the lights of the house guided her, and their reflection made a path in the water.

Old Samuel was in the hall when she entered. "Mistress want you in the drawing room. She worry about you, missy."

The Duc du Braille had returned. He had received a communication from the Marquis de Lafayette, asking the Duc to join him and bring Raoul.

Raoul's face was beaming. This news, she knew, was what he had been waiting for for months. He went across the room to her, apparently oblivious of the fact he had left her in anger.

"Rejoice with me, dear Penelope," Raoul said ecstatically. "Rejoice that I will have the chance to strike a blow for freedom. I have thought lately that the opportunity would never come. Doesn't it make you happy too?"

Penny looked at him quietly. "Yes, it makes me happy that you are having the chance to join your people. It does not make me happy that you are going to war." Her lips trembled. "I hate war. I wish we would never have wars to kill off our young men."

The Duc de Braille sighed. "Ah, yes, war is hard on the young. As you must have heard it said, old men don't fight the wars, they only make them. Yet the old grieve too for the young."

Raoul said eagerly. "I don't care who makes them or who fights in them, so long as I do. Now I must go to pack. If I work until late, I can get it done tonight."

Stephen Cabarrus smiled at his impetuosity. "Remember you are going to war, Raoul, not on a holiday. You won't need anything but your uniform."

"Yes," Marianne said. "You will come back to us. Soon, I hope. We will keep your things just as you left them."

"Then I must at least put them in order," Raoul said. "Pray excuse me." He ran upstairs, singing.

Penny's eyes were misty. Long as she had known that some day this moment would come and Raoul would ride away, perhaps never to return, she found it hard to bear now that it had arrived. She turned to her aunt.

"Perhaps I shouldn't have spoken," she said. "It was not for Raoul alone. It was for all the young men who go to war to fight old men's battles."

Marianne put her arm over the girl's shoulder. "There is another view of this war, my dear. This is a fight for freedom, not alone for the old, but for the young as well. Think of that a little. They are fighting now for all generations to come."

When Penelope was going to her room, Raoul came from his to meet her in the hall.

"I am sorry I was angry this afternoon," he said. "Forgive me, please. I could not bear to go away thinking we were not friends."

"I forgive you," she said.

"We shall be gone before you are up in the morning. May I kiss you good night—and goodbye?"

"Only good night," she said. "I shall pray to see you again."

He bent and kissed her gently but tenderly, his hands on her shoulders.

"My little friend," he said. "You are growing up fast. Don't grow away from me entirely."

When Penelope reached her room, she discovered to her surprise that she was weeping. Her heart was singing.

Raoul and the Duc de Braille reached Horniblow's tavern just as the Baron von Poellnitz and his equipage were setting out. No one had come to bid the Baron farewell. The rumors about his wife had made the people of Edenton think good riddance to them and all Tories. Only James Iredell was there.

"Write to me," he said to the Baron. "I don't wish to lose touch with you, my friend."

The Baron grasped Iredell's hand. "I will," he promised. "As soon as we are settled in New York, you shall hear from me."

Lady Anne sat in her coach, her head held high, a supercilious expression on her finely chiseled features. She had seen Raoul ride into the courtyard of the tavern and when he had dismounted, she beckoned to him.

"You are leaving so suddenly," he said. "I insisted on stopping here to bid you adieu, but I did not think to find you going also."

"My husband has pressing business in New York," she said. "So you are off at last to—where is it you told me you were to be assigned?"

"Williamsburg first, I believe. Then straight on to Yorktown. The Marquis has sent for me."

"How handsome you look in your uniform!" she said, smiling at him radiantly. Then she added slyly, "Yet I prefer you in the armor of love."

Raoul smirked at her naughty pun. Then his face grew serious. "I shall never see you again?"

"Nonsense, dear boy," she said gaily. "We stop at Williamsburg tonight. Will you do me the honor of calling on me?"

The Baron came up the coach. He shook Raoul's hand and congratulated him on his commission.

"We are ready to leave, my dear," he said to his wife. He opened the coach door to admit Dawkins.

The Baroness leaned forward to toss a purse to the hostler to pay the tavern slaves. As it left her hand, she managed a little parting wave to Raoul before returning to her imperious position.

The coach clattered out of the courtyard, the Baron and Sayre riding ahead of it, and the Baron's valet, behind.

When James Iredell reached his home, Hannah greeted him with a tender kiss. "So that woman's gone," she said. "She brought disturbance wherever she went. I'm glad that she is no longer in our little village."

James nodded. "You were right about her all the time."

Hannah kissed him again without words. She was too wise to say, "I told you so," to a contrite man. What she said was "Janie has blueberry muffins and applesauce for your breakfast, darling."

James lay awake for a long time that night, thinking of the Baron von Poellnitz. He had come to like the man exceedingly, as much as he had grown to dislike his wife. He thought of the effect of the Baroness on their little village. Whatever she touches turns to evil, he thought. He wondered how it was that Hannah had known about her from the beginning. Never again would he doubt a woman's intuition. It is superior, he concluded, far superior to man's reason.

The gossip ran from Edenton to the county and over into Perquimans. Lady Anne was a woman who followed Black Magic, took part in the Witches' Sabbath, had been known to worship at the Druid stones on Bodmin Moor, to have had a dozen lovers. With each telling the tale grew until Lady Anne became as notorious as a Restoration actress.

Someone in Edenton came up with the information that among others, Lady Anne had had a serious affair with a law student, John Hippisley. She had been discovered stealing into Hippisley's chambers in the Inner Temple at unconventional hours. It was learned that her family had repudiated her. Even her father, Lord Bute the Prime Minister, would not allow her to enter the Ministry. Her sister, Lady Augusta Corbett, with whom she had lived at Ash Park, was dead, and the rest of the family refused to have Lady Anne visit them. Some of this information came through Penelope Barker, whose husband, Thomas Barker, had spent eighteen years in London as agent for the colony. Mr. Barker had, in spite of the war, several English correspondents, who wrote to him via neutral Holland.

So the gossip ran from one country to another. A notorious woman of high society, it did not take long for Lady Anne to become an international figure.

James Iredell commented drily to his wife that if the war had not touched Edenton, at least Lady Anne had. That would provide them with enough to tell their grandchildren about.

"I should never mention her name in front of a child," Hannah Iredell said sternly.

Iredell put the Baroness out of his mind easily. He had heard disquieting news. The reports at Horniblow's were that the marauding British under the traitor, Benedict Arnold, had destroyed quantities of tobacco in the warehouse at Petersburg. It began to look as if the British did not intend to keep possession of Virginia. Something was agitating the minds of Cornwallis and Arnold. Their councils were fluctuating.

There was other news at Horniblow's that morning. Charles Johnson reported on his trip to Pitcher Landing on the Meherrin River, just over the line in Virginia. "The English are in North Carolina again, in Halifax," he told the Edentonians, "the British Light Horse, Arnold with them. Where is the French fleet and the troops that Congress expects under Admiral de Grasse? I hope we will be able to confound the schemes of our enemies, and that Americans will become a free and happy people. It is the next thing to hell to live in a country that is conquered."

Johnson, usually so sedate and composed, put his hands to his face as though overcome. A moment later he recovered. "If Cornwallis wins in Williamsburg, and Washington is defeated, the British will swarm over our village like a plague of locusts."

Johnson left shortly for Bandon. The men about the table were silent for a moment.

"I have never known Charles Johnson to be so disheartened," James Iredell said. "He must have had news that he has not disclosed to us. I do not like to think of Arnold in Halifax. I had rather he were farther north where General Washington can suppress him."

He thought of the information Dr. Williamson's last letter to him had contained, that there were more Tories in Philadelphia than in the two Whig parties combined. What would happen if Washington and the French allies conquered Cornwallis at the York River? There were plenty of Tories in North Carolina. Would they be strong enough to bring on another civil war?

He walked slowly home. He was disheartened. He wished they could get accurate reports about the situation on the York River. He tried to envisage the country —Williamsburg, Yorktown, the French fleet supposedly lying across the York River, guns pointed toward the shore and toward the entrance to Chesapeake Bay to hold off wandering British cruisers. What would happen? But was the fleet really there—or only in their hopes?

Questions raced through his active mind. He was no military strategist, but he had read enough military history to have an idea of the situation. The crux of the matter would depend on the land force. The fleet was a deterrent. It would not cause the war to end, but it would equalize it. The land force under General Washington must finish the war.

But, he thought with a chuckle, at last Edenton had got rid of Lady Anne, Baroness von Poellnitz. Perhaps the town had thus won its single battle of the war.

XII

Welcome and Unwelcome

After passing through Suffolk the von Poellnitz coach
traveled over muddy roads checked with marching soldiers. That small town was struggling to recover from
the devastation left by General Cornwallis' army when it
marched up from Wilmington on its way through Virginia to the York River.

Lady Anne sat straight with head held high, the
picture of an aristocratic lady of fashion. She relished
the soldiers' whistles and words of praise of her beauty.
It was almost equal to passage through London streets,
where the people used to cheer her as she rode by.

Dawkins now sat on the box with the coachmen,
for Lady Anne had remarked that morning to her woman that the air would be purer if she removed herself. "I
don't think you bathe enough, Dawkins," was her comment.

The woman climbed out of the coach and up to the
box. Tears were running down her cheeks. "And after
all I have done for her. Left my home and my family
and came to this savage country. God will punish her."

The coachman got out his kerchief. "Here, take
this, Maria. Don't you care, she'll be punished some
day."

Dawkins ceased weeping. "I don't see how the
good Baron stays with her, and him so kind and gentle."

Toward evening they crossed the James River to James Island. Before they landed they heard sounds of shots in the distance. The Baron and Sayre were off the ferry first. The Baron gave instructions to the coachman to drive into the churchyard by the ancient church and wait while they invesitigated the shooting. It was almost an hour before they returned. Sayre spoke first, a smirk on his face. "We saw your friend, the Comte de Polignac. He was marching with Lafayette's brigade."

"You saw Raoul? Why didn't you bring him to me? You know I would want to greet him."

"Madam, one does not take a man from a marching army even to greet the Baroness von Poellnitz."

The Baron interrupted. "Raoul did not see us. A man marching into battle is not looking to left or right."

Lady Anne sank back. "Poor Raoul! He is so young, so very young to go into battle."

Sayre grinned. "He's been in a sort of battle for some time. I don't think artillery fire will disturb him."

"Why don't we move on?" Lady Anne cried impatiently.

The Baron said, "We will wait here in the churchyard until the regiment has moved to Gloucester Point. Come, look about you. You are on historic ground, my dear. This is Jamestown, the spot where your English forebears made their first lasting settlement."

"I wish they had never settled America. We would have been better off. No wars."

Sayre had a sardonic expression on his face. "Tut, tut, your ladyship. What about the Low Country wars? The eternal wars with France and with Spain. You forget your history."

Lady Anne did not reply. She sat in her coach and would not set foot to the ground.

The Baron and Sayre went into the church to inspect the brasses, but she stubbornly refused to look at the spot that was the beginning of permanent America. "I'd rather go to Roanoke, where the English settlement failed than here where they succeeded."

Her husband either ignored her words or did not

hear her, but Sayre grinned provokingly. "What sentiments from an Englishwoman!" he said.

Lady Anne leaned back against the cushions of her coach and closed her eyes against the quiet beauty of great trees and of the church where the ancient planters had brought their wives and children to worship and give thanks to God for preserving their lives against Indian raids.

Her mind turned to Raoul. How golden was his youth and vigor, almost like that first youth who had deflowered her! She thought she actually preferred Raoul to Sayre. At least she did not have to fear Raoul. Now she imagined him marching to battle, perhaps to his death. As she indulged her reverie, she felt a little sorry for herself and the passion she might miss. If only she could get rid of the Baron and marry Raoul de Polignac! He was of a good family, and he had a fortune almost equal to the Baron's, besides being young and vigorous and beautiful. She thought herself a most unfortunate woman.

An hour passed before the Baron gave the signal to ride on along the wooded road to Williamsburg. They passed a company of militia encamped by the roadside. Their insignia showed they were from Georgia, country boys, rugged and browned by the sun and weather. They were shouting and laughing with no thought of the morrow—or when they would be called to go into battle. Living for the day—perhaps it was better that way. Real war would come soon enough.

Lady Anne looked out of her coach window, smiled and waved to them. They rose to their feet and bowed or saluted as the coach moved by. "They are so young, so very young," she said aloud. Startled by the sound of her own voice, she sank back against the cushions and closed her eyes.

It was dusk and the lamplighter had already passed along Duke of Gloucester Street when they arrived in Williamsburg. After Edenton it seemed a metropolis to Lady Anne. She wondered how long the Baron proposed to stay there.

The coach stopped at the King's Inn but there was no accommodation. Officers under General Lafayette occupied all the available rooms. The Baron sent his coachman to an inn farther up the street, but it was crowded also.

"Try the Raleigh Tavern," Lady Anne said. "I've been told it is the finest."

"It's sure to be crowded," Sayre remarked. "No doubt General Washington himself is billeted there."

Lady Anne leaned out of the window. "Baron, oblige me. We may be fortunate."

They turned back and the coachman pulled up in front of the Raleigh Tavern, a long, low building with a second half-story and dormer windows. Crowds of men in uniform stood outside on the brick sidewalk. Many paused to gaze through the window of the coach at the beautiful woman inside.

The Baron dismounted and went in. Sayre put his head in at the door of the coach. "I'm afraid we shall have to sleep in the fields under a haystack tonight," he said with a grin. "Will you join me in my hay bed?"

"Be quiet, you fool!" Lady Anne snapped. "Have you no sense at all?"

"I think I have plenty when I choose you for my bed mate."

The Baron came out, smiling. "We are fortunate. There is a small annex at the side with accommodations for us all and the servants. You were right, my dear. One should always go to the best instead of the second best for lodgings."

They drove down a lane to a small house set in a garden, blooming with purple asters and yellow marigolds and Michaelmas daisies. They walked along a box-lined path to the white clapboard house with green shutters. A smiling buxom Negro girl curtsied low and said, "This way, your ladyship."

The room was spotless. The chintz curtains at the windows matched the counterpane on the bed. There were comfortable chairs. The maid lighted a fire in the corner fireplace with a flint and some shavings.

Dawkins helped Lady Anne off with her wraps. "Order a hot bath for me at once. I want to wash the dust of the road from my body."

"Your ladyship, it will be laid at once." She left the room to attend to the matter.

Lady Anne sank into a chair by the blazing fire. "This is delightful. I hope we linger here for days and days."

The Baron came into the room. He kissed his wife lightly on the forehead. "I've ordered some tea and refreshment. We will have supper in the general dining room at nine." He looked about the room. "This is like an English coaching inn, isn't it? It was a lucky chance that General Anthony Wayne moved out yesterday and went on a raid."

Lady Anne said, "I have never heard of General Anthony Wayne, but I am delighted that he went out on a raid."

" 'Mad Anthony,' they call him. He is one of General Washington's high generals."

"Stephen, you always know everything," Lady Anne said. "If Mad Anthony Wayne moved out yesterday, who is living here? An American general?" There was a touch of sarcasm in her voice.

"Certainly, your ladyship. Some of the French officers are still here. General Lafayette and the rest of his staff are near the York River in the cantonments but I understand that they still eat here."

Lady Anne looked at Sayre, a twinkle in her eyes. "Again I say, you always have information."

"I try to. After all, I have two eyes and two ears. They used to say at Princeton that I was moderately intelligent."

The Baron and Baroness were finishing their roast beef in the tavern when Lady Anne discovered Adam Rutledge. He was about to sit down at a small table across the room beside a window. "Stephen, go tell him to join us."

Sayre grumbled. "We have only to eat our sweet and we will be leaving."

"Go fetch him," she ordered. "I want to talk to him. Besides, I like him very much. I want him to show me this delightful Williamsburg."

The Baron said rather sternly, "Do ask him to our table. I want to talk to him about the corn crop."

Sayre rose reluctantly.

"Always agriculture! Manure and plowing!" Lady Anne said. "I'm sick of the whole thing. Please, Bruno, let me talk to Adam some, too."

Sayre came back shortly with Adam Rutledge. He greeted the Baron with pleasure, and Lady Anne with a whimsical smile, and sat down at their table. The host of the tavern himself came to take Adam's order. "The beef is extraordinarily good today, Mr. Rutledge. The Yorkshire pudding is superb. Would you like a glass of arrack punch first, I brewed it myself this morning."

"Indeed I will—and the beef very rare." Adam turned to the Baron. "I hope you have tried the punch. It is famous all over the colonies."

The Baron turned to the host. "Bring us a small bowl so we can all taste it, after the sweet." The Baron smiled. "We do not want to overlook such a famous drink, especially when Mr. Rutledge recommends it. And now, sir, may I ask what you do in Williamsburg, Mr. Rutledge?"

Adam looked surprised. "Why, I'm here with my regiment. Didn't you know?"

Lady Anne said, "Why must you talk of war? It would be more pleasant to talk about this charming town of Williamsburg."

Adam looked at her coldly. "I did not know you were so interested in our towns."

"La, Mr. Rutledge," she exclaimed, putting on her most winning smile and making her eyes sparkle, "I love America. Since it is to be my home, I wish to know all I can about it."

She felt a sharp kick on her shin from Sayre. His face was dark.

"I am sure you do, my lady," Adam Rutledge said.

"And you, Mr. Sayre, you are new to this part of the country, I believe. Have you the same interest as the Baroness?"

Sayre quickly changed to his most jovial manner. "If one truly wants to know a place, he should find out for himself, not merely listen to accounts of it. He should stroll about and poke and pry. When I was first in London I roamed for a week by myself exploring that labyrinth of a city, stopping in taverns to talk with the people, taking a boat up and down the Thames and asking the boatman to explain what the great buildings and palaces were . . ."

The Baron cut him short. "Mr. Rutledge has been to London, Sayre."

Stung by the rebuke, Sayre glowered at his plate, and applied himself diligently to his sweet.

"You are quite correct, Stephen," Lady Anne said. "Tomorrow I shall walk about Williamsburg myself, and poke and pry, as you say. Like Doctor Johnson I shall let observation with extensive view survey mankind from China to Peru."

"I am sure you will survey mankind," Sayre muttered.

"Ah, well," she quipped, "the proper study of mankind is man."

The Baron looked bewildered. "I am not sure your Doctor Johnson is very acceptable to Mr. Rutledge, my dear. I have heard he does not favor the American cause, to put it mildly."

"I do not think your plan advisable, my lady," Adam Rutledge said. "As you must already have observed, Williamsburg is full of soldiers. A beautiful lady like you has been a rarity to them for so long, you might find yourself embarrassed."

"They look such handsome youths," Lady Anne said. "The ones we passed on the road seemed gently bred. Is not our friend the Comte de Polignac stationed here?"

"I do not know where he is at the moment," Rutledge said evasively. He turned to the Baron and began questioning him about what land he might have been able to purchase.

"You are fortunate indeed, sir," Adam said when the Baron had described his new acres at some length. "Now you are one of us." He raised his glass of punch. "I drink to welcome you to our company of landholders."

"I am deeply touched, sir," the Baron said with emotion. He raised his own glass. "May I love the land as much as you."

Adam spoke slowly and rhythmically, a faraway look in his eyes, his voice intoning like a bard's. "This I learned from a Quaker. Before he taught me, I loved the land only to possess it, only the feel of land under my feet. Then I loved the land for the way it locks in its embrace the beginnings of all life and receives at last their discarded forms. It will outlive all the works of man, transcend all human thought. It is dumb, yet it speaks of the imperishable storehouse of eternity."

For a long moment no one at the table spoke. Lady Anne felt a certain vague embarrassment she could not account for. Across from her, she saw her husband's eyes were misty. Strangely, she did not think him sentimental now. Even Sayre's insensitive features seemed quickened. Suddenly she understood her emotion. This Adam Rutledge, whom once she had coveted, she hated now. He had flouted her before, now he had as good as insulted her. She looked at him as she might have looked at the headsman on a scaffold she was condemned to mount.

Rising to her feet, she said: "I am very tired, and bruised from riding over these rough roads. Pray excuse me."

The men also rose. The Baron asked Adam Rutledge if he would join him in the taproom of the tavern.

"Forgive me, sir," Adam said. "I must report to headquarters."

He waited for Lady Anne and the Baron to pre-

cede him. Then he spoke quietly to Sayre. "Can you pre-
vail on the Baron to leave Williamsburg in the morning?
I do not think it will be pleasant for him if the security
officers learn that Lady Anne is the daughter of Lord
Bute."

Sayre was startled. "Who would have that information?"

"I, for one. There are many soldiers here who live
in Edenton or the nearby country. They all know about
Lady Anne. Gossip moves swiftly in a village. You are
the Baron's business man. Persuade him it is wise to
continue his journey in the morning. The Baron is a fine
gentleman. I should not like anything to disturb him."

Sayre spoke. "It would not be too hard to persuade
the Baron," Sayre said. "It will be Lady Anne. She is a
stubborn woman. She wishes to remain."

Adam looked straight at Sayre. "But you have influence, Mr. Sayre. Perhaps she needs a firm hand such
as yours."

"But who will report her to the security? Surely
there is no one—"

"I might be the one, Mr. Sayre. I am an officer of
the American army."

"You are not in uniform."

"Not at present, when I am on a certain mission.
Does that give you any ideas, Mr. Sayre?"

Sayre nodded. "I will do what I can. I promise."

"She must be out of Williamsburg by noon tomorrow or I cannot answer for the consequences."

Adam nodded abruptly, and walked swiftly up
Duke of Gloucester Street toward the Capitol. Sayre
watched him out of sight before he followed the Baron
and Baroness into the cottage.

He approached the Baron first and told him what
Adam Rutledge had said. The Baron was surprised.
"The authorities allowed the Baroness to enter America.
Why should they make restrictions now?"

"Did they know that she was the daughter of Lord
Bute?"

"They did not ask. She came as my wife. That was guarantee enough," he said stiffly.

"From what I see here and deduce, sir," Sayre said, "they are on the verge of a great battle, one that may finish the war. They have Lord Cornwallis surrounded on the land by Rochambeau's troops and General Washington's troops, and on the water by the French navy. It is a critical time. Their security officers will not permit anyone with Lady Anne's background to be in the town. You must persuade her to go on."

The Baron shook his head. "The Baroness told me that she wishes to stay here a week or two. She likes the place. It has a metropolitan flavor. She has read the *Gazette*. There is talk of a performance of 'Midsummer Night's Dream' at the theater. She desires to witness it."

"She will have to be persuaded that she must leave here by noon tomorrow. That is the time limit set by Mr. Rutledge. Believe me, Baron, he meant what he said."

"But Mr. Rutledge is my friend. Surely—"

Sayre interrupted. "He is also a patriotic American. He let it be known that he himself would act if you do not leave. Sir, I beg of you. I do not desire to see the inside of a jail."

The Baron shook his head. "You talk to her, Sayre. Perhaps you can make her see the necessity of leaving."

Sayre knocked on the door of Lady Anne's sitting room. He found her dressed in an apricot silk negligee, her hair in curls down her back. She looked very young and lovely. She ran to him and threw her arms about his neck. "Darling, darling, what brings you here tonight? Has the Baron departed with his friend Rutledge? Can we be alone for an hour?"

Sayre unclasped her arms. "We have other things to think about besides tumbling. We must leave Williamsburg early in the morning."

Lady Anne shook her head until her curls flew over her white shoulders. "No, no, no! I shall not go. I like it here. I want to stay and give dinners to some of the lovely men I have seen."

Sayre sat down on the couch. "Listen, woman, pay attention to what I say. You will have your clothes packed so that we can be on the road before noon."

"I will not go," she said.

"You will go or you shall be in the Williamsburg jail by nightfall. If you want that you may stay. The Baron and I are leaving."

"The Baron can appeal to his friend Rutledge. He won't allow us to be ordered out of town."

Sayre gave a short laugh. "Rutledge is the one who is ordering you out. Don't let him clap you in a filthy jail inhabited by criminals and fleas and lice."

Lady Anne shuddered. "You say such rude things, Sayre."

"Jails are rude things. I am but telling you what will happen if you persist in staying."

Lady Anne was silent a moment. In a wheedling tone she said, "I'll bargain with you, Sayre. I'll go if you'll come back and . . ." She looked at him archly. ". . . help me pack."

Sayre laughed. "You are a vixen. But you are also irresistible." He kissed her hard on her lips and slapped her buttocks. "A thorough vixen," he repeated as he went out the door.

In the morning, before the clock struck eleven, Lady Anne's coach was on the Richmond road, the Baron and Sayre riding ahead, the valet behind, Dawkins on the box. Dressed in a wide-skirted, trim-bodiced blue taffeta, Lady Anne lounged in the coach, looking out the window. Suddenly, as they turned into the Richmond road before the College of William and Mary, she called to the coachman to stop. The smartly uniformed Comte de Polignac was walking along the street. "Raoul! Raoul!" she cried out.

He turned at the sound of her voice. The Baron and Sayre rode on.

"Get in, Raoul," she said. "Get in and ride a little

distance with me. I have missed you sorely. It is God's kindness that allows me to see you once again."

Raoul came to the coach. "I will not get in," he said coldly.

The Baroness pouted. "How cross you sound, my boy . . ."

"I am not a boy, madam. I am a soldier."

Lady Anne laughed. "Aha, so you have become a man, you think? But you still love me, do you not? Don't think that any man can learn to put away childish things at once."

"Madam," Raoul said, "I have learned that you are a wicked woman, and a spy. I do not wish to see you again." He walked abruptly away.

On the box, Dawkins nudged the coachman. "Drive on," she said.

XIII

Liberty for All Men

As Cosmo de' Medici rode down from Richmond at the head of his troop of cavalry, the route was crowded with refugees leaving Williamsburg and the area around Yorktown. Devon carts, each drawn by one mule, piled high with household goods hastily assembled, carriages and coaches of the rich, carts and wagons of the poor jammed the road. All had the one objective, to get out of the sounds of the guns.

De' Medici stopped an old man trudging along, leading a few goats. The man talked excitedly. "Cornwallis is taking Gloucester Point. They say he will move on to Williamsburg. No one is safe. The British are looting and killing, ravishing women and young girls. Worst of all, they are spreading pox and other dread diseases. The cooped-up soldiers have gone wild. No one is safe. Old women, young girls, it makes no mind." Tears fell from his rheumy eyes. "I've lost my womenfolk. Maybe Cornwallis or that rascally Tarleton has captured them." He moved on, pulled forward by the lead ram.

De' Medici shook his head. He had heard such tales before, tales that always run ahead and behind an army.

The next man he approached had a different story. "It isn't the British, it's the Americans, the young militia men, looting, and ravishing women." He himself had

165

seen one act, a young woman bare as a jaybird, with a soldier astride her. The woman was laughing and kicking up her heels. Shocking, shocking. What was the world coming to when young girls enjoyed being ravished? The girls were as bad as the soldiers. Now when he was young such things were private. They weren't above snatching a little fun in the barn or the hayloft, but it was private, not out on the roadside. He too moved on along the road to Richmond.

After de' Medici had entered Williamsburg, his troop rested in an open field across from the College of William and Mary while he followed Baron Steuben's aide to headquarters for orders. From the aide, a young redhead, Cosmo got the true story of how General Washington had outsmarted Clinton and left him defending New York while he took his own troops by forced marches to Virginia. He heard how Lord Cornwallis would not receive the traitor Benedict Arnold, even after he had conducted a successful battle on the James River, but had sent Arnold to New York so that he would not have to see him. He heard that Count de Grasse now had his fleet in the Chesapeake.

Von Steuben's aide was enthusiastic about the Commander in Chief's strategy. Washington had no sooner arrived in Williamsburg than he had moved his troops to hem in Cornwallis' army at Yorktown.

"A great man is Washington," the aide said. "He stopped at his home in Mount Vernon for only two days, after having been away for six years. A dedicated man, Washington!"

De' Medici finally stopped the enthusiastic admiration of Washington long enough to get the position designated for his cavalry. He was to be stationed opposite Tarleton's cavalry on the south side of Yorktown. Having ascertained where he was to march, de' Medici left headquarters and returned to the encampment near the college. After a scratch meal he led his men down the road to Yorktown.

When de' Medici's troop had marched sixteen miles to its assigned place he found that he was to be camped between the French position and the American redoubts. The first person he saw after his men had set their tents was Adam Rutledge. They grasped hands firmly.

Since Herk had come from Edenton to join Adam at camp, the meals had been good. Adam asked de' Medici to supper. "Our old friend Raoul de Polignac is here," Adam said. "He is one of General Lafayette's aides. He has proved himself a good soldier."

De' Medici said, "That pleases me. It is good to have him away from the Baroness. She was an evil influence for a young man. In London she was involved in a scandal that shook society. It takes a first-rate scandal to close London society's doors against a beautiful woman. But you must have learned all this from the divorce proceedings I gave you in Edenton."

Adam sat down on a campstool and lighted a clay pipe. "Raoul is really out from under the woman's influence now. The Baron and Baroness, with his obnoxious man of business, Sayre, came through here last week. It was my unpleasant duty to order them to leave Williamsburg—not because of the Baron, but on account of Lady Anne. 'We are at war,' I told Sayre. 'We do not want Lord Bute's daughter here when a major battle is not far off.' I set a time for them to leave. . . ." Adam smiled at the recollection.

"What happened?"

"They departed at the time set. She met up with Raoul along the way, but he refused to ride with her in her coach up the Richmond Road, as she asked him to do. Our young friend has become a man."

De' Medici's classic features, his large dark Italian eyes showed his relief. "In the old days in my country she would have been called a creature of Satan. Perhaps she is."

Adam nodded. "I think she may have met her match in Sayre. I've heard him talking to her. He gives her no quarter. His talk is rough. She falls under the spell of his brutality. She is one of those creatures who likes to be beaten by words and by acts, and Sayre is her master, without doubt."

De' Medici said, "I feel for the Baron, a kindly, intelligent man. I'm sure he cannot cope with her."

Herk came into the tent and set up a table for supper. "Bwana, the Bwana Raoul will dine with you. I tell him I have found a fine fat fowl in henhouse down the road. He say he will be here to help you eat."

"Good! Set a place for him, Herk."

During Herk's chicken supper, gunfire began in the distance. Adam went to the entrance of the tent and fastened back the canvas flap. Far off toward the river they could see the flash of cannon, not a steady fire but intermittent flashes.

"Cornwallis is trying to break out of the trap Washington has set."

"He can't break out," Raoul said. "He is helpless in a circle of the French and the Americans. General Lafayette says he has not a chance. The French fleet has bottled him up, and will hold off any English fleet that Clinton can send down from New York."

De' Medici returned to the supper table. He sat silent a moment, looking thoughtfully at the floor. "I do not think that Sir Henry Clinton will send help to Cornwallis," he said. "Clinton hates him."

Raoul was horrified. "You mean he would sacrifice an army because of personal feelings?"

"Oh, he would rationalize his actions. He would say that holding New York was more important than any Virginia action."

"Do you agree with that, Captain?"

"Certainly not. When the British army in Virginia is defeated the war will be over. At least its back will be broken."

Adam took a cup of coffee from Herk. He turned to the men. "I feel that the next few days will settle the outcome. After that, freedom for the Americans, more freedom than man has ever experienced in the world."

The others were silent for a moment. Cosmo de' Medici walked to the entrance and looked out into the darkness. He spoke seriously. "Freedom. What a wonderful word! But it is much more wonderful to live under freedom." He turned to Adam. "All my adult life I have dreamed of this. You cannot know my feeling at this moment when I think that I have played a part, even a small one, in giving men freedom. I, an Italian, descended from generations of men who did not know the meaning of the word. I, Cosmo de' Medici, have helped make men free!"

Adam Rutledge watched de' Medici's dark medieval face alight almost with ecstasy. He thought of the de' Medici family—a long line of ruthless men, seeking only self-interest. What had happened that Cosmo talked of freedom for individual men he did not know and had never seen, men not even of the same race or country? His concern was for the welfare of unknown men. A universal thought was this man's conception of liberty, set down by Jefferson, implemented by General Washington, a man who loved land, his own land. Was the whole world entering into a period of brotherhood? Was this war changing the thoughts of the world? He thought of the German Baron, the eager young French volunteers, this Italian before him—all imbued with the spirit of liberty of the individual. An abstract idea to show the way?

His thoughts were interrupted by a heavy burst of cannonading. All three men sprang to the entrance of the tent. The sky to the east was alight with flashing gunfire. The bombardment of Yorktown had begun.

Adam Rutledge sat in his tent before Yorktown, thumbing through a mass of papers. The allied French and American Continentals had been assembled. He was completing the design for the investiture of Yorktown. The last order he wrote down was that detachments of artillery with seige guns and fieldpieces and other units were to be assigned to Brigadier General Knox of Massachusetts. As the light began to fail, he sat back in his field chair, and stretched out his long legs. It had been a monumental task to make the design and set it on paper so that all the commanders would have the plan before them.

He was interrupted by General Lafayette's orderly, who entered the tent and saluted. "Would Colonel Rutledge come to General Lafayette's headquarters within the hour?"

Adam returned the salute. "Tell the General I will be with him shortly." When the orderly had gone, Adam took a quick bath and dressed himself in the blue and buff of the Continental Army.

He found Raoul in the tent. "How often we talked of this in Edenton!" the young Frenchman said. "I was afraid I would never get word from the Governor to join the army."

"But now you are here," Adam said. "This was your aim, was it not—to fight for democracy?"

General Lafayette entered the tent in time to catch the last word. "Democracy—what a beautiful word! The people are sovereign. Pray God we will some day have democracy in our country, Raoul." He paused for a moment, deep in thought. "Ah, my unhappy country! When will she have a constitution?"

Only briefly was he in a dark mood. He turned to Adam and spoke energetically. "Come, Colonel Rutledge, let us look over the papers you have brought. Raoul, you had best go to the American headquarters and get me the information about the disposal of the fieldpieces. Tell them that the trenches are all dug and in good order. Tell General Knox that we are ready to visit Count de Grasse on the *Ville de Paris* to discuss joint operations whenever General Washington gives the word."

The two men discussed the plan of seige for two hours. Lafayette said, "The French have approximately one half the total land forces which will oppose Lord Cornwallis." He consulted some papers in his files. "Count de Rochambeau has seven infantry regiments grouped in three brigades. The cavalry is under the Duc de Lauzun, the artillery under Colonel d'Aboville. The

French engineers are headed by Colonel Desandrouins and Lieutenant Colonel Querenet. I think they have prepared an excellent plan of seige. The design you have drawn will be of great help to them."

Adam asked, "Will General Washington have time to prepare his full plans?"

"General Washington will be ready. He has already approved the plan. Count de Grasse will, as you know, be consulted in the morning."

It was suppertime before the conference ended in General Lafayette's quarters. An orderly brought in a large tray of food covered with a cloth.

"Sir, a nice country supper of ham and greens and grits," the man said. "Mrs. Mulvaney sent it over from her farm. She hopes you will enjoy it and not fire off cannons to frighten her chickens so they won't lay eggs for your breakfast."

The men laughed. "I fear that Mrs. Mulvaney's chickens will be frightened a good many nights in the near future," Lafayette said. He put his hand to his mouth to cover a yawn.

Adam rose at once. "I must be going, General. I think we both understand the plan perfectly."

It was almost dark. From the woods came the sounds of night. An owl hooted as Adam walked along the path to his camp. Swallows swooped across the sky, showing black against the last rays of a red sunset. Voices in the distance indicated the site of the American camp, to the right of the French.

Adam paused for a moment before entering his tent. Dark shadows covered the sprawling army, pricked by pinpoints of light, some fixed, some moving. A far off bugle sounded the call to mess. For a moment Adam felt depressed and very lonely. Tomorrow the rifle shots and the mortars would announce to Lord Cornwallis that the fighting had begun. He wondered how many of the gay laughing boys of the army would see another sunset.

Adam laid his papers in his foot locker and ordered his horse. He would ride to Williamsburg to shed these gloomy thoughts. At the hospital in the Palace was

Mary Warden. She had left Queen's Gift on the Albemarle two months before and followed the army as a nurse for Dr. Williamson. Adam felt the need of her, her calm, her understanding. Ever since the death of her husband, and especially in the last month, he had found himself thinking of her. She had been gallant when Warden had been proved a spy for the British and hanged, and afterward she had managed her plantation, Queen's Gift, as well as any planter in the Albemarle. He wanted to be near her tonight.

He found Mary Warden walking through the Palace garden, a lighted lantern in her hand.

"I was just going over to Wythe House. How glad I am to see you, Adam! We have just had a contingent of wounded brought down from the army around Richmond. We have made them comfortable, changed their bandages, fed them and given them their medicines. I felt that I must get away from the smell of blood."

Adam sat down beside her on the stone bench. "Dear Mary, I came to you because I thought you would brighten my mood, but you put me even deeper into gloom."

She laid her hand on his arm. "What is it, Adam? Is General Washington about to begin the attack on Yorktown? The rumors are flying about the hospital that he will call on Admiral de Grasse to close in from the river while he shuts off from the land. 'The great nutcracker' will clamp its jaws. That is what they are saying. Is it true, Adam?"

Adam looked down at her wide eyes, her little heart-shaped face, her sensitive mouth. How could he tell her that the rumors were true and that the armies were about to come together in a duel to the death?

"You know rumors, Mary. Come, let us walk to Raleigh's Tavern. I long for a mug of ale and a plate of roast beef."

She laughed. "How typical of a man! I ask you a question of vital interest to me, and all you think of is food."

Adam grinned. "A man fights better if his stomach

is full," he said lightly. "Come, my dear." He put his hand under her arm and guided her along the dark path between the box bushes. "Confess you are hungry too."

"For a pot of tea and a muffin perhaps."

"And a glass of Madeira. I insist on that."

She lifted her face to him. "I never can resist you, Adam. Madeira it is."

He bent over her. In the quiet of the garden she was so close to him, so dear. His lips touched hers. As he kissed her sweet lips he thought, What if I should die tomorrow—and never see her again? He held her close as though he could never let her go. "Mary, Mary, you are very dear to me!"

She loosened his arms gently. The sentry was walking down the path swinging his lantern. They walked sedately forward at the side of the esplanade. The lights of Raleigh's Tavern beckoned them to enter and partake of its abundance and its gaiety.

The British had been in Yorktown since August. Cornwallis' task was to fortify the little town of about three hundred houses and Gloucester Point, just across the York River. He established a line of fortifications around the town and surrounded it by earthworks or redoubts and batteries. Ahead of the fortifications he built two positions to command the high ground, Redoubts 9 and 10. Along the York–Hampton Road he strengthened the main road to form a point, called the "Horn–Work." The redoubts and fourteen batteries, sixty guns in all, with some eighteen pounders, constituted his defense.

The Royal Welsh Fusiliers Regiment was near a star-shaped redoubt where the Williamsburg road crossed Yorktown Creek. On the opposite side of the river, at Gloucester Point, Cornwallis had a single line of entrenchments and three batteries. Behind the line Cornwallis had at least seventy-five hundred troops, for the most part veterans accustomed to fighting. He also had two supply boats in the York River, the *Charon* and the *Guadalupe*. He had blocked all roads, and cut trees and obstructions out of the way so that the troops had clear vision. Seated in his tent on the night of the 30th of September, General Cornwallis wrote to General Clinton in New York:

> I have received your letter of the 24th which has given me the greatest satisfaction. I shall retire this night within the works and have no doubt if relief comes from you, in any reasonable time, York and Gloucester will both be in possession of His Majesty's troops.

This decision to retire without a fight may have been Lord Cornwallis' undoing. Many of his officers felt that General Clinton, who hated Cornwallis, had no intention of coming to his assistance and leaving New York undefended.

Adam Rutledge rode into Williamsburg again the following night. A crescent moon hung in the deep blue of the sky. A young fawn leapt across the path as he rode by the mill, frightening his horse and almost unseating him. He muttered a curse as his thoughts returned to the road ahead of him. The dark form of a man glided across the road. He drew rein and guided his horse into the shadow of an oak tree.

The figures increased in number. They were walking now two abreast. Adam saw the flash of light on a gun barrel. Already fifty or more men had passed by, and still they came. What was happening? Was Cornwallis moving a regiment? Retreating from his forward poistion? If that was so, he must get word to General Lafayette. He would wait a little longer until he had counted a hundred or more. Presently he was sure Cornwallis was evacuating his front line of defense. Men were dragging fieldpieces instead of carrying rifles. Adam turned his mount. The horse seemed to feel the urgency of his rider. He tried to move without sound along the dirt road.

Adam scratched on the canvas of General Lafayette's tent. "The enemy has evacuated the exterior line of works," he shouted as he entered at the General's call. "I saw them marching—men and fieldpieces. They were crossing the road below the mill."

Lafayette jumped to his feet. He called for his officers. "Make ready to move in the morning at daybreak," he cried in excitement. "We will be in possession of ground that commands almost all Cornwallis' lines of defense. What do you think has come over Cornwallis? This will give the French line and the American a real advantage."

"I have heard that he wants to retreat to the opposite side of the river," Adam said. "He thinks that is the best side to fortify. Besides they say there is much smallpox amongst his troops."

Lafayette did not seem to hear him. He was busy looking at maps, and giving orders for the next day's battle.

Adam left hurriedly. He wanted to inform Colonel Scammell of Cornwallis' move, for the Americans as well as the French were in a position to move into the redoubts that the British had evacuated.

In the morning a unit of the French from St. Simon's command drove into the British pickets near the redoubts occupied by the Welsh Fusiliers. In the skirmish that followed several casualties occurred, and Alexander Scammell was wounded, but the French and Americans took a more advantageous position. Adam went with the small detail that carried Colonel Scammell to the base hospital at Williamsburg.

The Colonel did not live to know about the taking of the redoubt. He died before the week was out. When Mary Warden told him, Adam shook his head sadly. "We could not afford to lose him. He was one of the best."

The French and Americans now occupied what had been the British forward lines. They prepared to lay siege and maintain it.

On the Gloucester side of the York River the British were now in a position to halt the large foraging parties and they had opened a possible escape route if General Clinton sent down his rescue fleet as he had promised.

The allied force was fifteen hundred militia and was reinforced by six hundred men from the French fleet and eight hundred marines, while the British at Gloucester had Simcoe's regiment and Tarleton's cavalry and ground units as well. A respectable number of fighters.

On the 8th of October, the French moved down toward Gloucester Point to force the British into a fixed position. A spirited engagement took place between Tarleton's cavalry from the British and the American cavalry units. Tarleton for the British and Laurens of South Carolina for the Americans. Sixteen casualties for the Americans and fifty for the British. The British withdrew behind their works and remained during the rest of the siege.

The first week in October saw the Americans marching to their assigned positions, ready for the opening of the first allied siege line. They had an advantage, for they completely surrounded the British works with men and artillery within firing range of the enemy, from the York River to Yorktown and west to the York-Hampton Road to Yorktown Creek.

Early the following week twenty-eight hundred men lay on the ground, their arms at hand to repel an attack. But it did not come. The night was dark and cloudy, an aid to the troops under General Lincoln and Baron de Viomenil. By daylight the trenches were ready, a protection for the allied troops from the British gunners. General Washington fired the first round for his battery. For two days the incessant sound of guns was over Yorktown.

The effect was shattering. Enemy batteries were silenced, Cornwallis' headquarters all but demolished. The General, himself, narrowly escaped being made a prisoner.

During the bombardment Adam Rutledge was with

Von Steuben's men. During the forward movement he stopped to aid a wounded British soldier, tying up his wounded hand and giving him water from his canteen. On him Adam found a half-finished letter:

> Tonight [October 9th] about tattoo the enemy began to salute our left wing and shortly afterwards our entire line with bombs, cannon and howitzers . . .
>
> Early this morning [October 10th] we had to change our camp and pitch our tents in the earthworks on account of the heavy fire of the enemy. One could not avoid the horribly many cannon balls either inside or outside the city.
>
> Many are badly injured or mortally wounded by fragments of bombs which exploded partly in the air and partly on the ground. Arms and legs are severed or men struck dead. Fragments and pieces of these bombs flew back and hit houses and buildings and did much damage. The event of all was to see bits of men, and arms and legs scattered about . . .

By the time Adam had folded the unfinished letter and put it in his pouch, the man who wrote it had suffered the fate of his companions. He composed the dead man's arms and covered him with a cloak. There was no time to do more. The troops were advancing.

The bombardment moved to the British ships in the river. Redhot shot were used to ignite the heavily tarred rigging and ship timbers. Two transport vessels were set afire, and two ships of war were burned completely. The other ships sailed to Gloucester to put themselves out of range of the devastating fire. During the night a British fire ship, designed to ignite American ships, caught fire from a shell and burned with a brilliant blaze.

Now the time had arrived when Washington thought

to open the second allied siege line which would put his troops within striking distance of the enemy earthworks. Adam Rutledge asked to join this foray, which was led by Colonel Alexander Hamilton, Colonel John Laurens, Major Nicholas Fish and two French officers.

They attacked the British redoubt after dark, when a burst of six shells gave the prearranged signal. The soldiers carried unloaded muskets, for it was to be a matter of bayonets, not guns. They charged without waiting to remove the pointed stakes that surrounded the redoubt. The British were caught by surprise. In ten minutes the position was in American hands.

Cornwallis was now in bad case. Old campaigner that he was, he knew there was no hope for his embattled troops, hemmed in on every side. He had already sent a last desperate appeal to Sir Henry Clinton for help: "If you do not send aid quickly, you must be prepared for the worst." Grave of face, dressed in his fine uniform with its bright red coat, he stood on the bank of the York River, his hands clasped behind him, looking up the river to the north from whence help might come. It was a forlorn hope, yet he knew he must attack again.

That night Cornwallis made a last-ditch attempt. He ordered all his fighting men across the river to Gloucester Point. This diversion might give him the opportunity to break through and open a road to march his troops north toward New York. But even nature was against him; a heavy storm swamped boats and drove others back to the Yorktown shore. Cornwallis had been beset by storms; storms and swollen rivers had been also his undoing at Guilford Court House.

Early the next morning, disheartened, weary and despondent to the point of illness, he called a council of his officers.

"We have not powder to fire a single gun," he told them. "I therefore propose to capitulate." He turned his face away from them into his pillow.

His officers filed slowly from the tent, leaving him to his dark thoughts.

At ten o'clock a drummer boy in a fresh red uniform, accompanied by an officer, went to a high-point of the parapet on the south side of Yorktown and beat a "parley."

Adam Rutledge was the first of the American officers to see the British flag of truce on the morning of October 17. He sent Herk running to Cosmo de' Medici's tent to inform him that something unusual was happening. Shortly afterward de' Medici joined Adam. They climbed to the top of the redoubt nearest to them, where they found General Lafayette and Raoul. The general was looking through his field glasses.

"They are approaching General Washington's headquarters. We are about to see history made, gentlemen. It will be one of the greatest moments in the world."

"Let us move over to Wormley Pond," Adam suggested. "We can see better from there."

Lafayette said, 'No. I may be called to a council. It will be better for me to be at my headquarters, but don't let me deter you. Raoul, you had best come with me."

As the two Frenchmen walked back toward the French headquarters, Adam and de' Medici made their way across the field strewn with the dead of both armies.

The drummer boy in his gay red coat had been joined by two subalterns, the flag of truce held high above them. The men of the American army watched from the redoubts they had taken the day before from the British. Every one was silent. No cheering, no expression of triumph came from their lips, as though each man sensed the tragedy of the downfall of a great army of a great nation, led by a proud general, whose military accomplishments far exceeded those of his superior generals, Sir William Howe and Sir Henry Clinton. His exploits in the operations of war were superior—his capture of Fort Lee, his pursuit of General Washington through New Jersey, his victory on the Brandywine, and occupation of Philadelphia and his defeat of Gates at Camden, showed his military genius. Perhaps the soldiers remembered that Lord Cornwallis had defended the Americans in Parliament against the obnoxious Stamp Act.

Cosmo de' Medici's large dark eyes were brilliant with unshed tears. "I grieve for him, Adam," he said. "His heart must now be breaking."

Adam nodded. He did not want to put into words the thoughts that crowded his mind. "I am glad that our men do not cheer. Victory is not always a time for joy, but sometimes sorrow for a fallen foe."

The silence was like a noise in itself, hanging heavy in the still, crisp October air.

Early in the afternoon, two days later, his throat full, Adam watched the British army, in a new issue of uniforms, march out from Yorktown to the sound of a band playing an old English tune, "The World Turned Upside Down." When they reached the place appointed for the surrender, their column marched between the Americans on one side, the French on the other. One after another, the regiments laid down their arms, and stacked their muskets in the open meadow.

General Washington's general orders were read, commending both armies. General O'Hara, on foot, presented the British Commander's sword, hilt first, to General Lincoln on horseback. The American general accepted it, saluted and immediately returned it to General O'Hara. Then the troops retired.

Riders on fast horses galloped from the camp to speed the news along the Virginia, Maryland, New Jersey and Pennsylvania roads to villages and cities, on to New York. "Cornwallis has surrendered" replaced the old terrifying cry of "Cornwallis is coming." In the minds of the people the war was over.

Adam Rutledge and Cosmo de' Medici rode into Williamsburg that night. Adam went to the hospital to find Mary Warden. She was just leaving the Palace with Dr. Armitage. When she saw Adam she ran to his arms. Tears were streaming down her cheeks.

He kissed the tears away. "Come, come, sweet Mary! This is no time for tears, but for rejoicing."

"I cry for happiness," she said, "not for sorrow."

They walked down the esplanade to Raleigh's Tavern. "I'm meeting de' Medici," Adam said. "He asked to join us in our victory dinner. You will be interested in the depth of his feelings. 'The whole world is moving forward into the brotherhood of man. You Americans have raised the banner of freedom for the whole world to follow,' Cosmo said to me."

Dr. Armitage's expression was profoundly serious. "I wonder, Adam, whether we are old enough to uphold this banner. The responsibility is great and fearsome. Have we the stamina and the courage?"

Washington's army marched slowly along the road to Williamsburg. The general had given orders that as many soldiers as wished could visit their wounded comrades at the General Hospital in the Palace.

Outside the town the soldiers rested in a field. Many of the men gathered bunches of late flowers along the roadside, Michaelmas daisies and black-eyed Susans. These tightly-held bouquets were to present to the sick in the hospital. A touch of autumn color to cheer their comrades.

Cosmo de' Medici rode at the head of his dragoons. He was glad he had been chosen to ride north with Washington rather than south to join General Greene. He had had enough of Charleston during his year's confinement at Haddrell's Point. He had no idea what the general's plans were. Clinton still held New York. The word had come that his fleet had turned back when he got the word that Cornwallis had given up Virginia.

As he rode along the Williamsburg Road de' Medici was quiet in mind, relieved of the anxiety that comes with battle. The woods were glorious in their autumn splendor of yellow and red, set off by the dark green of the pines. The marching troops engaged his attention. They were tired men, their faces drawn and weary from the siege and the battles they had fought. The contrast with the British, who had drawn fresh uniforms for the

surrender, was so great as to be almost sad. They were
faded and ragged, and some were in homespun, for the
last levy had had no time to draw uniforms at all. They
had fought in the clothes they had worn on their march
from their homes. Many were farm boys to whom drill
was unknown but who had borne rifles since childhood
and who could shoot straight. They were disciplined to
meet danger without flinching.

A surge of pride swept over de' Medici as
he looked at their tired young faces. Now the war was
over, or so they thought. They did not know that this
was only a phase; the great war was not finished. All
they wanted was to get back to their farms and prepare
the land for spring planting. If they thought at all, they
would believe that they would march with the general to
Philadelphia, surrender their arms to Congress, receive
thanks and perhaps a gift of land in the west, and go
home.

De' Medici knew that it would be a year or more
before New York was occupied and Charleston relieved.
Perhaps it was good that the men did not know as they
marched along, carrying bright bunches of flowers to
give their wounded companions in the hospital at Williamsburg. He himself understood. He wanted, in time,
to ride south again. Near New Bern there was land to be
had that could be the basis of the plantation he dreamed
of. He thought of his friend Adam Rutledge, who had
gone home for a short time.

The army came to the outskirts of the town.
Officers were riding up and down the ranks, trying to
make the weary troops look like a conquering army as
they marched down Duke of Gloucester Street. Cosmo
was fortunate. His dragoons looked smart and soldierly.
It was the foot soldiers, who had borne the brunt of the
battle, who could not be whipped into line. The officers
realized their plight. They called a halt before the Capitol to give their men a period of rest before they marched
into Williamsburg as far as the College.

But once in Williamsburg the men moved more
swiftly and straightened their weary backs. It was not

the end of the march that caused them to quicken their stride, but the crowds of men and women and children who stood by the side of the road shouting and waving flags. The glow that came to the faces of the marching soldiers when they heard the cheering press of people was something to warm the heart. Even de' Medici's dragoons straightened in their saddles. The jubilant voices of the townsfolk sounded sweet to their ears after the din of battle. This was the glory of war that comes seldom to the ears of tired soldiers. These people standing by the roadside were the people they had saved. Their efforts had been of some use, after all.

XIV

Philadelphia

The journey north of the Baron and Baroness von Poellnitz was, so far as the Baroness was concerned, utterly tedious. The autumn weather brought rain that turned the roads into sloughs of mire, and the cold, damp winds chilled her to the bone. They chilled the Baron, who continued to ride horseback, until he had contracted a fever by the time they reached Richmond, and they had been forced to stay in that city until he recovered.

The time passed slowly for Lady Anne. They knew no one in Richmond. She could not go calling, or expect to be called upon. The Baron sent Sayre on ahead to engage rooms in Philadelphia. He had heard that it was difficult to get suitable lodgings, for Congress was in session, and most of the desirable rooms were occupied by representatives and their wives.

Lady Anne had heard in London of the excellent society in Philadelphia, the balls, the gambling. The routes during the British occupation had given the city a reputation no other American city enjoyed. Philadelphia was said to be gay in spite of the war—gayer even than New York.

"We will stay at least a month," she told Sayre before he left. "Find rooms in a fashionable house. I want three rooms and rooms for the servants as well. I intend to do some entertaining while we are there."

Her husband made no objection. He had long ago found it useless to oppose her when she had set her mind to a thing. Besides, he looked forward to meeting some of the renowned scientists and members of scientific societies connected with the University.

With Sayre gone, Lady Anne had even less to divert her. She fell to brooding over the blows she felt an unkind fate had dealt her. Here in America everything had seemed to go against her. She had virtually been chased out of that revolting village of Edenton. She had definitely been chased out of charming Williamsburg. Adam Rutledge, whom she coveted, had insulted her. Raoul de Polignac, whom she loved, had spurned her cruelly. Such rejection she had never experienced before or dreamed it could happen to her.

Was it possible she was losing her charm? She spent most of a gray, blustery day at her dressing table, scrutinizing every pore of her skin. She could find nothing that might have changed her from an irresistible woman to a repulsive one, nothing that could not still compel and command the heart and body of any man she chose to entice. Yet, here she was, alone and, what was worse, with a gnawing sense of aloneness. It was the most painful affliction with which she had ever been visited, far worse than her chronic migraines.

"Do you think we shall ever have company again, Dawkins?" she asked her woman one night as she was preparing for bed. "Will this wretched isolation ever end?"

Dawkins patted her shoulder. "As Noah said to Mrs. Noah when she asked if it would ever stop raining, it always has."

"Do you never feel very alone, Dawkins?"

"No, madam."

"How do you avoid it?"

"I keep too busy to think about it," the maid replied.

"Yet you seem to have no one to love you."

"The Lord loves me, madam, and I love him, and that is quite sufficient."

One of these new-fangled Methodists, Lady Anne thought. What an utterly ridiculous sentiment! She had long been convinced that once God had created the world like some master clock-maker, and had wound it up to run forever, He had let it alone and probably moved on to construct some other ingenious mechanical device.

"Humph!" she exclaimed. "That may be well enough for you. I like a more tangible love."

"So I have observed, madam. But that is not very lasting, I fear."

Lady Anne was about to consider Dawkins' rejoinder insolent, and scold her, but she was too dispirited even for that. She could not help discerning a grain of truth in what the woman had said. Someday the clock—her clock, at any rate—would run down. At best, she might be like blind old Madame du Deffand. At worst . . . She refused to think of it. When she got into bed, she turned her face to the wall, and drew the coverlets up around her ears.

Finally the Baron felt strong enough to move on. As they neared Philadelphia, Lady Anne's spirits brightened. She seemed to recover her former gaiety and exuberance. The weather, too, had changed. It was almost as warm once more as in summer, but the early frosts had touched the trees and shrubs by the roadside, and the woods along the river were blazing with red and yellow and orange hues.

Dawkins she had permitted to ride inside the coach again. "Who knows what may transpire?" Lady Anne remarked to her. "Philadelphia will be filled with the great men of the colonies. It will not be London but it may be as gay as Bath, perhaps, or one of the other watering places, what with its legislature and army and navy men. I am glad I did not waste all my gowns in the village of Edenton."

"You met some fine men in Edenton, madam. I think you managed to enjoy yourself."

"Oh, I suppose so, after a fashion, but not the fashion of a cosmopolitan city like Philadelphia."

"Madam, remember there is a war and these people take their war very seriously," the maid spoke grumpily.

But nothing could dampen Lady Anne's blithe spirits. She sang as they rode along—gay French songs and old Scottish ballads which sounded good in her liquid pleasing voice.

The coach pulled up at Mr. Cochran's fashionable boardinghouse at noon. Stephen Sayre was in the common room waiting for them. He attended to the unloading of Lady Anne's many boxes and portmanteaus, and escorted the heavily veiled Lady Anne and the Baron to their quarters on the second floor.

Lady Anne passed the many people waiting in the common room for the opening of the dining hall. She walked swiftly with a great rustling of wide taffeta skirts about her. A sable fur piece drooped from her neck. A faint trace of French perfume followed in her wake. Her air of importance was unmistakable. The tall, erect figure of the Baron with his military bearing created almost as much attention as Lady Anne.

"Who are they?" was the whisper that passed about the room as they mounted the wide stairs. "He must be one of the French officers on Washington's staff," someone said aloud. "You know there are dozens of foreigners here in the army."

"He's not in uniform," a woman whispered. "Wouldn't he be in uniform if he were an officer?"

A man came in from outside. "The coach has a crest. I couldn't make it out but it's someone important."

Lady Anne walked into her sitting room and lifted her veil. She wore a look of satisfaction. This was just what she wanted, to create an atmosphere of mystery, almost as though she were royalty incognita. She tossed her cloak and sables on the divan and took the pins out of her bonnet, which she tossed on top of her cloak.

"Sayre, order our luncheon. Something extraordinary, a dish that Philadelphia has made famous."

Sayre called a waiter. "Sea food?" the waiter said.

"If madam will permit me I would suggest a well-liked dish of Philadelphia—terrapin stew. This city is famous for terrapin."

Good! I would enjoy a famous dish the Philadelphians like."

"A cut from a joint for me," her husband said, "and good Yorkshire pudding."

Lady Anne laughed. "My dear, you are being too British. This is America. Remember?"

The Baron smiled. "Perhaps I should say baked ham with sweet potatoes." He moved out of the sitting room into his bedroom.

"Hurry the waiter, Sayre. I'm starving. I haven't had a decent meal since Williamsburg."

Lady Anne walked to the window and looked out on the square. The ground was covered with leaves that had drifted from the trees. The sun was bright, the sky vivid blue. This was autumn at its best. She had no time to dream of autumn in England or to remember Ashe Park and William Bird.

Sayre laughed. He was watching a crowd of sober Philadelphians which had gathered about the Baron's coach and were trying to decipher the crest. He descended, and told one of them that it belonged to the Chamberlain of Frederick the Great. His information spread awe among the crowd. One man said, "I wouldn't be surprised if we had a royal king in our city one day."

When he returned, and reported this, Lady Anne clapped her hands for joy, like a little girl.

"I shall take my rest this afternoon," she announced. "This evening we will dine out and visit some club where there is gambling. I feel lucky today. I will wager a golden sovereign or two and test my luck."

The Baron looked up from the table, where he was writing to a prominent member of the Philosophical Society, asking to meet him at supper.

Sayre caught his eye. The Baron's look meant that Sayre was to deal with her. After the Williamsburg incident the Baron had told him that henceforth he would be

charged with the unpleasant responsibility of changing
Lady Anne's mind.

"I have other plans, my dear," the Baron said simply. "Sayre will take care of you."

For the moment Sayre said nothing. Not until the
Baron had left for his appointment did he approach
Lady Anne with tidings of disappointment.

"There will be no repetition of the scene in the
common room at Horniblow's in Edenton," he told her.

As he had expected, she protested shrilly and violently. Sayre sat watching her, a sardonic expression on
his face, until the storm had lessened its fury.

"Philadelphia is not to know you are the daughter
of Lord Bute," he said finally. "Not, that is, until it finds
out on its own, as it doubtless will before long. Samuel
Johnstone is here from Edenton. His cousin Charles was
no great admirer of yours, if I remember correctly. He
will soon be informed of your character and behavior,
if, indeed he has not been so already. You can still be
useful to me, and to your country, but not if you invite
trouble."

"You think only of yourself," she cried.

"It is a habit I have picked up from you," he said
with a grin.

"Sayre, you go too far. Have a care!"

"I have a care—for myself. And, in quite a different way, for you."

She paced the room furiously, her mouth set in a
grim line, her eyes flashing. Then she wheeled on him.

"You cannot stop me. I am going out."

She strode to the door and flung it open. But before she could cross the threshold, she felt Sayre's
powerful arms around her, pinioning her own. She
kicked at him, only to find her legs grasped, herself
turned face down, her rigid body lifted from the floor,
carried to the bedroom, thrown on to the bed. Before
she could struggle to her feet again, she heard the key
turn in the lock on the far side of the door.

Stephen Sayre dusted off his large, thick hands,
smoothed down his elegant, light blue coat, and ar-

ranged the ruffled stock at his throat. He stepped to the table where the Baron had been writing. Some of the many letters awaiting his arrival in Philadelphia had been opened, but others the Baron had obviously not had time for. Sayre read the opened ones. He found nothing in them of any interest to himself. He looked through the unopened letters. A vaguely familiar handwriting caught his eye. In a moment he recognized it as that of the planter in New Bern from whom the Baron had bought land. Sayre recalled that the planter had asked him from what persons in Europe he might get information and credentials about the Baron. Sayre decided quickly that this missive might well interest him. He broke the seal and unfolded the single sheet of paper.

I have learned what I think you should know, [Sayre read]. Your man of business, Mr. Sayre, is reported to be something of an adventurer. At an early age he got involved in land schemes and married an heiress. He was once a sheriff of London. In a short time he was arrested for an alleged plot against the King but was released.

He sued the Earl of Rockford for false imprisonment and won his case with negligible damages. He traveled through Europe as an American emissary, sometimes acting as such. His business in London went bankrupt. He has a wife and son although he pays little attention to them. It might be well if you personally were to examine the documents he has prepared for your signature. . . .

Sayre took the letter to the fireplace, stooped and held it over the coals until it was completely black. Then he waited until it had turned to gray ash. Then he stole out of the room and closed the door noiselessly behind him.

It was near midnight and Lady Anne was in her

first sleep when the noise of bells ringing and cannon booming awakened her. She jumped from her bed and sped to the window to look out on the street below.

The watch was passing by, swinging his lantern and crying out at the top of his lungs: "Twelve o'clock and all's well. Cornwallis is taken! Cornwallis is taken! All's well. Cornwallis is taken!"

The Baron was at the door of her bedroom, calling to be admitted. Finally it occurred to him to turn the lock. He was too excited to notice that the key was on the outside of her door. He rushed to join her at the window.

"Freedom and liberty are safe," he kept repeating. "Praise be to God for His mercy."

Lady Anne was silent. Her thoughts were on the land of her birth. England had been defeated by rebels in America. A sad blow for her father and for her countrymen.

She left the window and the delirious crowds below and crawled back into bed.

In the morning the crowds still thronged the streets, shaking hands, cheering, some shedding tears of joy. Congress met in the early morning. The dispatch sent by General Washington, which Lieutenant Colonel Tench Tilghman had brought, was read before the assembled body.

At two o'clock all the representatives marched together to the Dutch Lutheran Church and returned thanks to Almighty God for crowning the allied armies of America and France with victory.

The following day the Congress voted the nation's thanks and fitting thanks to Washington, Roachambeau and de Grasse and their officers, and resolved that a marble column be erected at Yorktown to commemorate the event.

All morning long Lady Anne stayed in bed with a migraine, her head bound up with a bandage dipped in vinegar. The Baron stepped into the room at noon. The shutters were closed and he could barely make out Lady

Anne's form under the covers. He backed out of the room quietly and went off to dinner with his Edenton friend Samuel Johnstone, and Pierce Butler.

The latter talked of the advantages of living in the South, the superiority of the people of the colonies, and the richness of the land. As they were dining, Tench Tilghman came into the room. Pierce Butler bowed to him and beckoned him to their table. "Sit down, sit down. I want to hear first hand about Cornwallis' surrender." He put his hand on the young Colonel's shoulder. "This man is the one whom George Washington selected to bring the message of Cornwallis' surrender to the Congress. He made a powerful ride, gentlemen. I tell you we are proud to have a Southerner—a Marylander —chosen for such an honor."

Butler turned to the Baron. "The Congress are going to honor him at a dinner tonight. We would be happy to have you attend, sir."

"I shall be happy to attend," the Baron replied, "and thank you for inviting me. I do love the land, gentlemen, though I am at present endeavoring to procure an estate in New York."

"No matter, no matter," Pierce Butler said heartily. "We'll have you in South Carolina before you are through. Why, you can't resist our climate—a proper climate for all growing crops!"

Colonel Tilghman excused himself, and presently, after the others had finished, the Baron went to his rooms. Lady Anne was still sleeping off her migraine. He went out into the street. The celebration of General Washington's victory was continuing. People were walking about aimlessly, laughing, singing, greeting strangers in the height of good humor. The Baron rejoiced in the joyousness of the people of Philadelphia and the Congress. It was almost too good to be true. It did not occur to him that his wife's migraine came because of General Washington's victory and Lord Cornwallis' defeat until her woman suggested that Lady Anne had taken to her bed because of her great disappointment.

"Sir, she never for a moment dreamed that the rebels would win a victory over the King's army. It has hit her hard, but she will never admit it to you or to anyone else."

Late in the afternoon, Lady Anne, dressed in one of her elaborate gowns for supper, came into the sitting room. She was smiling. "I've got rid of the migraine. Dawkins dosed me up like Mother Goose's rhyme, in vinegar and brown paper."

Sayre let out a big guffaw, but the Baron looked at his wife searchingly, wondering if Dawkins could be right.

"I am going out, my dear," the Baron said. "A dinner is being given by the Congress for Colonel Tilghman, who brought the message of Cornwallis' surrender."

Sayre looked at the Baron searchingly, as though to ask, "How did you get the invitation?" but he said nothing. Neither did the Baron. He left the room shortly to dress. When he had gone, Lady Anne smiled at Sayre. "What fortune. We have time to ourselves. We will eat here."

"Not I," said Sayre. "I have a yearning to eat at an old tavern I know by the river."

"I'll go with you, Stephen."

He eyed her speculatively. "In that gown? I think not, my lady."

"I'll change. I want to go out and see Philadelphia."

He looked at her. "I'm not sure that you will like Philadelphia when the people are celebrating a great American victory. You might not be able to control that temper of yours, madam. The British have lost. I remember an old song of another defeat that went:

> 'We're marching up to old Quebec
> And the drums are loudly beating
> The Americans have gained the day
> And the British are defeated.'

You wouldn't like to hear that, now would you?"

Lady Anne flared. "Indeed I would not. I don't believe they are defeated."

"You don't think Cornwallis has surrendered? Come now, madam, be sensible!"

Lady Anne spoke quickly. "Sir Henry Clinton still holds New York. He has not surrendered yet."

"He soon will. Do you think that because I did a bit of spying, I'm a Tory? Perhaps I did lean somewhat to your side—once. But events, and one in particular, have caused me to believe that it will be for my own good to remember I'm American born. A bit of gold is useful, and its color does not change with the hand that gives it out." He took up his tricorn and made for the door. "Au revoir, dear lady."

He had left the room before she could protest. She picked up the first thing her eye lit upon, a plaster statuette of Apollo, and hurled it after him. It shattered against the closing door.

Dawkins came into the room at the sound of the crash. "Oh, madam, what a sadness!" she exclaimed. "I'll get a dust pan and tidy up before any guest comes."

"No one is coming, Dawkins. We are left quite alone."

XV

The New House

Lady Anne had no wish to remain in Philadelphia as a virtual prisoner. Angry as she was at the reason for her confinement, she yet saw the practicality of Sayre's admonitions and restrictions, and she was not angry at him personally. Instead she took out her spleen on the Baron, who was too delighted with the new friends he had made among the Philadelphia savants, and the acquaintances he had revived among the delegates to Congress, to be in any great hurry to move on.

For over a week she had forbidden him her bed on the grounds that she was unwell, both by nature and by dint of the migraines from which she suffered worse than before. The climate of Philadelphia she declared was most unsalubrious.

In sober garb, however, she and Dawkins would saunter forth in the city, which was still celebrating the victory at Yorktown. They even ventured out one evening when there were to be fireworks.

They had gone but a little distance from their establishment, when they found a street full of roisterers. Dawkins held back, and tried to keep Lady Anne from proceeding, as the roar of the crowd in the distance smote their ears. It was like the sound of waves beating against a shore.

Dawkins held back. "Come on, woman," Lady

Anne said in her ear. "Come on or I'll leave you behind."

"Oh, no, madam," said the frightened maid. "Don't. I would be swept away."

Lady Anne grasped Dawkins' arm. "Come on. I want to see the crowd. I want to know what victory means to these Americans."

They turned the corner into a tree-lined square filled with laughing, singing, joyous people. The strong light of the flambeaux played on the faces of men and women, making grotesque masks of happy countenances.

Lady Anne held back only a moment, then pressed forward, dragging Dawkins with her until she was at the verge of the crowd. A man on a platform was haranguing the crowd in a loud, hoarse voice.

"They are whipped at Yorktown," he was shouting. "Their proud commander has bowed his head and surrendered his sword. Our general sits on horseback and receives the British sword, but he is a kindly man, our General Washington. He hands the sword back and invites Cornwallis to a meal with him." With this there came a roar from the crowd: "Why did he do that?" "Why did he ask Cornwallis to eat?" "He's our enemy, isn't he?"

The speaker disregarded the remarks. "He invited the general to dinner to show the world that he is a generous man who bears no grudges. A noble man, General George Washington."

The people clapped and cheered as the speaker got down from the platform. The crowd marched off down the street, Lady Anne and Dawkins with them.

Dawkins whispered, "Where are we going, madam?"

"I don't know. Does it matter?"

A woman next to them turned around. "We are going to see the victory celebration." The crowd moved them on to a large open space with trees like a park.

Lady Anne felt a pressure against her. She turned her head. A handsome young soldier in blue and buff had slipped his arm about her waist. She struggled to get free as the clasp of his arm became more insistent.

"Don't try to get away, my girl. You want this, or why are you out in a crowd like this?" He stopped her protest with a strong, hard kiss.

Lady Anne ceased resisting. She even responded slightly. The soldier, encouraged, drew her close to him and slightly away from the crowd. "You know you like being kissed. Now, don't you?" His eager mouth covered hers closely. Suddenly he felt a hard blow on the back of his neck. Dawkins had attacked him with a piece of wood. The soldier jumped backward in astonishment.

"Let go her ladyship, you oaf," Dawkins cried. "Let go."

The soldier stepped back quickly, his arm upraised to fend off another blow. "I meant no harm. A pretty wench out here alone, what was I to think?" He faded away in the crowd.

Lady Anne slapped Dawkins sharply on the cheek. "I'll thank you to attend to your own affairs, Dawkins," she said, furious at the interruption.

Dawkins rubbed her cheek. "No harm to you, madam, but what about the young soldier?"

"You've spoiled the evening for me, Dawkins. We may as well go back to Mr. Cochran's."

That night she dreamed about the young soldier, and tossed as she imagined the delights he might give her until she had thrown herself out of bed. Awake, she knew she needed a man, even the Baron. When she got to New York, Sayre could not possibly be so cautious, and so distant. There would be delicious nights with him again—and with others.

The only event that enlivened her stay was the Victory Ball, to which the Baron had procured invitations.

She had with her a ball gown that she had never worn, a heavy white brocaded satin over a petticoat of cerise, ruffled to the pointed bodice with fine Mechlin lace. It was cut with a square neck, low to show her rounded bosom, pushed high by tightly laced stays, with a tantalizing strip of lace across to half conceal her beauties. The short sleeves were finished with ruffles of lace.

She wore cerise satin shoes laced over her slim ankles with the same vivid color. The barber dressed her newly touched red-gold hair high on her head with long curls, and powdered. The latter process took some time, as the barber had a new invention to blow the powder on with a pair of bellows. Lady Anne sat on a stool set on a sheet, covered with another sheet, while the barber wielded the bellows. Dawkins hovered around to keep the powder from blowing on the furniture. Lady Anne watched the process with interest from her vantage point in front of a cheval glass and announced that she was highly gratified with the result.

She applied the black court plaster patches herself: one below her left eye; the other near the right corner of her mouth. They heightened her natural color but she added a touch of bright rouge to emphasize the effect.

The barber, a bold fellow, patted her shoulder and announced that she would undoubtedly be the most beautiful woman at the ball. "I know all the Philadelphia beauties and the wives of the officers. I assure your ladyship there will not be a woman in the hall who will touch you in beauty or elegance." This little speech brought forth a gold piece which the barber put into his pocket with an exaggerated bow and fulsome thanks.

The Baron was almost as fulsome in his praise when he came into the sitting room and discovered his wife preening before the glass. "My dear, you are ravishing!" he exclaimed. Kissing the slim white hand she extended, he added: "There will be no one at the ball to compare with you."

In spite of herself she smiled at him. "You are rather elegant yourself, in your full court costume. I always like a man dressed in pearl satin. Your orders and ribbons show so well."

The Baron made a leg. "Thank you, my dear. In reward for your compliment I have a little news for you on this festive night—a dispatch from New York. We now own Governor Elliot's residence, Minto, in the Bowery, a house with twenty rooms and twenty-one acres of fine garden. The deed has been signed. A suitable present for you on this auspicious occasion."

Lady Anne clasped her hands together in delight. "How splendid! Now we can entertain properly in our own home."

They were interrupted by the entrance of Stephen Sayre, splendidly attired in pale blue satin. His hair was curled and powdered. Lady Anne beamed at him. "Now I shall be escorted to the ball by two handsome gentlemen. I am enchanted at the prospect."

They went down the stairs and out to their carriage. A crowd surrounded the crested vehicle. "Oh's" and "Ah's" greeted their appearance. With her usual air of not seeing the citizen, Lady Anne paused a moment on the curb, waiting to be handed into the carriage. Her long, fur-lined cape almost covered her elegant gown.

"A queen at least," a woman called out. "Your majesty, drop your cloak so we can see your handsome gown."

Lady Anne smiled and obliged. While the people praised the beauty of her costume, Lady Anne stepped gracefully into the carriage followed by her escorts. The coachman cracked his whip. The two spirited bays moved off swiftly toward Carpenter's Hall.

North Carolinian acquaintances of the Baron were waiting in the anteroom. Together they all entered the ballroom and joined the line moving to the far side of the room, where the Philadelphia dignitaries and a few Army officers and their wives formed a receiving line. The room was ablaze with innumerable candles in chandeliers and wall sconces, their flames reflected in the highly polished floor. Sheraton chairs, placed side by side around the room, were occupied by gaily dressed women, whose escorts stood nearby.

The hall was decorated in flags and bunting. Vases of fall flowers filled the window sills under the velvet curtains. The room buzzed with conversation which rose over the music of violins, cellos and a harpsichord.

There was a hush in the crowd when Lady Anne, on the Baron's arm, walked slowly down the line. A few of the nearest people caught her name as she was announced.

Whispering began; heads were close. The name Von Poellnitz—was it Swiss or German or Prussian? Perhaps even Polish. The Baroness was beautiful, surely she was not foreign like her blond husband. In no time the story was whispered around the room: The Baron was Chamberlain to Frederick the Great, almost royalty.

Lady Anne was by no means oblivious of the sensation she had created. It had been so long since she had been equally admired that the sensation thrilled her almost as much as if she had never experienced it before. After the first minuet, which she danced with the Baron, gentleman after gentleman was introduced to her, including the handsome hero of the day, Colonel Tench Tilghman. To him alone did she consent to dance.

Sayre claimed her next. After the minuet, he was leading her to a chair when he whispered: "You are magnificent tonight, more beautiful than even I have ever believed."

She pressed his hand. "Do you still love me, Stephen?"

"I have never ceased loving you since the first time we set eyes on each other."

The Baron met them. "We should go, my dear," he said to his wife.

She pouted, and was about to protest, when Sayre intercepted her.

"The people here think you are royalty," he said. "You therefore should follow the example of royalty, and leave before supper."

Lady Anne looked at him quizzically. For a person as crude as Sayre could be, he had some strange sense of the appropriate. Doubtless, she thought, he has another motive. But his suggestion pleased her. She acquiesced gracefully. With never a backward glance at the glittering ballroom, she left with the Baron, her head imperiously high, her eyes glancing neither to right nor to left.

All the way from Philadelphia to New York, Lady Anne could think of nothing but the grand new house they would invest. It was something of a disappointment to her to find that the Baron had purchased it with most of the furniture, for she had hoped to furnish it herself with brand new pieces and china. But the Royal Governor Elliott, former owner of Minto, had taken ship for England so suddenly that he had left his things behind, and the Baron had willingly acquired them.

Nevertheless, the Baroness was ecstatic about the mansion and about New York. The British still occupied the city and the surrounding country. There were Redcoats on all the streets, and she felt at home and among her own kind for the first time since she had come to America.

By December she had the great house staffed. She opened it to the officers stationed in and near New York. Sir Henry Clinton, the British general and governor, was the guest of honor. Minto had never seen so much gaiety and excitement as on that night. Champagne toasts were drunk endlessly to the hostess, to her beauty, to her hospitality, to her loyalty.

All the rooms on the ground floor were opened. The long drawing room was brightly illuminated. The gay silks and satins of the women vied with the flames of the candles for brightness. The elite of New York were there, the many Loyalists as well as the military. Lady Anne glanced around at the company. She was pleased. Surely no more exciting company could be seen in London itself than were gathered under her roof that night.

The name of Lord Cornwallis was never mentioned, and no other word was spoken to spoil the gaiety of the evening. Lady Anne, her eyes bright, her voice high, toasted Sir Henry, the defender of the British Crown. Nothing was mentioned about the precarious position of Clinton's army on Long Island.

No one even spoke of war. No one save Stephen Sayre, who followed Lady Anne into a withdrawing room. He closed the door, and taking a glass of champagne from her hand, set it on the table. "You've had enough wine, my lady," he said. "Enough of silly celebration. Don't you know that General Washington is marching north—is practically at the gates of the city? What is there for these poor fools to celebrate? Except their own folly."

She drew away from him. "You talk like a rebel, Sayre. I'm tired of hearing about Washington and his army. I hear enough about that traitor from my husband. Don't spoil a happy evening. I've had little enough happiness in this wretched country."

Sayre came close to her and put his arm around her shoulders. "Don't tell me you have had no fun here in America. What about your young Frenchman, de Polignac—and, madam, what about Stephen Sayre?" He closed his arms about her and kissed her hard, pushing her down on a couch.

"No, Stephen, not here with all these people about."

Sayre only held her more tightly. "You silly husband goes tomorrow over the Post Road to Boston. He will leave very early in the morning. He has already retired." He brushed her cheek with his lips, then nibbled at her ear lobe as he whispered, "We shall have tonight, and tomorrow, and tomorrow . . ."

Gradually she yielded to him, thrilling to the pressure of his warm thick body upon her, the heat of his kisses, the animal scent that rose from him as his ardor increased. How long it had been since they had been together like this! At last she was in her own house, among her own people, free from prying eyes and gossiping tongues and hostile minds. She felt no longer alone, no longer rejected and unloved.

Her hands explored the hard muscles of his back, straining through the taut fabric of his scarlet coat. So great was the intensity of her desire that she did not hear the opening of the door to the room, only, as she relaxed for a moment, the clicking of the latch as it shut.

Sayre seemed to have heard it too. He sat up abruptly. "What was that?"

Lady Anne's hands flew to her curls to straighten them. "Some footman, no doubt," she said, her voice trembling a little as she hoped against hope that she was right. "They are all new servants here. I have not had time to train them properly."

Sayre seemed satisfied. He laughed. "It wouldn't be the first time a servant has caught you in the act of bundling. Remember young Dicky Bird."

She seemed not to have heard him. She was sitting bolt upright now, staring wildly before her.

"Stephen," she said faintly, "I have a terrible feeling it was not a servant."

He laughed again. "Who then?" His arms started to creep about her waist.

She pushed it away. "Stephen, what if . . . what it it was . . . Bruno?"

Sayre guffawed heartily. "So my lady has a conscience after all! But don't be absurd. I told you he had already retired. Besides, what if it was? Surely you don't believe the good Baron thinks you utterly faithful. He can't be that much of an idealist."

"You are coarse, Stephen. I do have some sensibilities. A woman may deceive her husband, but need not be so gross as to flaunt her infidelity in his very face."

"A delicate distinction," Sayre said. Then as she got to her feet and was smoothing her gown, "Where are you going?"

"To find the Baron," she said, stepping to the door.

His sardonic laughter followed her as she stepped across the sill, and before she closed the door behind her she heard him say: "You'll never know."

The words echoed in her ears as she stepped briskly through the other rooms, bowing to a guest here, smiling at another there, actually seeing none of them as her eyes roved over the company for a glimpse of her husband.

When she had traversed every room and still not found him, she was half willing to believe what Sayre had said about the Baron's having retired. But she had to be sure. Going into the hall of the mansion, she summoned the footman at the entrance door.

"Have you seen your master?"

"Yes, madam, he went upstairs a short time ago."

"What do you mean, 'a short time'?"

The footman stammered. "I—I do not know, madam. It was but a little while ago."

She moved to the foot of the stairs to continue her search, but as her foot was on the first step, Sir Henry Clinton emerged into the hall.

"Ah, there you are, gracious lady. I have been searching for you to take my leave. My poor officers may not depart till I do, and they must be up betimes. So I must tear myself away from your beautiful house and—," he kissed her hand, "your beautiful self."

As soon as he had gone, the other guests trooped into the hall to say good night.

It was a long time before Lady Anne could go to her room. On her way there she paused at the Baron's door and listened. In a moment she heard a snore that she knew unmistakably was his. So, at least he was asleep now, but how long had he been so?

The irony of this question she put to herself troubled her long after she had crawled into her own bed. Sayre was right, she would never know. The Baron was not one to reproach or accuse her openly. He would let her be tortured by doubt and, yes perhaps even by conscience. And he would act, if act he did, quixotically. Already she was wild with anxiety, imagining what he might do. What if he were to divorce her? Or leave her here alone in this wild, wretched country, perhaps to have her hair shorn or be tarred and feathered as some Tory women had been treated?

"Oh God," she moaned into her pillow, "what have I done to be punished so cruelly?"

XVI

An Icy Hand

Lady Anne, after sleep finally came to her, slept badly. When finally she awoke, it seemed to her that the whole night through, she had had but one continuous evil dream. Red-coated soldiers had been marching and marching along a wooded path, their boots thumping like the beat of a troubled heart. Then the red coats would blur into ones of blue and buff, and those, in turn, into many ships at sea with guns firing bursts of bright shells at turreted forts along a wooded shore. All over the ground red coats were lying—dozens, hundreds of men in British uniforms, dying. She wandered amongst them alone, no living soul anywhere about.

There was a late look in the wintry light that seeped through the panels of the shutters. Though the windows themselves had remained shut, the pale light itself chilled her. Presently the anxiety that had kept her tossing returned. This was no time for there to be any disturbance between her and the Baron. She wanted many new things for her new mansion—French furniture, and fresh brocade hangings for the drawing room were among the first items that occurred to her mind. She had already arranged credit at half a dozen shops in the city.

The more she thought about the joy of having money to spend on luxurious things, and of the balls and

205

smaller entertainments she would give, the further retreated from her consciousness the fear that such might
not be possible for her. It would be pure delight to be a
great hostess again. Here in the British-held New York,
she, as daughter of Lord Bute and wife of the Baron von
Poellnitz would be supreme in the society of the city.
Even the fabulous Madame Jumel would have to bow to
her. And it was more than apparent to her that Sir Henry Clinton did not find her unattractive. For that matter,
what man did? Except such rustics as the so-called patriots of Edenton. What a pity it was that she had to
waste so much of her time and her charms on them
when the only woman who could interest them was
some dowdy housewife!

She stretched out luxuriously between the fine linen
sheets of the bed. How silly of her to be worried! she
thought. After all she was the Lady Anne Stuart, and
had been the Duchess of Northumberland. If Bruno
made any fuss, she would remind him quite forcefully of
that. Who was he, after all, to question her conduct?

Feeling considerably restored, she rang for Dawkins.

"I shall have my breakfast here in my room," Lady
Anne told Dawkins. "You may lay out my brown silk,
and brush my furs. We are going shopping later. Then
you may tell that new butler that I shall be dining quietly here with Mr. Sayre. He is to serve us a fine bird and
champagne."

"Begging your pardon, madam," Dawkins said,
"but the Baron has already given orders."

"The Baron has gone to Boston, you goose."

"Begging your pardon, madam," Dawkins said,
"but he has changed his plans. He told me to advise
you, as soon as you were awake, that he had gone to his
lawyer's and wished you to be at home when he returned."

Lady Anne felt as if an icy hand had seized her
heart and was squeezing it until she could scarcely
breathe. She swallowed hard. Her arms grew suddenly

rigid. There was a hollow feeling in her stomach, as if everything within her had turned to water.

"My lady," Dawkins exclaimed, "is anything wrong? You look so pale of a sudden." She sprang to the dressing table and rushed back to the bed with a vial of smelling salts which she held under Lady Anne's nostrils.

Feebly the Baroness waved her aside. "Leave me," she gasped. "I shall rest a little longer."

"Madam, I dare not. Shall I send for a doctor?"

"No, you fool!" shouted Lady Anne. Then, after a moment, she said faintly, "Send for Mr. Sayre."

When the maid had left the room, Lady Anne found that she was still gasping for breath. Hundreds of bits of thoughts were flying about in her head like leaves in a gale, each belonging to some rooted tree, but so mingled in confusion that she could trace none to its origin. From time to time she moaned from the sheer exhaustion of trying to sort these whirling notions into some sort of order.

After what seemed hours Dawkins returned with a tray. Lady Anne managed to swallow a little tea.

"My lady," Dawkins said, "you told me yesterday I might go up the river today to visit my cousin. The boat leaves soon. Will you need me further?"

"Did you reach Mr. Sayre?"

"Madam, he is with the Baron. They have gone to the lawyers."

After a moment Lady Anne said, "You may go, Dawkins."

Eventually Lady Anne hauled herself out of the bed. Feeling still too shattered to dress, she put on a dressing gown and lay on a chaise longue in her dressing room to wait. It was impossible for her to concentrate on the book she picked up from time to time, only to let it drop on her lap. Try as she would, she could not think of anything except that something dreadful was about to happen to her. If only she knew what it would be!

She remained in that almost semi-conscious state

until midafternoon. Then she heard a gentle scratching on the outside of the door to her dressing room. "Come," she called weakly.

A parlormaid entered and curtsied. "Sir Henry Clinton is below, madam. He wishes to pay his respects to your ladyship."

As if a charge of electricity had shot through her, Lady Anne felt herself galvanized into action. She sprang up. "Go and tell him I shall receive him at once. Then hurry back and help me dress."

Even before the maid returned, Lady Anne had brushed her hair and arranged it in loose ringlets. She tied a blue ribbon about her head. Then she found a simple blue gown in her wardrobe and had it in readiness for the maid to help her on with it. About her shoulders she threw an India shawl. She tripped down the stairs as gaily as if her morning had been a pleasant and completely rewarding one.

She found the General pacing up and down the drawing room, and walked toward him, both her hands extended in warm greeting.

His face lightened as he raised her fingertips to his lips. "Beautiful lady, your entertainment last evening was completely delightful. It does my heart good to see you again. What a pleasure after a long disagreeable morning of talking with stupid officers about exchange of prisoners before we really know whether the war is over or not."

"Sit down, Sir Henry. I'll ring for tea. There is nothing so invigorating, especially as I have secured some real China since we came to New York."

"Tea is all right if you put a generous dollop of rum in it."

"That you shall have. Come sit near the fire. It grows chilly toward evening." She shivered a little and drew the scarf closer about her bare shoulders.

Sir Henry relaxed against the high back chair. "You have acquired the fine art of making a man feel comfortable so that he can forget the troubles of the day. What a wife you would make for a busy man!"

She smiled demurely.

"Pardon my stupidity. I was thinking of a wife for a Member of Parliament or an Ambassador—or even a weary general."

A servant brought in the tea tray and set it on a small dropleaf table. Lady Anne's slim hands fluttered as she arranged the cups and lifted the cozy from the teapot. "I always insist on my tea in a china pot. I imagine that it has a metal taste if it is steeped in silver." She passed him the hot buttered scones. "Now tell me your troubles, General. One always feels better if little annoyances are talked out."

Sir Henry sipped his tea and settled back in his chair. "You are quite right, Lady Anne. I can think of no one I had rather talk to than you." He watched her to see if his words had pleased her. He pretended to take her into his confidence.

"I am greatly troubled by General Washington's demands," he continued. "He wants to exchange his prisoner, General Cornwallis, for a Brigadier General, seven Colonels, two Lieutenant Colonels and, as an extra, the Tower prisoner, Henry Laurens of South Carolina. This is absurd. His lordship is certainly not important enough to offset that many men—at least, not to my mind. There was no need for Cornwallis to surrender at all."

Lady Anne smiled slyly. "You did not send him any help, did you?"

"Cornwallis is a coward! Damn him, why did he surrender his troops without consulting me? I am his superior officer."

"Surely you received my letters," Lady Anne said.

"I did not realize the significance of Lord Cornwallis' capture, or of the capture of the British army of Virginia. Charleston was still ours, and the army of the South."

"But I advised you to send aid to Cornwallis," Lady Anne said.

He ignored her remark. "I cannot move my troops effectively now," he said. "I am completely surrounded by General Washington's army. Surely you know that he has troops on Long Island, and is himself encamped at Newburgh on the Hudson, thus blocking any escape I might plan to the north."

Suddenly Lady Anne realized that here was a man in trouble, obviously coming to her for aid. She glimpsed, as it were, in the distance, the raft that might carry her to safety from what she feared was the shipwreck of her own fortunes. Here was a situation that required all her skill to manage successfully. At the moment she did not know what her strategy should be. To gain time she said, truthfully: "I am unfamiliar with the geography of this region, Sir Henry."

"You will learn in time," he said brusquely. Then, asking permission with his eyes and a nod of his head, he rose and walked to the drawing room door and closed it softly.

"Let me come to the point," he said as he returned to his chair by the fire. "I must know whether Lord North in England intends to send me more troops, or to abandon the war."

Lady Anne felt a glow of contentment flood through her. He knew that her family in England had great political power. She could forsee that this circumstance would make him think she could not only get him secret information, but that it might be of use to him if he should be recalled to England. She smiled to herself. What he obviously did not know was that her family had practically rejected her after the scandal of her divorce by the Duke of Northumberland.

"I have had no news from England for many months, Sir Henry," she said.

"I think you soon may have," he said pointedly. He waited for her to speak.

She looked at him levelly for a long moment. "I believe I understand you, Sir Henry," she said at length. "You remember, however, that my husband, the Baron, is very sympathetic to the American cause."

"I am well aware of it, madam," Sir Henry said. "For that reason I have this morning canceled his passport. He may no longer remain in New York." The trace of a smile appeared on his face. "I trust his absence will work no great hardship on your ladyship."

"My place is at my husband's side," she said. "If he goes, I must go with him."

Sir Henry Clinton laughed. "I should advise against it," he said. "You should have to travel through country held by the Americans. They are not, I am sure, unaware of your correspondence with me. I know for a fact that one of your letters to me was intercepted. The messenger bearing it was ignominiously hanged. Need I say more?"

Again Lady Anne stared at him. Finally she said in a toneless voice, "So you have trapped me here?"

Sir Henry Clinton laughed again. "But what a pleasant trap!" He waved his arm. "This lovely house? The companionship of your countrymen? Surely you should not object. I shall consider it a privilege to see to it personally that you will not want for company."

"Or for protection?" she asked.

"Of course."

She considered the situation as carefully as she could, sipping at her tea, not taking her eyes from the decorations that sparkled on the scarlet tunic that encased the General's deep chest. It was hard for her to stomach being his pawn, his virtual prisoner. Or, for that matter, anyone's. On the other hand, if, as she was now sure he did, the Baron knew of her affair with his man of business, there was no telling what he would do to her. And, of course, with him away—he would doubtless leave Sayre to look after his interests—there would be interesting times in the future. But to be a prisoner . . .

Eventually she understood that she had, for the present, no alternative. Later, in that future . . .

Rising, she made a slight curtsy to Sir Henry Clinton. "I am at your service, sir."

He bowed and raised her hand to his lips. "At your country's service, dear lady."

Bowing again, he left the room.

Lady Anne sat before the fire, watching the logs crumble into coals. So deep was her reverie that, though she heard a person come into the room, she vaguely assumed it was a footman to remove the tea things. Only when she was aware that the person was close to her did she look up to find the Baron standing by her chair

She gave a little jump. "Bruno, you startled me."

"I am sorry," he said. "Were you drowsing?"

"I must have been. I am tired from last night's reception."

He gestured toward the tea table. "I see that, as usual, you have not been alone."

"I feel very alone, Bruno."

He gave her a long look that seemed to say what she knew all too well, that she had brought her aloneness upon herself, but he spoke no word of that. Instead, he said:

"I have little time, I must be brief. Tomorrow I leave for North Carolina again. I wish to be with my sons for Christmas, and I must tend to a matter concerning my new lands there that Sayre seems to have handled badly."

"Oh?" she said innocently. "I shall miss you, Bruno. I had planned a Christmas Ball here at Minto."

"I rather doubt that you will miss me," he said.

"That is unkind, Bruno."

"Kindness is a quality of which you are not capable to judge," the Baron said.

Lady Anne rose slowly to her feet. She looked at him icily. "I do not care for your remarks," she said.

He stepped before her.

"You are in my way, Bruno. I wish to go to my room."

The Baron did not move. "You would be well advised to attend to what I am about to say," he said.

He looked at her so steadfastly and so coldly that, in spite of herself, she found herself sinking into a chair. She could not endure his gaze. She lowered her eyes.

"I have spent the day with my attorneys. I have informed them that I shall not return. They will make you

an allowance for the remainder of your natural life on
the condition that you make no attempt whatever to join
me or to importune me in any way. This house will be
offered for sale, and the first reasonable bid made for it
will be accepted. If you do not know the reason for my
action, I am sure you can guess at it. Whatever else you
may be, you are not unimaginative."

He started toward the door. He had almost reached
it before Lady Anne could find her voice. "Bruno!" she
cried.

He turned back to her.

"You have made your intentions very clear," she
said, her voice, to her embarrassment, trembling a little,
"with one exception. Do you plan to divorce me?"

"I do not," he said: "There is a limit to my gener-
osity." He took a few steps toward the door. then turned
again. "I forgot to say that I have dismissed Stephen
Sayre from my employ. Since I have been in New York I
have learned several things about him that have caused
me to distrust him. It may interest you to know that he
is married and has a son. His wife is a tavern wench in
Princeton."

With an ironic nod of his head, the Baron left the
room.

XVII

Good Fortune to Pembroke

The Edenton Company assembled at the waterside of the Court House Green—a group of almost a hundred, bound for the south to join the army around Charleston. They were young men from the county of Chowan, from the farms and plantations. They had had no military experience, but every one of them knew the art of shooting a rifle or a pistol, and they were hardened to outdoor living. They were to sail south to a point above Charleston on one of the Chapman ships bound for the Indies.

Captain Bembury was in charge of the company. He had been trained at the Institute in Virginia and he needed only a little time to whip them into shape.

The whole of Edenton was down to see them off. The fife and drum corps of the Home Guard marched ahead of the company down Broad Street, over to the Green. Flags were flying from the houses. It was a gala day for the village.

Since Yorktown the people had grown used to the idea that the war was not over with one great battle and had settled down to the idea that Charleston in the South and New York in the North had to surrender before the war was completely won.

By the time the company had been escorted to the dock, and drummed aboard Chapman's ship, the *Saucy Susan*, the sun was low in the western sky. The crowd was silent as the last of the young soldiers went up the ramp onto the ship. Tears were in the eyes of mothers and sisters and lovers, but they made a brave show of flags and kerchiefs as the Captain ordered the lines cast off. The ship moved out of the bay to catch the westerly wind that would drive it down Albemarle Sound to the open sea.

Raoul de Polignac stood beside the cannon. Penny Cabarrus was beside him, wiping her eyes with a tiny lace handkerchief.

"You weep to see them go away, perhaps—some of them—not to return," Raoul said. "Yet they are not your countrymen."

"Ah, but they are," Penny said. "I am truly an American now."

Taking her chin in his hand, he turned her face up to his. With his finger he flicked away the last of her tears. "Did you weep when I went away?"

Penny nodded. She dropped her head. "And when at last you came back to us after Yorktown. But that was for joy, Raoul, that you were safe."

Raoul reached for her hand. "I am very touched," was all he said.

He sighed. She had made it clear that she cared for him. He knew he cared for her. It troubled him deeply that she might still be too young to feel for him more than what she felt for any one of the young men who had just sailed away. Her emotions might easily be those of any patriotic young girl, in love with the idea of boys going off to fight for their country, not with any individual himself. Besides he knew that her aunt wished an American husband for her, and that at any time now he might be summoned back to France by his father, never to return to North Carolina.

He sighed again. "Come, my dear," he said, "it is late and we must return to Pembroke."

When they arrived, the afterglow of the sunset was intensely red.

"The whole world is afire," Penny said, watching a flight of birds show black against the flaming sky.

"It is like Vesuvius in eruption," Raoul said. "I remember as a child, the family went to Italy when the volcano was in action. I was frightened. I began to cry and hid my face in my mother's skirts. 'The world is ending! The world is ending!' Everybody laughed but mother. She said, 'You are quite right, son, that is the way it looks—like the end of the world. But I don't believe it will end tonight.' She was quite right. In the morning there was no blaze, just smoke. Before night we were on our way to Venice. I never knew whether it blazed again or not."

Penny laughed. "You must have been an imaginative little boy, Raoul."

"That's what the family said. I was always making up little tales about the cats and the dogs. I was sure that they could talk and that they had a life of their own when human beings were not around."

Stephen came in from the plantation and sat down with them on the gallery. Marianne joined them also. Stephen began to talk about the crops. It looked like a good year for the planters. That made him happy.

"I am growing to be a very industrious planter," he told them. "I go to bed very early; I am always up before the sun; I exercise nearly all day; avoid reading and thinking as much as possible and hope soon to arrive at that degree of stupidity and insensibility which I begin to think can only make people happy. I have observed that the greatest fools have not only the most pleasure in life but are generally the most respected—they have a greater share in good fortune than men of the best understanding."

Raoul beat on the gallery railing. "Hear! Hear" he said loudly.

Marianne said, "Are you rehearsing a speech for the legislature, my love?"

Stephen joined the laughter. "How wise you have become, my dear! I always say that women are our betters. They think faster and see farther. You are right, I have to make an opening speech at the next meeting of the legislature. I am trying it out on you."

The dressing bell cut in on their conversation. They all rose to go to their rooms.

At the table, Stephen had just finished saying grace when Penny glanced up and saw Adam Rutledge standing in the doorway. She clapped hands with delight. "Oh Mr. Rutledge, how nice that you are in time for dinner."

Stephen got up from the table to greet his friend. Adam bent over Marianne's hand, and gave Penny a quick kiss on her cheek.

The butler laid a place, and Adam sat down. The ham and sweet-potato pudding were passed and the Madeira poured before Adam told his news. He and Mary Warden would be married in three weeks. "As soon as Parson Earle says the banns."

"Oh Adam, how wonderful!" Marianne said. "It is what we all have been hoping for. I can't imagine any two people who are better suited than you and Mary."

"Will I be invited?" Penny cried. "Where will it be? Are you going to have bridesmaids?"

Adam laughed. "Question number one, yes, you are invited. Number two, it will be at St. Paul's. Number three, no, we will not have any bridesmaids or groomsmen. We will just get married in the simplest way possible."

Raoul, who had been silent, said, "I wish you would tell me how you find out if a girl likes you well enough to marry you."

"In spite of custom," Marianne laughed, "it's not the man who does the proposing. I believe the girl has a lot to do with it. It is the girl who leads the man gently down the garden path."

"Did you lead Uncle Stephen?" Penny said.

"That I did. I really believe that if I had waited for him to propose, we would not be married yet!"

Stephen's eyes twinkled. "Don't listen to her, Penny. The first time I saw her I made up my mind that she was the girl I was going to marry. It was a garden party at my uncle's. She had on a pale pink dress with lots of ruffles."

Adam leaned forward. "I confess I was worried,

Raoul. I wasn't sure that Mary would have me. She is a very independent woman, and a successful one. She has managed a big plantation as well as any man in the Albemarle. You know that Queen's Gift is famous in both the Carolinas. Since the Loyalists burned the main house at Rutledge Riding, I've been living in one of the tenant houses. I couldn't ask her to live there—and I did not want to invite myself to live at Queen's Gift."

"Where will you live?" Penny asked.

"At Queen's Gift. Mary invited me to live there after she told me that she would never leave the Plantation. It has been in her family for three generations."

Marianne had been thoughtful. Finally she spoke. "Adam, you have much to make up to Mary Warden. It must have been a difficult time for a proud woman like Mary to have her husband hanged as a traitor to his country."

Adam's face was grave. "It will take the years of my life's devotion to make up to her for what she has suffered. Pray God that I can do it!" He got up from the table. "I must be going on into Edenton. I want to see if there is any news from New Bern."

"Do you hear anything of the war, sir?" Raoul said. "I understand that most of the French officers have returned to France. I am afraid my father will be wanting me to come home. I've been away almost three years now."

Marianne looked at him a moment. "I suspect he will, Raoul. I don't doubt that he will have a bride picked out for you before long."

Penny looked stricken. She dropped her napkin on the floor to hide her face.

Raoul laughed. "I have different ideas. I like the American way of marrying for love, not having your bride chosen for you because her father's land adjoins yours or some such silly reason."

After Adam Rutledge left, Penny walked out on the gallery. She watched the ducks on the creek, a long line sailing serenely along, their bodies reflected in the black water. She was thinking of what her aunt had said.

Raoul's father would be selecting a bride for him. He would go back to France. Tears came to her eyes. She could not bear to think of him sailing off to France, or of a girl waiting there for him.

She heard the laughter of the Negroes and the children in the quarter line. She wished that she could be as happy and free as they. Oh Raoul, Raoul, she cried in her heart, why can't you love me as I love you?

She got up and went to her room. She threw herself on the bed and began to weep. She could not help wondering whether Raoul had really forgotten about Lady Anne or was still grieving for her. How could she say anything? In spite of Marianne's talk about leading a man on to proposing, she did not know just how it was done.

The next afternoon Raoul asked her to go out on the creek with him. She consented gladly, and ran to her room for something warm. When she came down to the landing she was wearing a crimson coat and a hood, tied under her small pointed chin with crimson ribbons. She still looks like a little girl, Raoul thought, too young, much too young to think of marriage.

Raoul laughed. "I have different ideas. I like the stream that led to the hidden lake. It had been a long time since they had been in that secret spot.

Penny's heart was beating swiftly. Why had Raoul brought her here? Why? Suddenly she knew what to say. "Raoul, I think this is the loveliest place I ever saw. I wonder why? Is it because I was so happy when we came here, you and I together?" For a moment he did not answer. He helped her out of the skiff and led her toward the mossy bank under the tall cypress trees. The cypress had shed its leaves, but the Spanish moss was hanging from the bare limbs.

He turned to her, pushing back her little crimson hood until her hair shone in the sunlight that slanted through the trees. He stood tall above her, looking down into her eyes. "Were you happy here, Penelope? Tell me, did you find happiness here with me?"

Her red lips trembled. "Happier than I have ever

been in my life, Raoul." Her voice was low. "Oh Raoul, so happy, so happy!"

He put his arms about her and drew her close to him. "My dear one, you are the world to me." He touched her lips gently, then with mounting passion. They stood close without speaking. Then he said, "I have been filled with fears since I have come back that you might no longer love me."

Tears stood in her eyes. "Oh Raoul, I've loved you so long, so very long, never anyone but you."

For a moment he did not speak but held her close, kissing her. "My dear, you are so sweet, so young— your lips are so sweet. I could kiss you forever and never tire."

He drew her over to the mossy bank. "As soon as we return to Pembroke, I will talk to your uncle and ask his permission to marry you, Penny. If he consents, we will go to France for a visit, so that my family may meet my wife. Then we will come back here to live. I have an inheritance from my grandmother and I can buy land, a plantation. I want to live in America."

"So do I, Raoul," Penny said. "I am glad you want to live here."

He kissed her again. "I have been planning this for a long time, ever since I came back from Yorktown, but I was afraid . . ."

Penny smiled. "Oh, Raoul, it has been you for a long time. I was terrified that Lady Anne . . ."

He put his hand over her lips. "Don't talk of her. I was a young fool. Shall we forget it?"

Penny nodded. "Nothing will make me happier than to forget the whole thing."

The light of the setting sun fell upon the creek, turning the water to gold. The white herons waded out knee-deep in the water. Raoul rose to his feet and held out his hands. "Come, Penny. Let us go home so we may tell your people that we love each other and want to marry."

When they returned to Pembroke, they found

Adam Rutledge and Mary sitting by the fire in the library. Raoul could not wait to ask Stephen to come with him to his room. "I must ask him at once," he whispered to Penny. "I want to have his permission so that I may tell our friends the good news."

Penny smiled at his eagerness. "I'll tell Aunt Marianne," she said. "I'll signal her to come out."

Penny did not have to tell her. Her own glowing face, her bright eyes were enough. Marianne opened her arms.

Penny clung to her. "Oh, Aunt Marianne, it is I he loves. I'm very happy."

When Raoul and Stephen came down the stairs, Raoul went to Marianne and put his arms about the two women. "Stephen has said yes," he said. "Come, Penelope—come let us share our joy with our friends."

It was a gay dinner that night. Many toasts were drunk. Stephen sent bottles of ale to the quarters for the slaves to drink to the health of the young folk.

"A marriage and Christmas at the same time—" old Dulcey told Penny—"that will be good fortune to all of us at Pembroke."

The days went by swiftly as the plantation prepared for the holidays. The smell of spices was in the air; Dulcey was making small ginger Christmas cakes and Christmas pies by the hundreds. Marianne herself mixed the Christmas punch, and put it away in the cellar in stone jars to ripen. Plum puddings were made and set away, and cakes for the children of the slaves, cut in shapes of animals and people. The field hands went hunting in the forest, and came home with bags of rabbits and squirrels for Brunswick stew, which the slaves always cooked for Christmas dinner, together with the wild turkey they shot in the woods close to the pocosin.

One of the really great events that came in December was hog-killing time, when the slaves were up before dawn to set up the racks, make the fires and get the water boiling in the great iron kettles that swung from tripods.

Stephen Cabarrus always supervised the killings himself. His overlooker, Tubbs, attended to the actual killing, driving the grunting pigs from the pens to the barnyard, where the killing took place. Instead of the old method of hitting the hogs over the head with a sledge-hammer, Tubbs slashed each animal's throat with a sharp corn knife, a quicker and more merciful death.

This was a great event for the slaves. Everyone from the quarters was in the barnyard, from the smallest child in arms to the grownups. Besides the excitement of preparing the swine, certain parts of the animal belonged by custom to the slaves: the head, the feet and the internal sections—with the exception of the intestines, which were cleaned and used to stuff sausage.

The morning was clear and cold. The slaves looked like scarecrows from the cornfields, their legs and feet bound with straw wound round with tow sacks, scarves tied over their heads to protect their ears and faces. All, excepting the men who were cutting the meat, wore woolen mittens.

The fires were blazing; the water in the great iron kettles was boiling, giving off steam. Since it was early in the morning, the frost of the night still hung thickly on trees and bushes and turned the ground almost as white as snow.

All twenty swine were killed, skinned and hanging on the racks before Marianne and Penny came out of the plantation house. Marianne watched the grinding. Seasoning the sausage she did herself, as no one else knew the amounts but she. Penny helped her. In another year she would learn the well-guarded recipe.

She went to the door of the carriage house where the sausage was being made to watch the children playing and singing a song brought from Africa by their elders.

"The crane flies with long legs dangling.
The antelope jumps high over the hill.
The alligator bites off a woman's arm

and swallows her copper bracelets.
I hope the bracelet bewitches the alligator."

To accompany the song one of the small boys beat a little drum that swung with a cord about his neck. The children began to dance to the steady rhythm of the drum, circling around the racks as they chanted: "Aye, aye, ayee-ee, ayee-ee—"

Christmas celebration began at daybreak. At every plantation along Albemarle Sound and up all the rivers and creeks the slaves, some lately come from Africa, were at the great houses to celebrate John Canoe. No one knew how the custom started, but thought its beginning must have come from Africa like the songs they sang. The sun was just rising in the east when the sound of drums and pipes and trumpets came from the quarters line.

Marianne wakened everyone with the dinner gong. "It's Johnny Canoe! Rise to welcome John Canoe!" By the time the procession arrived at the great house from the quarters line, everyone was out in the gallery waiting. Marianne and Penny, wrapped in heavy capes, had boxes of gaily wrapped gifts. Stephen, with Raoul beside him, had a keg of rum open, ready to ladle it out in little cups.

The procession had formed below the stables near the quarters line. Horses decked with wreaths of holly and mistletoe and with colored streamers flying from their bridles, carried the older slaves. Next came the plantation mules; they too had wreaths of pine and holly, and streamers of colored calico dangled from their bridles.

Behind the riders trooped women and men and children, wearing clothes of bright calico and streamers of varicolored cloth, their faces covered with tight-fitting grotesque masks made of goatskin stripped thin and painted to resemble animals. The small boys had shrill whistles and cow bells which they sounded as they marched. Everyone else was singing an old African song:

"Hah, low, here we go!
Hah, low, here we go!
John Canoe comes from Dohema,
He came from Mombera—
He return to Dohema."

The women and girls clapped their hands or beat on squares of wood. Two men had little gamba boxes, wooden frames covered with stretched sheepskin, which they shook violently or scraped with little sticks.

Two slaves not in costume came to where Stephen and the two guests were standing by the rum keg. They sang a little song to the rhythmic clapping.

"My massa am a white man—juba.
My missus am a white lady—juba.
De children am de honey pods—juba.
Chris'mus come but once a year—juba.
Pat juba all ye chillen, pat juba, heigh ho!"

The patting continued until every one had his presents from Marianne, and a coin from Stephen and a cup of rum. Then the slaves formed two long lines and began an intricate dance to the rhythm of the drums. Children patted juba and shouted at the top of their small voices. Dogs barked and the donkeys brayed until the noise was like bedlam.

Suddenly, all the noise stopped at once. The slaves moved silently away until they reached the quarter line. Then the noise broke out again. All day it went on: shouts and screams and drum rhythm. All day and into the night the dancing went on until the men fell down with weariness. Then the masks were wrapped up and put away in the barn loft until another Christmas day.

Raoul and Penny stood arm in arm on the gallery watching the dancing down on the quarter line. "I never say anything so pagan before," Raoul said. "Do the slaves do this on all the plantations?

"All along the Albemarle at least. I think it is ex-

citing even if it is pagan. Maybe we are a bit pagan ourselves, here in this new world. Pagan, but free."

That's the most important thing of all," Raoul said,
as they walked into the house together. "And in love!"

XVIII

The "Natural Charms"

The exit of the von Poellnitzes had left a vacuum in Edenton life. There was no longer any scandal to relate at morning teas, nor was there any speculation as to which man would be the next to fall under the spell of Lady Anne. The departure from Edenton of the Frenchmen to join the army as well as the young men of the Battery left a wide gap in the social life. The village settled down to its usual small talk and the sparse reports that drifted in from Williamsburg.

The population of Edenton—for the most part, women and children—who had fled to Windsor at the beginning of the war, began to return home. The usual family life of the village fell into its old pattern. The only person to regret the return of the women was the tavernkeeper, Horniblow, for the men who had come so regularly to his common room for a mug of ale and supper now took up family life again. They continued to gather, however, in the late mornings for their customary discussions of politics and finance.

The women and girls paid little heed to affairs at Philadelphia, but whenever a group of them gathered they were bound to get on the topic of Lady Anne. No news had come from her since Philadelphia, where some of the Edenton men had seen them, and had spoken of her gaiety and beauty at the Victory Ball. They wondered why she had made up her mind to leave Philadelphia for New York in such haste.

"Of course she wanted to leave," Marianne Cabarrus said. "She is English, for all the Baron has to say about a wife taking on the nation of her husband. He himself is only a very new American. He does not understand that she is cut to the quick by our triumph in Virginia. I suppose it doesn't occur to her that the British might be defeated in the rest of the country. She wants to get to New York, where the British army is still supreme. She would have high prestige with General Sir Henry Clinton, being Lord Bute's daughter."

"I wouldn't have thought of that," Hannah said. "Of course you are right. I'm sure the men didn't think of it either, they were too busy admiring her. That woman can bedazzle without half trying. My Jemmy tries to tell me he believes me when I say she is evil, but in his heart he still admires her."

Marianne shrugged her shoulders. "Don't you know that men never find out anything about women so long as they are beautiful and fascinating!"

There was no excitement in the village. After the defeat of Cornwallis, Edenton was almost barren of war news. The planters, now that winter was on its way, had no field work, save to prepare the ground for spring crops. Most of their field hands had been sent into the turpentine woods to work, while they themselves gave their attention to hunting. Every day the baying of hounds in the chase could be heard in the village. Business improved, as the blockade the British were keeping off Cape Fear grew looser, and naval stores could be shipped out on Dutch ships for sale in Europe.

Then there came a flurry of excitement when Hannah Iredell received a letter from her husband, who was holding court in Windsor, telling of Governor Burke's escape from the English:

The Governor, [he wrote], was guarded with vigor in the midst of a great number of refugee forces who had begun to massacre some of the prisoners and had fired on the house where the Governor was held. He made his escape by boat—and passed some sentries—which induces a suspicion that it was contrived.

Hannah at once sent the note to the tavern, where Horniblow read it to the men of Edenton. Their huzzahs and shouts of delight brought in half the town to hear the good news. People began to speculate that the British General Leslie, who still held Charleston, was afraid to keep the Governor any longer lest plans for his rescue cause trouble in uneasy Charleston, already on the verge of revolt since Cornwallis' surrender.

Hannah Iredell's sending the news of Governor Burke's escape gave Nancy Horniblow the idea that the ladies might be as interested in the war news as the men. She sent out invitations to tea in the Ladies' Parlor. She went even further than Horniblow. She had a blackboard installed, on which she wrote the news of the war from the southern, the northern and the western parts of the state.

The blackboard item about the Governor aroused considerable interest among the Edenton women who came to drink tea, but another report which Nancy Horniblow wrote out while the ladies were finishing their yaupon was even more exciting:

News comes from New York that Sir Henry Clinton still occupies the city and the surrounding country. The city is gay with entertainment. Plays are enacted in the theatre. Cricket is played by soldier teams. Bets are made on horse racing. The social life is excitingly gay. Some of the most splendid entertainment, teas and balls are given by the Baroness von Poellnitz at her beautiful country home Minto. The Baroness is the acknowledged beauty of New York society. When she rides out in her handsome coach she is always

accompanied by a British officer on horseback.

This item created so much chatter in the Ladies'
Parlor that it brought the men out of the common room
to find out what was happening. They, too, read the bul-
letin with interest.

Marianne Cabarrus and Hannah Iredell walked to
the Hewes and Smith corner together. "Well, she has the
whole British army to draw from now," Marianne said,
"but she will never bewitch Raoul again."

Hannah nodded. "We have seen the wicked and
have learned she is spreading like a green bay tree. Let
the English be infected with her. She was a poisoning
Tory. Thank heaven we were delivered from her."

At her beautiful country home, Minto, the Baroness von Poellnitz had been offering less and less splendid entertainment as the winter of 1782 wore on. The
furniture and draperies she had planned for the house
remained at the shops. She cut down the number of
servants to the fewest possible, and closed off many
rooms. The allowance the Baron had arranged for her
proved adequate for barely more than her necessities,
and she had no other income.

The Baron's attorneys had brought several different parties to inspect the property, and she lived in con-
stant terror that it would be sold. She tried not to think
of what would become of her when it was.

At first she had thought the surrender of Cornwallis an isolated event that could hardly affect the total
position of England in America. It had seemed impossible to her that the rebels might win, for she had no real
understanding of their concept of liberty, which was the
heart and soul of their cause. Now, even in Loyalist
New York, where the only persons she saw were the
military and other Tories like herself, there were rumors
of a peace treaty. If these should prove true, and the
British evacuated the city, she would be distinctly un-

welcome there and, for that matter, anywhere else in America.

To disguise her plight, and her poverty, she let it be known through Sir Henry Clinton that she was in poor health. She seldom went out, and then only in a closed carriage she hired, for she had had to dispense with the coach in which she had dazzled the town. She could not bear the thought of being seen in a less splendid equipage.

"It is royalty," a man had shouted when he saw the Von Poellnitz arms emblazoned on the door of the coach, and the coachman and the footman, and the pair of prancing bays, "foreign royalty!"

"To hell with them!" another man had answered him. "We want no royalty here. We are plain people, and we want only plain people in America."

The memory of the incident caused her a twinge. She had never been, and could never be "plain people." Yet that was what fate was forcing her to become. How she hated "plain people!" Was the whole world to be made up of them now? If so, she did not care to remain in it.

Sometimes she wondered whether she cared to remain in it at all. Death, which throughout her previous life, had had no significance whatever to her, now occupied her lonely thoughts to a degree that terrified her. She began reading essays and poems and plays on the subject. Addison's *Cato* deeply impressed her. It was, she concluded, nobler to die than to suffer ignominy. Had she been Lord Cornwallis, she knew she would have fallen on her sword rather than hand it to a victorious enemy.

As spring came on, she took to walking alone, plainly dressed and heavily veiled to escape recognition, along the lanes of the Bowery. On one of these strolls she found the harsh sunlight to have a touch of warmth in it at last. She sat on a milestone to enjoy it. But almost at once a chill and wind swept up from the river, and a cloud passed across the sun.

How tired she was of her existence, she thought, how hopeless it seemed! She shivered. Without looking to right or left she stepped into the lane and directly into the path of a horse that came galloping around a curve. The horse shied, almost throwing its rider, who yelled an obscenity at her as he tried to bring his mount under control and went curveting on down the lane.

Ah, she thought, finding herself not much shaken by the near fatal occurrence, it could have been so easy! Immediately she rallied her courage. Such foolish notions she would put aside at once. When she returned to Minto, she threw her melancholy reading matter into the fire.

She had had no word, no visit from Stephen Sayre. It did not surprise her. Sayre might have indeed been interested in her, even loved her in his own opportunistic way, but only when she was rich. He would not even think of her now that she was not. Her only visitor was Sir Henry Clinton, and he was poor company, depressed as he was with the outcome of the war and the insecurity of his position. He had nothing to do but sit out the winter, in a way as trapped as she was, waiting for a change in the weather and a possible spring campaign.

In addition to being poor company, Sir Henry was beginning to ask embarrassing questions about the news, or, rather, the lack of news, she was supposedly getting for him from England. She neither had any nor the means for getting any. If he were to discover this truth, he would withdraw his protection and, doubtless, cease his visits. After all, he was a man and his society was better than none, especially when he brought one or more of his officers to tea.

At first she had found him singularly unimpressed by her charms. Yet was it that, or was he too cautious or too preoccupied to succumb? At any rate, she had not been able to detect, as out of long experience with other men she had learned to do, the moment when his thoughts would be turning to her in passion. When Sir Henry came alone, they often ran out of conversation before he left.

On one such occasion, however, he did have something new to offer.

"By the way," he said, "we have an interesting prisoner that my officers took in New Jersey. He is an Italian, one of the de' Medici family. I am trying to find out just why he is here."

Lady Anne felt her heart skip a beat. She waited a moment before saying anything in order to appear calm.

"De' Medici? What would a de' Medici be doing here?" she asked.

"I don't know. If I send him here, will you try to find out? You are a clever woman."

Lady Anne smiled. "Send him here by all means." She settled back in her chair and began to talk of something else.

After Sir Henry left, she felt more lighthearted than she had for many weeks. There seemed to be a ray of hope for her in the pale twilight. If the British had to move out, as they might at any moment, Cosmo de' Medici could be a means of her getting to General Washington. At any rate, no matter what happened, she would be in a stronger position, whoever occupied New York. She even hummed a little tune to herself as she gathered up the tea things.

It was a week before Major Douglass, Sir Henry Clinton's aide, brought Cosmo de' Medici to Minto for tea, and introduced him to Lady Anne as if he were a stranger. Lady Anne welcomed him as if he were.

If Cosmo de' Medici felt any surprise, he did not show it. It was only after Major Douglass muttered an excuse that he had to leave, but would return, that Lady Anne crosssed the room and sat down at his side.

"Tell me what is happening? Why are you here? I thought you were with General Washington's army."

"So I was, but I have left the service. I am trying to get back to Italy. I thought it would be easier to leave on a British ship if I could get a passage."

He spoke so frankly that Lady Anne was taken in. What he did not say was that he was still in the American army and that he was here in New York to gather information about the number of troops and their condition. Cosmo volunteered for the task since he had a legitimate reason for being in New York. He well knew that there would be no ships sailing at that time. A couple of weeks, even less, in New York would give him the time he needed.

How handsome he was! she thought. His tall, robust figure, his long straight limbs, his classic features and dark Italian eyes—what a lover he would make! It might be a rich experience. Still something held her back, some little forgotten thing.

She questioned him. "Why was it that you never called on us in Edenton? Were you not there while we were living at Horniblow's?"

"Unfortunately, very little of the time, your ladyship. I was away with my troop."

"I am sure that I would have taken note of you. I have always been interested in Italy and Italians." She smiled at him. "Certainly one knows of your family in Florence. How do you come to be in America?"

"It is a long story, Lady Anne. I am afraid I do not have time to tell it now. I am on parole, you know." He smiled at her. "A very loose parole, to be sure, but still under observation."

Lady Anne laid her hand on his arm. "I must talk to Sir Henry. He is a dear friend of mine. Perhaps he will allow you to spend a few days at Minto. I should be happy to have you here."

Cosmo watched the change of expression in her face. "I can imagine nothing more dangerous," he said. "Let us not meet again."

Fortunately, Major Douglass returned for his prisoner, then, and they left shortly afterward.

When they were gone, she thought deeply about the two men—Sir Henry, cold, calculating, somewhat harsh; and Cosmo de' Medici, warm and pleasant and treacherous. She wondered. Sometimes harsh men were heavy with desire and gave great pleasure. If she could bring Sir Henry under her spell, she would be doubly—nay, triply—safe. Now his thoughts were on what he might get from her through her family. If she tried, might she not change those thoughts?

It was almost a week later when Lady Anne's servant reached Cosmo de' Medici to invite him to supper at *Minto*. He arrived at seven o'clock one rainy evening. He wore a long cape over his clothes to protect him from the rain. It gave him a dashing look of a buccaneer.

The butler removed the rain-splashed cape in the hall. Lady Anne all but gasped when she saw him, so elegant were his civilian clothes. She had seen him only in his rather faded dragoon's uniform and high dragoon boots.

Tonight he was a Florentine gentleman in a brocaded satin coat of rich wine color with an ivory waistcoat and satin small clothes. His long stockings were silk and he wore large paste buckles on his shoes. His dark hair was cued and puffed over the ears and tied with a black riband. He wore a small sword and a rich metaled sword belt. The lace at his neck and wrists was of the finest.

He bowed over her hand with easy grace. His dark eyes laughed at her as he smiled in a happy good humor. He said, "This is an occasion, madame. I hope I am worthy. I have been told that I am no longer on parole and the freedom of the city of New York is mine."

Lady Anne bowed mockingly. "Welcome, Citizen of New York. I hope that I can offer a welcome worthy of such an occasion. I am sure my cook has something to please your fancy."

Cosmo kissed her hand again. "Just the privilege of looking at a beautiful woman is reward enough for me."

Supper was announced. Cosmo offered Lady Anne his arm and they walked out to the small dining room where the table was laid for two. She had ordered an Italian dinner for them. Antipasto, fish, a fine sea trout, ravioli, a broiled pheasant, Chianti with the dinner, Lacrima Christi with the meat.

Cosmo was gay and the talk was delightful. It touched on London, Paris, and Rome, then went to

Florence and Venice. People and events, the opera and the sea resorts across the bay up to the seacoast of Trieste. Lady Anne was delighted with her guest. "Why *was* it that I didn't see more of you in Edenton?" she inquired when they were drinking their coffee and brandy in the little French drawing room.

Cosmo smiled. "There was a war, remember, and part of the time I spent as a prisoner of the British at Haddrell's Point opposite from Charleston."

"I remember. A foolish ill-advised war which will soon be over, I hope."

A sudden dark look swept over Cosmo's mobile face, gone in an instant. "Come, this evening is too vital to us both to think of war. Wouldn't it be more agreeable to you to talk of love instead?"

Lady Anne studied her guest. The thought that he might be making sport of her crossed her mind. Only for an instant. "Why not?" she answered. "What could be more pleasurable than to speak to an Italian of a subject always close to his heart?"

He crossed the room and sat beside her on the couch. "We Italians do have that reputation, don't we? But is that too bad? To play the game of love while we are young and gay? Surely you would not have us serious like Englishmen?"

"No, no. I like you exactly as you are. All I regret is that we wasted time when we might have been playing your game of love, as you say."

He lifted her hand to his lips, kissing her wrist, her fingers. "You are a divinely beautiful woman and you have all the power that beauty gives."

Lady Anne sank back against the pillows. "I have dreamed of a Latin lover but I have never had one."

"You have one now, my dear—." He leaned over and kissed her red mouth lightly. "What will you have of him?"

Lady Anne put her arms about his neck drawing him down against her. "Everything, Cosmo. Everything."

He laughed. "Not this way, my dear. Not this way.

I would never take love under the hedgerow or the haystack as a peasant does. No, love is for the chamber amid beautiful surroundings. An Italian lover would have his lady disrobe before him, garment by garment, so that he can savor her natural beauty." He got to his feet. "Come, surely there is a more suitable spot for lovemaking then this room, where at any moment a servant might interrupt."

Lady Anne looked at him, her eyes glistening. "Come with me," she said. She held out her hand. "Come."

It was almost dawn when Cosmo rose from Lady Anne's couch. "It is time for me to leave you, my dear. With regret, I assure you."

She lay quietly and watched him put on his clothes. "Don't go, Cosmo." She held out her arms, the lace of her robe fell from her lovely arms. "You make me so happy—don't go."

He smiled at her as he buckled on his sword belt. "But I must. It will soon be daybreak." He stood for a moment looking down at her, all the gaiety gone from his face. He drew a purse from the pocket of his coat and held it over her as she lay on the pillows. The gold pieces clinked in his hand.

"If you should think the payment excessive, my lady, there is something here also from my dear friend Raoul—payment for a fancy lady."

He dropped the purse on the bed. Some of the gold pieces fell out on the counterpane and rolled to the floor. He left the room, and closing the door, ran lightly down the stairs.

For a moment Lady Anne was motionless, stunned by his words. Then she leaped from the bed and ran into the hall. Cosmo was at the foot of the stairs. He looked up and waved his hand as she flung the purse over the rail. As it hit the gold burst out over the floor.

"Damn you! Damn you! Damn you!" she shrieked.

But Cosmo had already closed the front door, his parting echoing in her ears, "Arrivederci."

Two hours later at sunrise Cosmo de' Medici, mounted on a fast trotting horse, gave the password to a sleepy sentry at the outskirts of New York and took the road to Newburgh. There he would report the condition of New York to the commander-in-chief. He felt good. The morning air felt soft against his face and the smell of spring was in the air. The sun on the Hudson sparkled on the water and gave off a myriad of tiny flashes. He laughed aloud. "An old debt, a long time being paid —but now the slate is clean."

Lady Anne was sure that General Sir Henry Clinton would come to tea the following day, to learn what she might have found out about Cosmo de' Medici. She had Dawkins bring out gown after gown before she made her choice. She had laid her plans as carefully as any victim might have thought out a military campaign. She would move cautiously, play him on a long line, bring him in carefully.

"I think the turquoise taffeta over the apricot petticoat is the one, your ladyship," Dawkins said. "I have sewed lace ruffles in the sleeves and across the bosom."

"Rip them off entirely," Lady Anne ordered. "I don't want any interference with my natural charms today."

Dawkins held up her hands in mock horror. "Fie, your ladyship. Consider the poor General who is coming to tea today."

"That's exactly what I am doing, Dawkins. Considering the General."

Dawkins laughed. "I feel for him, madam. I feel for him greatly." She set about lacing Lady Anne into her stays. She gave the strings purchase over the bedpost and pulled the garment tight. "There, you've no more than an eighteen-inch waist." She laughed slyly. "And your natural charms show above the low cut bodice."

"Good, you are an understanding woman, Dawkins."

"I've learned since I have been with your ladyship," she said.

Promptly at five, Sir Henry Clinton came swiftly across the drawing room and kissed Lady Anne's fingers.

"A beautiful woman in a beautiful gown in a beautiful room! What could be more inviting?" he said.

Lady Anne bowed. The warm pressure of her hand was meant to tell Sir Henry she was pleased by his words. "Come sit near me on the sofa," she said. "I have much to talk to you about. But first, let me ring for your tea."

"If you don't mind, I'd rather have rum. I've had a wearisome day. I can stand a drink or two to bolster my flagging spirits."

"You may have anything you want when you come to Minto, Sir Henry." She paused and smiled.

Sir Henry did not seem to catch the significance of her words. Instead he began to question her about Cosmo de' Medici. Had she found out anything about him? Was he in New York for any secret reason?

Lady Anne reported that she had not been able to ascertain anything of importance other than that he had been in Washington's army, having organized the Light Dragoons. He had been captured by Colonel Tarleton near Charleston and been imprisoned for a year. Now he wanted to go home. That was all.

Sir Henry nodded. "That is the report I already have. I had supposed it was correct; now you have confirmed it. But enough of the Florentine. Do you have any news from London—more particularly from Lord Bute, your father?"

Lady Anne glanced at him sharply. "Nothing. Nothing at all, Sir Henry. I fancy you have all the news there is—the Peace Treaty, perhaps."

He frowned.

She saw the situation going against her plan. She must bring him over to thinking about her. She leaned forward. Her white breasts were close to him. His eyes strayed and were held, but the expression on his rugged face did not change.

"You have told me nothing that I did not know,"

he said. "And nothing that I wish to know. Perhaps that will come in time. Now, what did you tell our Italian friend?"

"Why—why, I told him nothing, Sir Henry. What do you mean? I had nothing to tell him."

Seeing that he had emptied his glass, she rose and filled it again with rum. As she handed it back to him, she leaned close to him.

"You seem tired, Sir Henry. Why must we talk of military things when you are so harassed?" She sat close beside him.

He sipped at the rum without looking at her, but staring at the pattern of the Persian rug at his feet. The only sound in the room was the ticking of the clock on the mantelpiece. Finally he spoke in a dull tone.

"I have failed," he said, "because others have failed me. England cannot afford to continue this war. She is too occupied fighting for her survival against the powers in Europe to care what happens to a strip of wilderness along a coast three thousand miles away. The Americans have fought because this is the homeland they have wrested from the forests and the rocks and the mountains. And they have won. We have failed. We had to fail. You as well as I." He rose and, bowing, took her hand. "These thoughts are too gloomy for you, dear lady. I shall not bore you with them more."

Slowly Lady Anne rose too, and stood close before him. She put her hands on his arms.

"Sir Henry," she said, "you must not say such things. You have not failed. You cannot fail."

He looked deep into her eyes. She heard his breathing quicken. Suddenly he had clasped her to him. His mouth was greedily on hers.

At the same moment there was a sharp knock at the door of the room, and then another short one, and another, long.

At last Sir Henry let her go. "That is a signal," he exclaimed. He rushed to the door and flung it open. His aide, Major Douglass, stood just beyond it. He saluted his General.

"A ship from England has arrived, sir. It has anchored in the river. Your replacement, Sir Guy Charleton is aboard. He has sent a messenger to ask that you attend him at once."

Sir Henry Clinton did not even turn back to Lady Anne. Snatching up his tricorn, he rushed from the room.

Lady Anne, the following day, ordered her carriage to drive to the British headquarters on Wall Street. She was about to step into her coach when Stephen Sayre rode up. He dismounted quickly from his horse and threw the reins to a groom.

"I have a matter of importance to discuss with you, Lady Anne. Will you dismiss your carriage?"

Lady Anne hesitated but the look on Sayre's face and the urgency in his voice decided her. She turned to the coachman and dismissed him and followed Sayre into the house. "What has happened?" she said.

He helped her off with her wrap. She unpinned her gay little bonnet. "Come into the library," he said shortly.

"What is it, Stephen? Why are you so urgent?"

He brushed her uplifted face with his lips—a fleeting kiss. "How soon can you be packed?" he asked abruptly.

"In a few days, I suppose, if I rush."

He interrupted. "I can get passage on a ship sailing for France tomorrow. Can you be at the pier by eleven in the morning?"

She sat down on a nearby chair. "Oh, Stephen! Tomorrow! How can I be ready by tomorrow?"

"Anne, it is either tomorrow or not for months. News has come from Paris. The treaty has been signed."

"Is this the truth or is it more rumors?"

"It is the truth. Benjamin Franklin, Jay, and Adams for Amerca signed; Shelbourne for England. It was signed in Paris on the sixth of September. You know what that means. The British Army will be leaving New York and then comes the exchange of prisoners. There will be no room on ships for civilians. So get ready—

take what you absolutely need and leave the rest of your luggage to be sent later."

He gave her no time to object. "Go upstairs now and have your maid start packing."

Influenced by the urgency in Stephen's voice, Lady Anne started for the stairs. He said, "I'll arrange with Hamilton's office to close the house and get a caretaker."

Lady Anne stopped at the foot of the stairs. "Oh, Stephen, I forgot. I gave Dawkins the weekend off to go upstate. What will I do?"

"I'll have her taken care of. Get one of the maids to help you. Hurry, now. Be at pier three by ten in the morning."

Lady Anne turned back. "Ten in the morning! Why you know that I'm never up by ten!"

"You will be tomorrow, never fear!" He took up his hat.

"Where are you going?" she cried. "Aren't you going to stay with me and help me pack?"

"No, my dear, I'm not going to help you pack. I've work to do in Wall Street."

He was at the door, his hand on the knob when she remembered. "Oh, Stephen, wait! My money. You didn't bring me my money!"

He paused, the expression on his face changed. "Oh, the money! I'll bring it down to the ship in the morning."

She leaned over the banister, "Stephen, don't you forget this time. I will need that money. The Paris shops are very compelling."

"I won't forget," he said as he closed the door. "I won't forget."

Promptly at ten in the morning, Lady Anne was at the dock. The only ship in sight was a small disreputable looking pacquet. She sent her groom to the ticket office to make inquiries. He came back after a time accompanied by the ticket agent.

It was the right ship. Mr. Sayre had made the reservation. Her ladyship could go aboard at once. The porter would see that her luggage was sent aboard. He was sorry that the accommodations were inferior, but he assured her that she had the best cabin on the ship—a deck cabin, and he hoped that her ladyship would be comfortable.

All of this information was poured out like a stream of fast flowing water over a mill race. Lady Anne thanked him and asked about Sayre.

"Mr. Sayre will be here shortly. He left a package for your ladyship in the cabin. Quite safe, I assure your ladyship, the door is locked and the purser has the only key."

Lady Anne said, "Thank you so much. I would like to go aboard now if I may."

"Certainly, certainly." The agent signaled to a cabin boy. "Show the Baroness to her cabin, Simpson. Get the key from Mr. Olney."

Lady Anne followed the boy on board. They went up the companionway to the cabin deck. The purser stood at the door, key in hand. He bowed to Lady Anne and said, "Welcome aboard the *Dolphin*, your ladyship." He opened the door wide. "Please enter, your ladyship," he said.

Lady Anne looked about. The cabin was small but quite neat. It had a porthole that looked out on the water. Lady Anne gave the cabin boy a shilling and thanked the purser.

She noticed a sealed package on the bed addressed to her in Sayre's writing but she did not open it. Instead she removed her wraps and threw them on the bed. She wondered how she was going to travel on the long journey to France without a maid to dress her, but Stephen would assist her. She wondered why he hadn't come, but there was still almost an hour before the ship sailed.

A knock at the door. She thought Stephen had arrived at last. She called "Come in," but it was not Sayre; it was two cabin boys bringing in her boxes. "Put them in the corner," she said and reached for her purse.

Her luggage filled almost one side of the cabin. She

was beginning to be annoyed by the accommodations and by Sayre. Why hadn't he come? He had been so positive that she must be there an hour before the ship sailed. She took up a light scarf to throw over her shoulders. She would go on deck to watch for him. But before she could open the door, Sayre arrived.

She ran to him. "Oh, Stephen, I was so alarmed when you weren't waiting for me!"

He kissed her and patted her shoulder. "I was delayed. There is so much business to be done that I have been about crazy."

Lady Anne kissed his cheek. "I'm sorry you have had to work so hard to get us off, but now you are here. In half an hour we will be on our way to your beautiful Spain! I can hardly believe it is true. We've waited so long, so very long, Stephen!"

He loosened his arms from her waist. "Come, my dear, let us go on deck where there is more air."

They went on deck. There was all the confusion of a ship about to sail. A few late passengers were running down the dock; the cries and calls of the sailors loading the last cargo; the officers giving orders to make sail ready to go out on the tide.

Lady Anne and Sayre leaned against the rail. She noticed that he was unusually quiet but she did not question him about his mood. Instead she said, "Is your cabin next to mine, Stephen? I didn't notice whether there was a connecting door."

Sayre did not answer. He was looking at the cabin boy who was walking down the deck striking a gong, crying, "All ashore that's going ashore! All ashore that's going ashore!"

When he came opposite, Stephen suddenly turned to Lady Anne. He put his arms about her. "Anne, I am sorry but I am not sailing today. I will follow on the next pacquet and meet you in Paris." He kissed her hard.

Anne pulled away. "What are you saying, Stephen? Of course you are going."

"No, Anne. I tell you I can't go. Things of importance have come up. I can't possibly leave. Business."

Anne stamped her foot. "Then I won't go. Get my luggage. I won't go a step."

"Now, Anne, be sensible. It will only be a short time. You can occupy yourself in Paris. You know many people—."

"Damn you! Get my luggage off the ship," she said, her face white with anger. She started to run to her cabin but the call came again, loud and final. "Last call, all ashore that's going ashore!"

Stephen broke away from her and walked swiftly away. She saw him descending the gangplank. She called to him, "My money. Where is my money?"

His voice came across the widening stretch of water as the ship moved out into the stream. "In your cabin, Anne. Look in your cabin—" He stood looking at her. She thought there was a curious look on his face as he stood on the dock. A strange look, almost a look of triumph.

She went to her cabin. She snatched up the package from the berth and tore it open. She found a package of worthless paper—and a note in Sayre's vigorous handwriting, addressed to her.

It is all over between us, Anne. There will be no honeymoon in Spain. I have given all this careful thought for some time. I am sure I don't want a wife that I cannot trust to be true to me. You could not be true to any one man. I could never be sure if I left you for a night that you would not be in some other man's bed. That I would not tolerate.

As for the money from the sale of von Poellnitz's property, I have reached the conclusion that I am as much entitled to it as you. At least I won't squander it as you would. When you think this over you will know that I am right. Be thankful for the pleasant times we have had together.

Goodbye, Anne, and good fortune in your next adventure.

                                        Stephen

Lady Anne sat frozen, unable to move. She had given her love to a man who only wanted to deceive her for his own gain. She didn't know how long she sat in stunned silence before the full indignity of Sayre's action swept over her.

She tore his letter into small bits and scattered them over the cabin floor. She took the papers he had cut into the size of treasury notes and threw them out of the porthole into the water.

She strode up and down the narrow cabin with swift steps, a stream of curses falling from her lips. He had betrayed her—the only man she really loved. Betrayed her, and now in sanctimonious words, dared to tell her that the fault was hers. How long she paced the floor in anger, she did not know.

Finally exhausted, she threw herself on the berth and burst into violent tears of anger. When at last she grew calmer she got up and went to the porthole. She saw the tow boat cast off and turn around to head back to the dock. The ship was at sea. On deck, sailors were hoisting sail to catch the breeze. The three weeks journey to France had begun.

A feeling of deep sadness came over Lady Anne. She had lost her lover. She had no maid to tire her. She had no husband's name to protect her. She realized that she could no longer put the truth away. For the first time in her life she was alone.

THE END

ABOUT THE AUTHOR

INGLIS FLETCHER'S greatest fame rests on her books about early North Carolina, although her first two novels, *White Leopard* and *Red Jasmine,* were about Africa. Travel was long one of Mrs. Fletcher's chief enthusiasms. With her mining engineer husband, or often alone, she journeyed to remote mountain camps in Alaska and into the interior of Africa, where she went to study witchcraft and native customs.

Once back in the United States, she began, haphazardly at first, to hunt through records in California's Huntington Library for information about her early North Carolina ancestors. As she searched through the colonial documents, her interest grew until the names became live, vivid men and women and eventually the characters in such stories as *Raleigh's Eden, Men of Albemarle, Lusty Wind for Carolina, Toil of the Brave, Roanoke Hundred, Bennett's Welcome, Queen's Gift, Cormorant's Brood, The Wind in the Forest* and *Wicked Lady.* The Fletchers lived in an old plantation house called Bandon, right on the scene of the historic events that come alive in Mrs. Fletcher's writing.